S0-BER-458

The Black Tent
and other stories

Other works by Robin Maugham

Novels

THE SERVANT

THE INTRUDER

LINE ON GINGER

THE ROUGH AND THE SMOOTH

BEHIND THE MIRROR

THE MAN WITH TWO SHADOWS

NOVEMBER REEF

THE GREEN SHADE

THE SECOND WINDOW

THE LINK

THE WRONG PEOPLE

THE LAST ENCOUNTER

THE BARRIER

Travel

COME TO DUST

NOMAD

APPROACH TO PALESTINE

NORTH AFRICAN NOTEBOOK

JOURNEY TO SIWA

THE SLAVES OF TIMBUKTU

THE JOYITA MYSTERY

Biography

SOMERSET AND ALL THE MAUGHAMS

ESCAPE FROM THE SHADOWS

ROBIN MAUGHAM

The Black Tent
and other stories

With an introduction by Peter Burton

W. H. ALLEN
LONDON AND NEW YORK
A division of Howard & Wyndham Ltd
1973

© ROBIN MAUGHAM 1973

© INTRODUCTION, PETER BURTON 1973

THIS BOOK OR PARTS THEREOF MAY NOT BE
REPRODUCED WITHOUT PERMISSION IN WRITING

PRINTED AND BOUND IN GREAT BRITAIN BY BUTLER AND TANNER LTD,
FROME AND LONDON FOR THE PUBLISHERS
W. H. ALLEN & CO. LTD, 44 HILL STREET, LONDON W1X 7FR

ISBN 0 491 01291 8

For Jeanne

Contents

Acknowledgements

Thanks are due to the following periodicals and publications where the stories in this collection first appeared: *Chamber's Journal* (*The Black Tent*), *Britannia and Eve* (*The Man who could Hypnotise Racehorses* and *The Prodigal Son*), the *Evening Standard* (*Stolen Tune* and *Le Père Auguste*), *Gay News* (*The Boy from Beirut*), *Transatlantic Review* (*Night in Cassis*), *M.D. Companion* (*The Last Gauguin*), *Best Short Stories of 1954*, Edited by John Pudney (*Broken Cellophane*), Michael DeHartington, Publishers (*Testament: Cairo 1898*), War Facts Press (*The 1946 Ms*), and the *Strand Magazine* (*Half Marks*), *Daily Express* (*School Curtains*). Thanks are also due to Karen De Groot who spent some time searching out copies of some of the older short stories—both at the British Museum Library and in the British Museum Newspaper Library.

Introduction

Robin Maugham has had a highly successful career as a novelist, a travel writer, a dramatist, as a journalist, a family biographer, and, most recently, as an autobiographer. He has written over a dozen novels, seven travel books, and more than twenty plays for stage and television. The *Selected Bibliography* of his work shows him as the author of more than seventy major items. Yet, for all this volume of work, he has written very few short stories. In fact, there can be few writers as prolific as Maugham with so few short stories to their credit.

The Black Tent and Other Stories are very nearly the complete short stories of Robin Maugham. The only things missing from the book are the adolescent pieces he wrote—whilst at Trinity Hall, Cambridge—for *The Granta* (1934–1937), and one long, comparatively recent story, *The Messenger* (1955), which no one connected with this present volume was entirely happy about, and decided to exclude from the collection. With these exceptions, this book forms an almost complete collection of Robin Maugham's short stories.

Though the stories are not arranged in any chronological order, they cover the years from 1943 to 1972. Thus, included is *The 1946 Ms*, Maugham's first important publication, which originally appeared in a slender volume from the War Facts Press in 1943, and his most recent essay into the short story field, *Testament: Cairo 1898*, which appeared in a limited, numbered and signed edition in 1972. Between these two pieces are nearly thirty years of short stories—and though the number is small, they are well worth collecting together and preserving between the covers of a book.

Most of the stories in this book have appeared elsewhere. Equally, most of them have been unavailable for some time. Some of these short works of fiction were first published in

English newspapers or magazines. Two appeared in book form—*The 1946 Ms* and *Testament: Cairo 1898* (the latter as a specially limited edition, the former, due to wartime paper shortages, in a *necessarily* limited edition)—one, *The Last Gauguin*, has only previously appeared in America, and two of the stories, *The Girl in Number Seven* and *The Guide*, have not been previously published. Each of the stories is interesting and immensely readable in itself. Taken as a whole they make a remarkably diverse collection of styles, themes and attitudes.

In this volume can be seen ideas and themes, plots and characters, which have contributed to the major stream of Robin Maugham's novels. Like Tennessee Williams, Maugham is not afraid to mine a seam of imagination or invention more than once. Like Williams, many of whose short stories have formed the basis for later plays, Maugham likes to work on a theme or character until he gets it, or him, exactly right.

Some of these stories are based upon true incidents, or on stories told to Maugham in his peregrinations around the world. For, like his distinguished uncle, W. Somerset Maugham, Robin Maugham always has his eyes and ears ready for some incident or character he can develop in his fiction. Some of the stories are extensions of personal experience, transmuted into the realms of art by the use of imagination, and the clarity of literary style for which he is justly noted. At least one story was developed out of the extensive research involved in the construction of an historical novel. Some of the stories are simply delightful; others delve deeper and have more to give than just a passing pleasure.

The 1946 Ms, Robin Maugham's first major contribution to literature, has an interesting history, and it is worth spending a little time explaining. The story was written in 1943, when Maugham was on the point of being invalided out of the army. He had heard dangerous talk of some kind of military *putsch* in England. Accordingly, he wrote *The 1946 Ms* as a warning. He sincerely believed that some popular and famous General, backed by his devoted officers and troops, might attempt to become Dictator in post-war, debilitated England.

The 1946 Ms is a fictional piece, running to nearly fifteen thousand words. It is, in fact, a *nouvelle*, belonging together with the author's distinguished *The Servant*,* *The Black Tent*, and the more recent *Testament: Cairo 1898*. However, it is also something more than a fiction—or certainly was meant as something far more drastic at the time it was written. The piece was written during the Second World War as a prophetic warning about what could happen if an overwhelmingly successful military leader were able to take complete control as a Dictator of Great Britain.

The publishers, War Facts Press, printed manuscripts which were 'a contribution to the social, literary or economic future of Great Britain', and which were written by authors with 'something to say about the world of to-morrow'. Even so, they were afraid of the implications of Maugham's anti-Establishment piece. At the time of publication *The 1946 Ms* was to be serialised in the *Sunday Chronicle*. Even as the paper went to press, suddenly *The 1946 Ms* was censored. It was due to appear on the front page of the newspaper. But the first page was blank. The editor of the *Sunday Chronicle*, James W. Drawbell, remonstrated with the powers-that-be. The following week *The 1946 Ms* appeared. It is interesting to note, however, that no copy was ever allowed in the Eighth Army area abroad.

Thus, more than a purely fictional piece, it must be considered as a semi-propagandist work, doubly interesting since it also contains the pattern for all of Robin Maugham's later work. In fact, though themes occur which are used throughout his later books, *The 1946 Ms* is most directly the parent of the novel *The Man With Two Shadows*.†

Two other stories in the collection evolved out of wartime experience: *The Boy from Beirut*—which appeared originally in a different form in the author's travel book *Nomad*,‡ and the *nouvelle The Black Tent*. This latter work was first published as a two-part serial, under the title *Desert Bond*, in *Chamber's Journal* in 1953. The narrative is sparse and clear—it is possibly one of the strongest pieces Robin Maugham has written—and shows the deep affection for the Arabs, and interest in Middle Eastern affairs which is so characteristic of his early work. It also has tones and patterns in it which Maugham first used in

* Robin Maugham, *The Servant*, Falcon Press, 1948.
† Robin Maugham, *The Man with Two Shadows*, Longmans, 1958.
‡ Robin Maugham, *Nomad*, Chapman and Hall, 1947.

The 1946 Ms, later in his war diary, *Come to Dust*,* in *Line On Ginger*,† and, most latterly, in his play *Enemy!*‡ *The Black Tent* was filmed, under the direction of Brian Desmond Hurst, in 1956. The film crops up, on television on both sides of the Atlantic, with positively alarming regularity.

The lighter stories, in which must be included *The Man who could Hypnotise Racehorses*, *School Curtains*, *Stolen Tune*, *The Girl in Number Seven*, and *The Last Gauguin*, are notable for sheer simplicity of storyline and observation and wit in the telling. *The Last Gauguin*, hitherto unpublished in England, is a small comic masterpiece of invention and imagination. It is also possessed, as all great comedy should be, of an underlying current of truth, sadness and humanity.

Both *The Prodigal Son* and *Broken Cellophane* belong with the mainstream of Maugham's fiction in which he expresses concern for the ill-used, the misbegotten, and those ill-adjusted to society. *Broken Cellophane*, with its ugly but gentle hero who can communicate with other people only by displaying the pretty toy horse he has bought, is carefully written—there's no hint of sentimentality about it—and infinitely moving. There is an interesting aside on this story too. *Broken Cellophane* represents the first time Robin Maugham appeared in print in a collection of stories side by side with his uncle Willie—Somerset Maugham. In 1960, *Broken Cellophane* was included in a Danish schools English textbook called *How Do You Do*.§ Amongst the other stories in the anthology was W. Somerset Maugham's *The Verger*.

In a similar vein, though written with a lighter touch, is *Le Père Auguste*, one of the stories in the collection which is based upon an incident which actually happened to the author. In fact, the friends whom the narrator goes to stay with at the opening of the story were Pamela Frankau and Humbert Wolfe.

The two most recently created stories in the volume: *Night In Cassis*, and *Testament: Cairo 1898*, show the sure touch that maturity brings to a writer. The middle-aged, and

* Robin Maugham, *Come to Dust*, Chapman and Hall, 1945.
† Robin Maugham, *Line on Ginger*, Chapman and Hall, 1949.
‡ Robin Maugham, *Enemy!*, in *Plays of the Year: Volume 39, 1969–70*, edited by J. C. Trewin, Elek Books, 1971.
§ C. M. Gyde Poulsen and E. Hvid, *How Do You Do*, III, Ejnar Munksgaard, Copenhagen, 1960.

over-weight hero of *Night In Cassis* has a sense of ironical humour. He doesn't become annoyed when his little plots go astray—he is, at the end, more or less content. Written by a less certain hand, this story could have lost all its simplicity and essential honesty. It is a story which a less experienced writer could have made loud and coarse. As it stands, it is ever so slightly self-mocking of middle-age, of lechery, of fallibility. Yet there is never a trace of self-pity. The story has a gratifying acceptance and positive joy in the freedom and happiness of youth. One feels, instinctively, that these sentiments spring not just from the story, but from the author himself. And, above all, at all times, the story remains human and true.

Testament: Cairo 1898 is a bleak and bitter story. There is little hope in it for the characters. But there is a very firmly stated moral message for the reader. This story, which evolved out of the intensive research which went into the preparation of Maugham's reconstruction of General Gordon's last months in Khartoum, *The Last Encounter*,* cries out loudly and clearly for tolerance and understanding. It says, in no uncertain terms, 'What is wrong with this young soldier? Nothing! What right has anyone to decree his desires criminal—and base? None!' Though it may leave the reader saddened, depressed, or even appalled, it cannot but leave him *thinking*.

The stories in this collection have not been arranged in the order in which they were written—for two reasons. The first, and most obvious, reason being that, had they been organised chronologically, this would have created a somewhat un-balanced book. The second, and more personal, reason is that they have been arranged so that there is a constant ebb and flow of moods, light to dark, dark to light, and a constant change in location from, for example, the South Seas to London, from London to New York.

The book has been organised, in fact, so that it is—as all books *should* be—a good companion, shifting in mood, shifting in feeling, changing in attitude. A good companion: a book or a person in whom there is infinite variety, and with whom there is never time to become bored.

PETER BURTON

*Robin Maugham, *The Last Encounter*, W. H. Allen, 1972.

The Black Tent

I

> The slaves of domestic tyranny may vainly exault in their national independence. But the Arab is personally free.
>
> Gibbon: *Decline and Fall of the Roman Empire*

Until to-day I have never kept a journal, because I have lived for thirty-three years without an adventure—with a capital A. I've had fun and games at school and at Cambridge; I've known the excitement and beastliness of war; but nothing has come my way which I considered sufficiently unusual to write down in a notebook. Even now, I cannot be certain . . .

However, I shall keep this journal, partly to please myself, and partly, I must confess, because I think it would please David, alive or dead. I can hear him chuckling and saying: 'My dear old Bill, adventure's come your way at last.'

When it started, four days ago, I was more bored than I'd ever been, and it's not hard to explain why.

By the time I was due to be demobbed at the end of the war I realised that I was too restless to go back to my job as junior partner in the family shipping firm. I was a bachelor without responsibilities. By joining the army in 1939 I had seen a good bit of the world; I reckoned that by staying on in the army I'd see some more of it. Poor dope. My regiment was sent to Egypt, where I'd been during the war, and we've been stationed for what seems like eternity in the Suez Canal Zone on a bleak, windswept, dusty stretch of desert near Quassasin.

When I first came out to Egypt as a Second-Lieutenant in the Hartland Yeomanry every stretch of desert looked the same to me. But now I realise the desert can be as friendly as the Sussex Downs or as grim as Dartmoor. God, how I hate the Canal

Zone! Dirty sand; lines and lines of tents; barbed wire; stores; trucks; signboards with letters which now spell gloom in my heart—'H.Q.R.A.S.C.', 'No. 127 R.E.M.E. Sub-Depot', 'G.H.Q.M.E.L.F. 59 Coy. C.M.P.'; closely-spaced rows of derelict tanks—German, British, Italian, American, side by side at last, parked in their rusty graveyard, awaiting the furnace; more tents, more barbed wire, all the clutter of equipment, the paraphernalia required for maintaining an army 'to protect vital British interests in the Middle East'.

How dreary it all looks, I was thinking to myself when I ambled towards the Officers' Mess last Monday morning for a cup of tea, and saw the orderly coming towards me.

'G.H.Q. wants you on the 'phone, sir.'

'Now, what is it?' I thought as I followed the man to the Orderly Room. 'A posting, or yet another course on map-reading?'

For once the line was clear.

'Is that Major Dawson?'

'Yes,' I said warily.

'My name's Croft. You probably don't remember me, but we once split a bottle of Chianti in Florence. I was in the Fourth Sharpshooters.'

'Of course. I remember.'

'I've now got an Intelligence job in this God-forsaken place. Weren't you a friend of David Holland?'

'Yes.'

'He was reported missing, and then presumed dead, wasn't he?'

For an instant a silly hope surged in my heart and I was so excited that I could hardly reply.

'Yes.'

'He was last heard of in May 1942?'

'Yes.'

'I thought so. Well, something rather odd has happened. I wonder if you could nip over and see me at G.H.Q.?'

'Nip' meant wangling a car and driving sixty miles to Fayed. 'Certainly,' I said, and we arranged to meet that afternoon at five.

<hr />

While I drove along the tarmac road which runs by the side of the sweet-water canal, past caravans of mangy camels, children washing in the filthy water near the village drains, the corpses of donkeys rotting under the clear-blue winter sky, my mind churned over the past trying to guess what it could be 'rather odd' that had happened to make an officer in the Intelligence branch of G.H.Q. telephone me about David Holland who was presumed dead over six years ago.

Feverishly I rehearsed the scanty facts I knew about his last patrol.

When, early on the morning of May 26th, 1942, Rommel burst through the Eighth Army defence line which ran from Gazala to Bir Hacheim, our armoured car regiment was stationed near a small, innocent-looking signboard perched on a mound of stones. On the plain wood were written unevenly the letters which spelt the worst defeat our army was ever to suffer in the Western Desert—KNIGHTSBRIDGE.

By the morning of May 28th the British High Command decided that the battle 'had become fluid'.

'Which means, as usual, that it's a complete balls-up,' David said cheerfully as he sat that afternoon on the top of his Daimler armoured car, munching biscuits, looking at the horizon.

I can remember him well at that moment, slight and wiry, hunched up like a little gnome. I can see his very blond hair matted with sand, his cracked lips, the skin peeling on his nose, the gleam in his light-blue eyes, the sweat trickling down his dusty thighs.

The scene is fixed in my mind like a photograph in a book, because that was the last time I saw him. An instant later he left on the patrol from which he never returned.

For the first half-hour he was in wireless communication with regimental headquarters, and I could hear him from time to time on the air. He had spotted a formation of German Mark IV tanks moving north-east and was keeping them under observation. As usual his information was accurate and clear. Then, suddenly, he came on the air and said: 'Hullo Bill, David calling. Squadron of Mark IIIs coming up from the south-east. I think I've had it.'

Even while he was speaking, I could hear the guns firing at him above the crackle of his transmitter. So far as I knew those were the last words he spoke. He was never seen again. Later that evening the other two cars in his patrol returned. His Sergeant reported that David had left the two cars six hundred yards apart in good positions for observation and had gone ahead himself to the west. The Mark III tanks coming up from the south-east had cut him off.

Through the usual Red Cross channels we learned that the men in the crew of his armoured car had been killed. But of Captain Sir David Holland there was no trace. He was posted missing, and then presumed killed. As soon as the men in his crew were reported killed, David's friends in the regiment decided that his armoured car must have had a direct hit from a Mark IV tank. If the shell had exploded in the turret it was probable that nothing remained whereby David could be identified—not even his disc.

'Poor David,' they said. 'What a grand chap he was.' And they ordered another round of drinks and tried in their clumsy way to be specially kind to me, for they knew that he had been my best friend. Yet I still cherished a hope—a silly, inexplicable hope—that David was alive. Somehow I could not think of him as dead. And now, as my car drew close to the tents of Fayed, that hope surged and pulsed like a drum in my brain. If he had been killed by a shell, what now, seven years later, could it be 'rather odd' that had happened?

———◆◆◆———

As Major Croft rose from behind a desk littered with maps and files, I recognised him. He was a gaunt, round-shouldered, red-faced man, with bleary eyes and a ridiculously large moustache, which seemed to have grown in proportion to his rank. The bristles had seemed rather long on the day I had met him by chance in a bar in Florence and we had lunched together. He was then a Captain, and I remembered that I had discovered he was not as dull as he appeared.

He greeted me warmly. I could hardly control my impatience while he rambled on and on about the good old days in the Eighth Army.

At last he got to the point.

'You knew David Holland pretty well, didn't you?' he said.

4

'Yes.'

'Would you recognise his handwriting?'

'Certainly.'

He opened a metal box on his desk and produced a grubby bit of paper which looked as if it had been torn from a field service pocket-book.

'Did he write this?' he asked.

As I took the piece of paper, the shape of David's writing danced and flickered before my eyes long before I could read the words he had written, and I felt sick with excitement.

I made myself read the words again, written in pencil in his clear, bold script. 'Pay bearer twenty pounds (£20)', the note said. And it was signed 'David Holland, Captain'. The figures which followed were his army number. The note was undated, but the top right-hand corner was torn.

Major Croft was speaking to me.

'Is that his writing?'

'Yes.'

'You're certain?'

'Beyond any doubt. How did you get this?'

Croft smiled at me.

'Through somewhat unusual channels,' he said. 'The bearer of it is waiting outside. But before we call him in I'd better explain the set-up. You remember that during the fighting in the Western Desert we were told that if we were captured and escaped we could always be sure of refuge in any Senussi Bedouin tent we might find?'

'Yes.'

'So far as I know they never betrayed our men even though the price of sheltering a soldier—if the Italians found out— was to have their encampment razed to the ground. They're fine chaps, the Senussi.'

'Certainly.'

Croft smiled at me. I think he was enjoying my impatience.

'You may also remember we were told that if we had been wounded and stayed in their tents for any length of time we could write them a promissory note for what we owed them which would eventually be honoured by G.H.Q.'

'So that note . . .'

Croft silenced me with a wave of his bony hand.

'Let me finish, please,' he said calmly. 'After Alamein, the British Military Government of Cyrenaica received and honoured several of these notes or chits. But few of them, so far as I know, were handed in here. Perhaps few of our chaps wrote them. Perhaps the Senussi were too proud to accept money for their hospitality. Perhaps no one from their tribe came this way. That's possible. Because long after the shooting match was over, stray Senussi types would turn up with these notes. There's one of them outside now.'

'He brought David's note?'

'Yes. But there are three curious points. First, it's several years since Holland was reported missing. Secondly, the note is for a large amount. Thirdly, as you can see, the note is un-dated. For these three reasons the Senussi who brought the note was passed on to me.'

'What's his story?'

'Unhelpful. He says that a man from a neighbouring tribe heard he was coming to Egypt and gave him the note to cash if he could.'

'Does he know anything about David?'

'Nothing. He can't read, of course. The man who gave it to him—he came from the Hiwari tribe—told him that an English soldier had promised it would be honoured.'

'Can we see him?'

'If you like. Do you speak Arabic?'

'Well enough to question him.'

Croft called for an orderly.

'Bring in old hairy-face,' he said.

The orderly returned with a small thin Arab of about sixty. He was wearing a shabby burnous, and his face was covered with dirty white hairs. Yet such was his dignity as he entered the room that we both rose quickly.

'*Salaam aleikum*,' he said.

'And the blessing of Allah be with you,' we replied.

Croft offered him a cigarette, which he refused with a slow, graceful movement of his hand. Then he sat down delicately on the chair Croft produced, and I began questioning him.

'What tribe do you come from?'

'The Atilah tribe.'

'Where do they pasture?'

'Near Bir Abu Zrail.'

'Where is Bir Abu Zrail?'

'South-west of Tobruk. In the direction of Agedabia.'

'How many miles south-west?'

'How many miles? I don't know.'

'How many hours or days on a camel?'

'Perhaps five days.'

'Riding by night?'

'Riding by day.'

'You know the man who gave you this note?'

'Yes. He is from the Hiwari tribe, near us.'

His replies were made so courteously that I felt I must apologise for questioning him. I explained that the Englishman who had written the note he had brought had been my friend.

He listened gravely. Then he said: 'I can only tell you this. The Arab who gave me the note is from the Hiwari tribe. His name is Salem Ben Youssef. He is an honest man. He is their Sheikh. He hears that I am going to Egypt. He tells me that an Englishman gave him this note for money. He asks me to find out where I can get the money. I am here.'

'Why did you come to Egypt?'

'Many years ago my son left the tribe to work in Egypt. He writes to my cousin in Tobruk telling him he is sick and will die. so I come to Egypt.'

'Where is your son?'

'In Port Said. He is very sick. I will stay with him now till he dies. Then I will go back.' His voice was flat, expressionless.

'Do you need money for your son?'

'No. I have money. It is Sheikh Salem who needs money. His tribe is very small and poor. The drought has killed many of his cattle.'

'When are you returning to Port Said?'

'To-morrow.'

'Where will you sleep to-night?'

'Where Allah wills.'

'I've told an orderly to see he's fixed up,' said Croft.

'*Inshallah*. I will see you later,' I said.

'*Inshallah*,' he replied.

We rose, and he departed.

'Remarkable old boy, that,' Croft said. 'I believe he's honest, don't you?'

'I'm certain he is.'

'So now, what?'

'How long ago would you say the note was written?'

Croft looked at me steadily.

'Seven years ago,' he said quickly.

'The writing looks quite fresh.'

'If you look at the way it's been folded, you'll see that at one time it was kept in a wallet.'

'Are you going to pay him?'

'That isn't for me to decide.'

'What is for you to decide?'

Croft gazed at me thoughtfully with his bleary grey eyes.

'Nothing,' he replied. 'I'm just here to find out things.'

'What have you found out?'

'For one thing I've found out that you still believe David Holland's alive.'

I stared at him in amazement.

'How can you know that?'

'Your voice on the 'phone, your impatience when you arrived, your face when I handed you the note. Besides, I'd got a clue already.'

'A clue?'

'You remember when we met on leave in Florence?'

'Yes.'

'That was two years after Holland had been presumed dead, wasn't it?'

'Yes.'

'Yet you were still convinced he was alive. Why?'

Suddenly his voice was crisp and hard.

'I'd just got a hunch, that's all.'

'Two years after he'd been presumed dead?'

'What are you getting at?'

'I happen to have a good memory. I was impressed by the obstinate faith with which you clung to what you call your hunch. But I'm beginning to wonder if your faith wasn't based on something more than a hunch.'

'What are you talking about?'

'You were his best friend, weren't you?'

'Yes.'

Croft began playing with a pencil which was lying on his desk.

'You see, *I've* got a hunch now,' he said casually.

'What?'

'I think you knew something which made you suspect he hadn't been killed.'

'You're quite mad. What could I have known?'

'Oh, I can think of several things. For instance, he might have told you he was going to quit.'

'Quit?'

'Supposing, only supposing, mind you, that he had some urgent reason for disappearing—debts, perhaps blackmail, perhaps fear of some kind—he goes off on patrol, his armoured car is hit, the crew killed. He manages to escape. What a chance fate has given him! Where does he go? Not back to our lines, not to the enemy, but to the only place where he can find oblivion—a Senussi encampment. He knows that Captain Sir David Holland will be reported missing and eventually presumed killed. He has only to stay with them for a while. And then . . .'

Croft paused and looked at me closely.

'And then would come the difficulty,' he continued smoothly. 'He might become converted, go native, and live in the desert for the rest of his life. Or he might try to reappear later with a different name—in which case he might need the help of someone he could trust.'

The grey eyes were ranging slowly over my face.

'Have you quite finished?' I asked.

'Yes. I can see now that my hunch was wrong.'

'If it's of any interest to you,' I said, 'David Holland wasn't in debt. His estate, which passed to his cousin, is worth nearly thirty thousand pounds. He wasn't being blackmailed. I had to go through his papers. And since he'd got an M.C. and bar I don't think he was particularly afraid. You couldn't be more wrong.'

'I know,' Croft said, quite unmoved by my outburst. 'But I told you it was only a hunch. Come, let's go over to the mess and have a drink.'

'All right.'

I liked him a little better after we had each had two whiskies.

'If you don't think he's dead, what do you think has happened to him?' he asked.

'I don't know.'

'It really is just nothing more than a hunch?'

'Yes.'

'How old would he be now?'

'Thirty.'

'What near relations had he got?'

'None. His parents died when he was young, and he was an only son. As I told you, the estate passed to his cousin.'

'If he's still alive, why do you think he's never communicated with you?'

'Perhaps he's lost his memory.'

'Possible, but improbable.'

'Perhaps the shock of the explosion which killed his crew deranged his mind. Perhaps he's now a harmless creature living with Bedouins too charitable to turn him out.'

'But not so charitable they won't cash a note from him for twenty pounds,' Croft said.

'The old man said the tribe was poor.'

'Shall I tell you what I believe now?'

'Yes, if you'll have a drink on me,' I said.

'The note was genuine and it was written seven years ago. When his armoured car was hit, Holland escaped, found refuge with the Senussi, stayed with them for a while—perhaps he'd been wounded or was ill—gave them that note in repayment of their hospitality, left their tents in order to regain our lines, and died on the way back. That is the report I shall make.'

'And leave it at that?'

Croft looked at me curiously.'

'I expect so,' he replied.

'I'm due for a spot of leave,' I said.

'Now isn't that just too fortunate.'

'Planes from here go to El Adem.'

'So they do. And the Western Desert's at its best in winter.'

'I'm going on one of those planes. I'm going to reach that tribe. I'm going to find out exactly when David wrote that note. Can you help me?'

Croft examined his fingernails as if he had never seen them before.

'You could get to El Adem without my help,' he said, after a pause. 'But I could certainly make things easier for you. For a start, I could produce maps. I might even give you a letter to a chap in El Adem who could lay on a guide for you.'

'That would be grand.'

'I think you are going on a wild-goose chase. However, it's not in my power to stop you. But if I help you, there's one thing I must insist on.'

'Which is?'

'You'll report to me immediately you return.'

'Certainly.'

The bleary eyes slowly searched my face.

'And I think I'd know if you were lying,' he said, draining his glass. 'Now let's go and find hairy-face.'

------◆◆◆◆------

That was four days ago. Since then we have made good progress. We saw the old Arab and found out all we could from him about the Hiwari tribe. It would be more accurate to describe it as a sub-tribe, small and impoverished, ranging the Libyan desert with its camels and goats and black, goat-hair tents. We located Abu Zrail on one of Croft's large-scale maps—most of the birs or wells were marked. It lay about a hundred miles south-west of El Adem. And, after some hesitation, we told the old man that I was going to visit the tribe myself to pay the money my friend owed them. We offered him money, which he refused to accept, and said goodbye to him the next morning, as he sat impassive and aloof, a tattered, proud little figure, squatting at the back of an army truck. Then I returned to my regiment to remind the Colonel that I was due for a fortnight's leave, and Croft set about wangling me a seat in a plane to El Adem.

I leave to-morrow, and my plan is made.

Though it looks from the map as if one might be able to reach Abu Zrail by car, I have decided to go with a guide by camel. Thirty years of Italian military occupation have given the Senussi Bedouin a distrust of anything European which their friendship with the British during recent years has not yet removed. The books which Croft has given me to read about Libya prove that, even before Fascism, the Italian domination along the coast was cruel and ruthless. Arabs were lined up and crushed by tanks, whole tribes were shut into concentration camps and left to perish with their animals, wells were sealed with cement.

Bir Abu Zrail lies in the eastern zone of Libya, called Cyrenaica, which borders on Egypt. It is a pastoral country. Almost all the Arabs who live outside the little war-scarred towns along the coast—Benghazi, Derna, Tobruk—live in tents and retain the characteristics of nomads. Almost all belong to the Senussi faith (which is a Moslem one, demanding a strict adherence to the Moslem code) and regard their Emir, Sayyed Idris, as their spiritual and temporal leader. They are a simple, primitive people, poor and proud, leading a hard life in the endless desert.

As soon as I reach the Hiwari tents, they will certainly question my guide about me. What shall I tell them? It is essential that they should not suspect that I know anything of David's note. I must have time to look around before I play that card. The old man, waiting for his son to die in Port Said, cannot reach them before me. He may not reach them for several months.

I shall say that I am an English officer on leave who wants to make a camel trip. But what is my reason for wanting to visit Abu Zrail? Why should I choose an isolated, unimportant well to visit? Surely that will make them suspicious? Perhaps Flight-Lieutenant Luke Baring may be able to provide me with an excuse. He is technical adviser—whatever that may mean— to the British aerodrome at El Adem. Croft has given me a letter asking him to help.

———————◆◆◆◆◆———————

It is late, and I must get up early to-morrow. Yet I cannot go to bed. The thought that within a few days I will hear news of David, the thought that, perhaps (what odds would I lay against it? A thousand to one?), that perhaps I may—I can hardly write the words—I may even see him, will not let me sleep.

What is it that I expect to find? Why have I always felt that David was not dead? Why is the picture of him so clear in my mind? I can even remember the first time we met . . .

The regiment had come back from the desert in October 1941 to re-equip and we were stationed a few miles away from Alexandria. A new officer was expected from a regiment which had been disbanded because of heavy casualties. All that was known of him was that his name was Sir David Holland, that he was twenty-two years old, a Lieutenant with an M.C. I was sitting in the officers' mess tent when he walked in, slight, wiry, gentle-looking, very blond, with a face which looked at once puckish and serious.

'I'm the new boy,' he said. 'Where can I find the Adjutant?'

'In the Hotel Cecil with a girl friend,' I said. 'But I'll sign you in.'

There were a few people in mess that night, and afterwards we sat in a corner chatting about the days before the war.

He had nothing unusual to say. His upbringing had been conventional—a public school, then Cambridge, where he read agriculture, intending to manage his estate in Essex had the war not come, then six months in an Officer Cadets' Training Unit and six months in the Western Desert. We had both had roughly similar experiences, though I was two years older. But he was amusing and easy to get on with, and I was delighted when he was posted to our squadron.

Gradually, as we became close friends, I discovered a quality in him which I find hard to describe. I would call it innocence, except that 'innocence' is probably the wrong word. Few people who have been through an English public school can be described as innocent. No. I think 'directness' is a better word. There was no deflection in his enjoyment of a binge in Alexandria, a sunset in the desert, a walk in the moonlight. He enjoyed it all without any reservation, like a child. And like a child he was easily awed—not by authority, but by his thoughts, the vastness of the desert, a star gleaming many years away. He was normally selfish and self-indulgent; he was not outstandingly intelligent; but he was without malice or cruelty, and there was a charming quixotic streak in his character. When I try to analyse why it was we all liked him so much, I can only suppose it was because of some animal vitality which radiated from him.

Although at the time I considered that Croft's hunch that David had some reason for disappearing was ridiculous, I've been wondering during these last few days whether there may not be some grain of possibility in it, and I've racked my brain to think of a motive, rehearsing our conversations together, considering his life and circumstances—but in vain. We shared our food, our drink, our lodgings, and our dreams—even our letters from home. He had plenty of money, a good reputation, and no entanglement that I knew of—sexual or other.

I am still baffled, and I shall now go to bed.

————◆◆◆◆————

I am writing this in the spare room of Baring's bungalow at El Adem. Baring, thank God, has gone to bed.

The flight was lovely. We crossed the desert trail south of Alexandria and circled north-west, passing low above the romantic courtyards of Burg el Arab, onwards into the Western Desert spread out like a dappled carpet under an azure sky, over slit-trenches and disused camel-sites, until, half a mile south of the coast road, we could see a small square of sand which seemed to be covered with white grass. Then, as we drew near, I could make out the neat rows of little white crosses trimly planted in the open desert. To that square of sand how many times must their hearts return—the woodman in the snows of Canada, the widow in her skyscraper in Johannesburg, the old man sipping coffee in his London club, the young girl behind the bar in Sydney, the farmer watching his sheep in New Zealand, the Jewess in her tenement in Tel-Aviv—to that small square of sand in the empty desert, El Alamein.

At El Adem I soon found Baring, who was most eager to help, once he had read Croft's letter. He was kind and efficient. Within a few hours he managed to lay on an Arab guide and two camels. The guide is a young, lithe Libyan, with a wicked sparkle in his eyes. He is called Ali. Until six months ago he had been working in Tobruk. However, Baring swears that he knows the desert and will be useful.

I like Baring. But heavens, what a bore! We Eighth Army people may be bad enough but we're scintillating compared to some of the R.A.F. types. You wouldn't believe that at this date people could still talk about wizard prangs. They do, they do.

———✦———

Although the sun is shining from a clear blue sky as I am writing this, I am muffled up in a greatcoat and scarf, because a bitterly cold wind is blowing from the south. I have insisted on halting for an hour to eat and rest. This has annoyed Ali, who seems tireless, the little beast.

He promised me that if we rode six hours the first day, and nine hours on the second, I would feel less stiff on the third. Like an idiot, I believed him. The result is that I am now in agony. I cannot think of any part of me which is not aching. Ali's camel is a white, delicate creature with fluffy ears and a smooth step. I wanted to ride it, but he maintained I was too heavy. My camel is a gaunt brown brute, with his hair worn away in patches like a child's old teddy-bear.

I am convinced Zen, my camel, disliked me at sight. As I approached him that cold grey dawn which seems an eternity ago, he rolled his long-lashed, bloodshot eyes at me, and groaned as if in anguish and blew out his tongue like a balloon, which was most disconcerting. The dislike is now mutual. He moves with a jolting, rocking movement, as if he were just learning to walk, and he is extremely lazy.

At first I thought that Ali was shy. But as soon as we got out of sight of the camp he took off his boots and socks with high solemnity, as if it were a symbolic ritual, popped them into his camel-bag, and from that moment became friendly and rather domineering.

'Colonel, Colonel,' he would shout, as I lagged behind on the wretched Zen. 'Beat him, beat him. We must ride together. *Sawa, sawa.* Side by side. Beat him harder.'

'All right,' I would say, 'And don't call me Colonel.'

'I once knew an Italian Colonel,' Ali would reply, looking at me sideways, through his slanting eyes. 'I knew him very well. That is why I call you Colonel.'

15

Then he would begin singing a tune to make the camels trot. It was a phrase repeated over and over again. I thought it would weary me. But somehow it seemed to blend with the flat desert stretching all around us, the cloudless sky, and the crisp dry air.

By the time we had reached the wadi where we intended to spend the night I was so tired that I could hardly get off my camel. I lay flat on the sand gazing at the red and gold sunset, while Ali unsaddled the camels and hobbled them. Even during the war I felt a great peace at evening time in the Western Desert. Idly and happily I watched Ali take the blankets out of the camel-bags and lay them in a soft place before preparing our big meal of the day. All his movements were alert and neat. With his tiny waist and feet, he might have been a ballet dancer.

After he had scooped out a hole in the sand he cut a few clumps of dry camel-grass, and within two minutes he had got a fire blazing into the dark blue sky. He waited until the twigs had burned down to hot embers, then he placed the can of water on one side while he baked bread on the other. The bread was hot and salty, and tasted most pleasant with bully-beef washed down by a mug of tea.

After we had eaten, we sat beside the fire watching the sparks fly up into the darkness around us. I gave Ali a cigarette.

'The Italian Colonel was very fond of me,' Ali said, rather regretfully, I thought.

'How did you meet him?'

'After the Italians sealed up the wells in the desert, many of us came to the towns for food and work. The Colonel took me as his servant.'

Ali puffed at his cigarette in silence for a while, then he looked up at me and smiled rather coyly.

'I was sixteen then,' he said. 'And the Colonel became very fond of me. He gave me a shirt and a pair of shoes, and even, after some time, a wrist-watch.'

'How old are you now, Ali?'

'Twenty-eight. But then I was sixteen, and I knew little. But the Colonel was a very clever man and he taught me. And when he went on leave to Italy he did not want me to be alone, so he took me with him.'

'Did you like Italy?'

'Very much. There were towns with many houses and much to eat, and there were many girls. I was very happy there.'

'How long did you stay?'

'Not long. Because there was trouble.'

Ali looked at me slyly and then bent down his head and stared at the thin gold ring on his little finger.

'It was very sad,' he said. 'The Colonel's wife became fond of me. She gave me this ring. And I was fond of her also. And one evening the Colonel found us. And he was cross. Very, very cross. And he sent me away. And when I was hungry I sold the shoes he had given me, and even the watch, for food. But this ring I have always kept though I have been very hungry—because she gave it me and I was fond of her.'

This morning when I woke at dawn it was bitterly cold and I was so stiff I could hardly get into the saddle. A well-trained camel will kneel patiently while you mount. Then, when you shout 'Hup', he will rise to his feet, rocking to and fro. Not so Zen. As soon as he feels my weight he begins rising before I have got my balance. This morning I fell off, and Zen bolted. This made Ali laugh so much that he did nothing about chasing Zen, and we nearly lost him.

For the last three hours I have been too conscious of my stiffness and weariness to talk, so Ali has carried on a monologue—mainly about the women of Tobruk.

'I have two women,' he said. 'And though I am no longer sixteen, they cost me nothing. The first one is good and fat—perhaps thirty years old. Her husband is a sailor, so she is alone quite often and needs me. When I come, she gives me chicken and raisins and sometimes a cake. And then I stay all night with her. The second one is very small and skinny—perhaps fourteen years old. She has only been married three months, and she does not love her husband. He is cruel to her. He does not care that she is very little. But me she loves because I am gentle with her. Of course, if her husband knew, he would kill her. So we are very careful. It is the little one I love best. I will tell you why . . .'

I soon got bored with his descriptions of girls he had known, and purposefully let Zen lag behind. For a while he prattled on unaware that I could no longer hear him. Then the old cry began again.

'Colonel, Colonel, beat him, beat him. We must ride side by side. *Sawa, sawa.*'

He has now packed our lunch things into the camel-bags and is lying on his back watching me write down these words as if he had never seen a man write before.

I suppose Ali is quite an ordinary product of the recent impact of the Western world on the Arab lands. We have exported, it seems, only the trappings of our civilisation—phonographs, frigidaires. The best things we had to give never left the wharf. The result had been unfortunate. Ali is virile and decadent, worldly and ignorant, amoral and religious, energetic and lazy. He is disintegrated, attached by habit to his traditional way of life, yet fascinated by the ways of Western countries. I believe that it is only among Bedouin protected by this sea of sand around me now that the positive vitality of the Moslem invaders can be found. The Bedouin whom I shall see to-morrow will be leading an existence scarcely different from that of their ancestors two thousand years ago.

To-morrow . . . to-morrow . . . I've tried hard to keep my mind from leaping ahead of Zen's jolting steps, and rushing into the Hiwari tents.

————◆◆◆————

What is it I expect to find? This may be the last time I shall write in this book before reaching the Hiwari camp, unless they have moved on to fresh ground for their flocks. I must force myself to contemplate the horror which may await me.

If David is alive, he may be witless, or obscenely deranged by shock or wounds. If he is alive, what other explanation can there be? Though his parents were dead, and though he had few friends in England, he was devoted to his property— almost ridiculously so. He showed me the photographs he always carried with him. And even now there is a clear image of his house in my mind. I can see the Palladian façade, the huge pilasters sliding up between base and capital past two tiers of pedimented windows. I can see the lawn rolling gently down to the tranquil river and the park beyond with its neat clumps of trees and open grass stretches. Even if David were prepared to forsake his friends, he could never make himself abandon Fanshawe. Either he is dead or he is mad. There can be no third solution. If he is dead, at least I shall have learnt how he spent some of the days since I last saw him—I may even discover how he died. If he is mad, at least I can take him back with me and let the doctors, whose knowledge of treating the human brain has been increasing rapidly since their experience in the war, do their best.

Whatever happens to-morrow, this trip will not have been wasted. I feel closer to David now as I sit here writing, looking up to see the empty desert stretching all around me, the flat sand dappled with blue-grey camel-grass, sniffing the keen, dry air, soothing my mind with the openness and solitude—I feel closer to him than I have ever felt since I saw his armoured car disappearing over the horizon.

The derelict vehicles have been collected from the desert. The eternal wind sweeping up grains and grains of sand has obliterated the tracks of our cars and trucks, which ran like a thousand pencil-lines across the flat places. But where the going was hard and steep, the marks still remain, and as I see them I feel the last seven years melt away. I feel that I am still young and ardent and unsoiled. I am in the turret of my car again. The black dots I can see in the distance are German tanks, and I am moving forward, one tiny unit in a vast crusade to free the world from want and fear.

How pathetic those words now seem!

II

When we reached Abu Zrail, which is nothing more than a well surrounded by five palm trees, we discovered that the Hiwari tribe had moved, and it was not until far in the after-noon of the following day that we approached their outlying herds—first a few mangy-looking goats, then a dozen camels, then a flock of ragged sheep. A few minutes later, we saw, to the south, smoke spiralling into the clean air, and presently we drew near to a group of about thirty Bedouin tents, low and oblong, with one side open, the black goat-hair cloths drawn taut by guide-ropes pegged deep into the sand. One tent, probably the Sheikh's, was larger than the others, and towards that we drove our weary camels, while the pye-dogs barked furiously.

As we entered the camp all my tiredness left me, and waves of excitement surged over me. Outside the larger tent three men were standing.

'*Salaam aleikum,*' we said.

'*We aleikum salaam,*' they replied. 'Welcome. Enter.'

I tapped Zen on the head with my camel-stick, and, groaning, he lurched to the ground. Then, leaving Ali to deal with the camels, I obeyed the polite gesture of a small, spare man who, from his authority, appeared to be the Sheikh, and entered the tent.

I had arrived at last.

Five minutes later we were sitting on rugs round the fire, drinking fragrant very sweet tea from tiny glasses, and all was going well. The small man with the short black beard was indeed Sheikh Salem. He was talking to me cordially, and without suspicion. I had explained that I was an English officer on leave, that I had always wanted to make a trip by camel through the desert, and that I wanted to see something of life amongst the Senussi Bedouin tribes. He had accepted my story. Indeed, he seemed most anxious to be helpful and friendly.

'My home is your home,' he said, in the traditional phrase.

As I talked to him, I glanced through the opening of the tent. The sun was slanting low across the desert turning the ground red-gold. There was only half an hour of daylight left.

I excused myself politely and rose from my place in the group round the fire, knowing that I would not be followed. Once the Bedouin accept you as their guest, you come and go as you please. Moreover, it is tactful for an infidel to leave them at the hour of prayer.

I then wandered slowly round the camp. The men and little boys were driving in the flocks. The women were preparing the evening meal. Everywhere I was greeted with politeness and cheerfulness. If I passed near a tent, a man would come over and invite me inside. And as I strolled round the full circle of the camp my heart sank, for I realised from the cordiality of everyone that there was nothing to conceal.

Sadly I returned towards the Sheikh's tent. Nearby, I saw two men skinning the tiny sheep which had been slaughtered in my honour. As I took my place in the circle of hairy faces round the fire I decided that I would say nothing of the real purpose of my visit until we had eaten. Perhaps some chance remark now as we sat sipping tea, waiting for the sheep to be cooked, might give me a clue. The tent was split in two by a heavy black cloth. In the other half were the women, but they spoke softly and fast, so that I could not hear what they said.

At first, I confess I was not impressed by Sheikh Salem. He was a wiry, dirty-looking man with a puckered face, delicate hands, and gentle black eyes. He looked tired and old, but I learned later that he was only fifty. As he sat by the fire with his shabby burnous he looked like a dusty puppet. He appeared to lack any vitality or distinction. We talked politely of pastures and of the drought, of camels and the price of sugar. Then, diffidently, I enquired if he would mind telling me about the Senussi faith.

'Are you interested?' he asked.

'Yes. And very ignorant.'

When he began to speak in a soft deep voice it was as if some hidden generator had cut in, so that his power, irresistibly, filled the tent.

'Our founder,' he said, 'was Mahommed ibn Ali El-Senussi, and he was born one hundred and fifty years ago in Algeria. When he was twenty he went to Fez and studied for ten years. There he became worried because we Moslems were divided into so many different sects. "Strife and division," he said, "have prevailed on all sides because the scholars and sheikhs do not have religious zeal for the spread of knowledge." Therefore he left Fez and made the pilgrimage to Mecca. Gradually his purpose became clear to him. It was to unite all the Islamic orders and so in the end to unite all the Moslems by returning to the simple teachings of the prophet.'

I watched Ali who was sitting three places away from me round the fire. A few minutes ago he had been pulling an imaginary black beard in imitation of the Sheikh, and winking at me covertly despite my frowns. Now, even he was half-fascinated by the immobile little figure and the deep passionate voice.

'We Senussi believe,' the Sheikh continued, 'that it is the right of every believer to return to the original sources—the Koran and the Sunnah—and to find from his own study the rules and beliefs which, in his own judgment, make up the religion of Islam.'

'What if he finds them wrongly? What if he makes a mistake?' Ali asked him.

The Sheikh smiled. 'We have this saying,' he replied. ' "If a man uses his own judgment and reaches a correct conclusion, he will receive two rewards. If he does so, and makes a mistake, he will receive only one reward, but his mistake will be forgiven".'

'I see that some of you smoke cigarettes,' Ali said, with a titter.

'Yes. At first it was forbidden. But now we may take tobacco or snuff if there is any. We also, as you can see, drink tea. Our life is hard, and these are our only luxuries.'

The hairy, worn faces intent around the dancing fire, the desert sparkling in the moonlight, somehow made it possible for me to ask my next question.

'Do you believe that the simplicity of your life brings you closer to God?'

'We believe that it is not only the great saints and teachers of our order who can see the prophet. All of us who will follow the road to that end, all of us who will imitate the prophet in word and deed, will see him. The man who repeats, forty times a day, every day, the prayer—"O my resource in every time of distress, the one who answers my prayers, my refuge in every difficulty and my hope when my own devices fail", that man will see the prophet every night in his dreams.'

A man came in carrying a bowl of water in which we washed our right hands.

'Food!' cried Ali.

Somehow I do not think Ali will see the prophet in his dreams.

Our meal began with bread, broken and baked in the embers and soused with liquid butter which tasted rancid. Then two

22

young Bedouin came in carrying a huge wooden bowl in which was the sheep, cut up and boiled, with a little rice. And we squatted round it and ate with our right hands, moulding the rice with our fingers into hard balls, scooping them into our mouths with our thumbs. From time to time the Sheikh would tear off a tender piece of meat and put it on the rice in front of me. I was extremely hungry, and the meal tasted delicious, though now and then in my ignorance of anatomy, and in the half-light of the fire, I would take a piece that looked rather odd.

When we had finished eating and washed our hands, we returned to the fire and sat smoking and drinking sweet tea. As we talked, I watched their faces—friendly, open, unguarded, unsuspicious. It was then that I decided to tell them the true purpose of my journey. I turned to the Sheikh.

'When I told you that I came here only because I wanted a camel ride through the desert I lied to you,' I said. 'You gave an Arab a note from an English officer called David Holland. It was a note asking for you to be paid twenty pounds. Your friend has handed in that note at Suez. I have come to pay the money which David Holland owes you. I know that he must have lived in your tents. I knew him very well. Please tell me all you can about him.'

There was silence. It was as if I had dropped my words like a stone into a well and now awaited the answering splash, but the well was bottomless.

I looked at the Sheikh. He was staring fixedly ahead at the blue desert outside, and in his eyes was an expression I could not understand. It was neither quite fear nor anger. I looked at the others. They were watching me closely, and, there was no doubt about it, they were now hostile. The silence became so heavy that I longed to repeat my last sentence.

'Please tell me all you can about him.' I could feel my lips framing the words. But to speak again would have been a sign of weakness. At last the Sheikh spoke.

'I would not have sent for the money if my tribe were not now very poor,' he said.

'I am sure of that,' I said quickly. 'But I know that my friend owed you the money. I know his handwriting, and I have come here to pay his debt.'

'We are grateful,' the Sheikh said, with cold dignity.

'David Holland lived here in your tents?'

'Yes.'

'Please tell me how he reached you.'

I longed to add, 'and what became of him.'

'It is a long time ago now.'

'But you can remember.'

Again there was silence.

'He was an English officer,' the Sheikh said after a long pause. 'He had been wounded. We took him into our tents and sheltered him for a while. He could not go back to his friends at once because Rommel had driven back the English. They were far away. Besides, he was not strong. Then, when he got well again, he said he must go back to his friends, and he left us. But before he went he made me accept the note you have seen. I would not have sent for the money if there had not been a drought.'

'When he left, you never saw him again?'

'Never.'

'How long did he stay in your tents?'

'Not long.'

'How many weeks?'

'It is so long ago that I find it hard to remember.'

The Sheikh turned to the others.

'How long did the Englishman stay? A few days only, was it?'

'Yes,' they said. 'A few days.'

'Perhaps it was two weeks,' said the Sheikh.

'Where had he been wounded?'

'In his left arm.'

'He wrote no other note? You've got nothing else in writing?'

'Nothing.'

'He was my best friend. Please tell me what you can remember about him. Was he happy? Was his wound completely healed when he left?'

The Sheikh stood up slowly, and the others scrambled up after him.

'Perhaps we can talk about that in the morning,' he said. 'It is late, and we rise early. Will these rugs be sufficient for you during the night?'

'Certainly. Thank you,' I said.

I was confused and angry.

The Sheikh turned to Ali.

'If there is anything your master needs you will let me know,' he instructed him.

Then he turned to me.

'Good night,' he said, and left the tent.

Long after Ali had begun snoring softly in his corner of the tent I lay awake looking at the red embers glowing, rehearsing all that had been said in the tent, trying to discover some explanation for the violent change in the attitude of everyone as soon as I mentioned David's name. It was impossible, surely, that David could be alive and living here. I had walked freely round the camp. I had watched everyone closely. I had been convinced that these people had nothing to conceal.

I had been convinced . . . But now?

If their story was true, if David had spent two weeks resting in their tents and had then left on the difficult journey to rejoin our lines, why should they resent discussing him? Why should they suddenly become hostile and suspicious? Why should the Sheikh end the conversation so abruptly? And if David had left them to rejoin our lines, why had nothing more been heard of him? Perhaps he had died on the way back. But his identity disc? He would have travelled in Bedouin clothes. Perhaps he had left his disc in their tents. Yet the one plain fact remained— the Sheikh and the others round the fire had got something they badly wanted to conceal, and that thing was connected with David's visit to their tents. Perhaps David had left them and was now living with some tribe further south. Perhaps they were afraid I would find some trace of him.

I do not know for how many hours I remained awake. And when at last I slept, it was only to dream of David. I was visiting him at Fanshawe. We had stayed late talking over the dinner table, and the room was full of smoke. We wandered out of the house, past the tall pillars, down the wide stone steps on to the lawn. In the moonlight David's blond hair looked white.

'Your hair's turned white,' I said.

He laughed.

'It's the terrible responsibility of being a landlord,' he said.

'Is it worse than being a troop leader?' I asked.

'Infinitely worse, because you can't shoot the Ministry of Agriculture,' he was saying when I awoke.

The rays of the rising sun slanting across the desert were glinting into the tent, and in the opening a small Bedouin child was peering in at me curiously. There was nothing unusual in that.

Suddenly I rubbed my forehead to make sure that I was no longer dreaming. Then I stared at the child again.

It was no dream. I could not see the child's face, for the sun was directly behind him. I could only see the shape of his head. His features were in darkness. But on his head were clustered thick curls, through which the sun was shining. And the curls were of the palest gold.

For a moment I gazed without moving at the blond head three yards away from me. Then slowly I pulled aside the rugs covering me and got up.

I had slept fully dressed, for it was bitterly cold. As I walked towards the tent opening, the child turned and ran away. When he turned I saw his face, and I could have laughed from excitement and joy. I had once seen a picture of David taken at Fanshawe when he was seven years old. There was no doubt whatsoever about it. The child skipping away from me across the camp was made in David's image.

The child was his son.

Taking care not to walk too quickly, I followed him across the open space between the lines of tents. The child soon realised that I was following him. He would stop and look round at me provocatively, and then skip away again. As he approached a tent on the outer edge of the camp a girl came out, saw us both, and cried something to the little boy which made him scamper into the tent and disappear. The girl remained at the entrance as if guarding him.

I went close to the tent and greeted her. She replied timidly. She was perhaps twenty-three years old, and very slender. Her face was unveiled. Even the faint-blue tattoo-marks on her chin and cheeks could not mar her beauty.

She stood there at the entrance, wild-eyed, breathing quickly, like a trapped animal.

'Is that your son?' I asked quietly.

'Yes.'

Her fear was so obvious now that it was painful to ask more. But I had to find out.

'Where is your man?'

'In the pastures.'

'Is he the father of that child?'

'No,' she said in a whisper. 'He is dead.'

I, too, spoke very softly now, in case the child was listening inside the tent.

'I knew the father of that child,' I said gently. 'He was my friend. He was an English officer, and his name was David.'

For an instant she swayed, and I was afraid she was going to faint. Then with a little sob she rushed into the tent. It was impossible to follow.

Thoughts were swirling round in my mind as I walked back to the Sheikh's tent on the other side of the camp, but in my heart was a fierce joy, for I knew now, certainly, that though David might be dead his son was alive.

When I arrived at his tent, the Sheikh was sitting round the fire with the same hairy faces I had seen the night before. He greeted me coldly and, I thought, suspiciously. However, the water-can was put on to boil and a few handfuls of tea were produced from his meagre store. Once again I determined to say nothing until we had eaten. Presently a cold platter of rice with rancid butter-oil in the centre was produced, and we ate in silence. Afterwards, I handed round cigarettes to those who smoked, and when the tea had been poured out I turned to the Sheikh.

'Last night,' I said, 'you told me that this morning you would tell me more about my friend David Holland. I am now most anxious to hear all you can tell me.'

'There is little more that we can remember,' the Sheikh said, looking straight into my eyes. 'He stayed with us two weeks. He was a good man and brave. We did what we could to help him. When he was well he left, giving me the note which he made me promise I would use if ever I needed it. I am sorry, we can tell you no more.'

'I am grieved that I must risk breaking your laws of hospitality by asking to be told more.'

'There is nothing else.'

'Yes, there is, ya Sheikh,' I replied, keeping my voice quiet and steady. 'O Sheikh, there is. May I tell you what it is when we are alone?'

The Sheikh muttered something, and the others left us.

'What is it then?' he asked, as soon as we were alone.

'David Holland's son is in your camp. I saw him this morning.'

His eyes never wavered as he stared at me.

'You are mistaken,' he said quietly.

'No.'

'Perhaps the child you saw was fair?' he asked.

'He was very fair, and he was about seven years old. I saw also his mother. She is a young girl living in the tent yonder.'

'You think that because her child is fair and we are all dark that the father must be of your race. That is not true. For centuries our tribes have lived near the coast. For centuries conquerors have passed across this land. For centuries sailors have sailed into our harbours. Our blood is mingled with the blood of the Phoenicians and men from the far north more fair than you. Therefore, sometimes it happens our children are born fair.'

'But you forget, ya Sheikh, that I have seen the child. I can see his father in him.'

'I knew the father of that child,' the Sheikh replied steadily. 'I knew him well. He died a few years ago, and the girl was married again.'

'Perhaps you knew the man who was the girl's husband. I know the man who was that child's father.'

'I tell you it is impossible.'

'How can you tell?' I said firmly. 'There are many girls in your tribe. Can you know all their weaknesses and all their loves?'

'No.'

'Then why should you be so certain? How can you know?'

His expression did not change as he spoke.

'Because the girl you saw this morning is my daughter,' he replied, rising to his feet.

I could feel the blood rushing to my face as I, too, got up.

'I am sorry,' I said. 'You have given me hospitality, and I have offended you. But, even if I had known what you have told me, I could have spoken little differently. I do not believe there is any shame attached. I only know that my friend was the father of the boy I have seen. I am only anxious to do all I can to help the child.'

'I have told you that you are mistaken,' the Sheikh said in his deep, strong voice. 'There is nothing more that I can say. You will find your guide and your camels waiting for you outside. Farewell.'

'Here is the money I came to pay,' I said, handing him the notes.

He would not take it from my hand, so I placed it on the rugs.

'I will leave now,' I said. 'I will leave, because I must think. But I will return.'

The Sheikh looked at me sternly.

'This time when you came we took you in as our guest. Next time it may be different.'

'I mean you and your people no harm,' I answered. 'I mean only to do good for the child. I do not believe you will harm me.'

'Farewell,' he said, and turned abruptly and left the tent.

I walked outside.

A few hundred yards away Ali was waiting with our camels. I suppose the Sheikh had given orders for them to be saddled when I had asked to speak with him alone. Until I had made a plan there was no point in remaining. Wearily, I mounted.

'Where are we going?' Ali asked in surprise. 'I thought you wanted to stay two nights in these wretched tents.'

'We are going back the way we came.'

'Were you uncomfortable last night, Colonel? Did the food make you sick? I can see you are not happy. What is wrong?'

Nothing,' I said shortly.

'Perhaps you hoped you would find a girl?' Ali went on irrepressibly. 'These people are no good for giving you girls. They are very strict. If you come with me to Tobruk, it will be different.'

'Ali,' I said firmly, 'if you speak again for another ten minutes I shan't give you a tip.'

Ali haunched up his shoulders and rode on in sulky silence—thank heavens—while I tried to make up my mind what to do.

What could I do?

I was convinced that the boy was David's child—first, because his features and fair hair were unmistakable; secondly, because I had realised even the previous night that Sheikh Salem and his friends had some secret they wished to conceal. But what proof had I got? None.

Our camels were now passing through the outlying herds of the tribe.

Suddenly I saw a girl running towards us. Long before I recognized her I knew instinctively who it was—Sheikh Salem's daughter. I halted my camel. In her right hand she was clutching what looked like a black stocking filled with sand. She ran up to me, threw the stocking into my lap; and then, without speaking or looking at me, she rushed away. I called after her, but she would not turn back.

From the feel of the stocking in my hands I knew that it contained papers. Carefully I untied the end and drew out a dozen or so pages. They were sheets torn from an army note-book and tied together with thin string.

Even before I had ripped off the string, the familiar writing was dancing before my eyes. Still holding the pages in my hand I made myself wait until we had reached a clear open stretch of sand, well out of sight of the camp, before dismounting to read what I already knew, from the few lines I had seen, to be David's diary.

This is what I read.

III

I am David Holland. I'm an Army Captain, and this is my diary.

I can't put the name of my regiment, in case the enemy ever

get this, though it's unlikely that anyone who can read it will ever get it. Anyhow, if anyone gets it who can read English, will they please send it to Rupert Holland, Fanshawe, Essex. He is my cousin, and the estate will pass to him if I don't get back. I would also like Bill Dawson to read it.

It's now nearly three months since I spoke to anyone who could understand English, and it's odd to be writing down these words when I'm so cut off from anything remotely English.

I feel awkward writing about myself like this, but there's a very good reason why I must tell my story—quite apart from the fact that I'd like Bill and the others, if they're still alive, to know what happened.

As soon as I left on that patrol on the afternoon of May 28th, I had a 'hunch', as Bill would call it, that something was going to go wrong. For a start, I could see that Bill thought I ought to let one of the younger troop leaders go. But it was an important moment for us to get information and, like a fool, I rather fancied myself. So I persuaded them to let me go, and then I made a mess of it.

A strong wind from the south was hissing across the desert, blowing up the sand. But the visibility was fairly good, and we soon picked out a formation of German Mark IV tanks moving north-east, which I reported over the air. There was no doubt that Rommel was putting all he had into the battle to get an immediate break-through.

I left my other two cars about six hundred yards apart in a position where they could report on the Mark IVs, and went on ahead myself to the west to see if I could discover anything more.

Then, to my horror, I saw a whole squadron of Mark IIIs coming up from the south-east. They were well fanned out, so I couldn't get back. My only hope was to go on west and make a loop round them. But they spotted me. I was bang in between the two squadrons, and I was pretty sure we'd had it.

I told Lucas, my driver, to go flat out, I said a little prayer and gave Deakin, my wireless-operator-cum-loader, a wink to cheer him up. I must record that he was calm and perfectly cheerful and efficient.

For a moment I thought we'd get away. Then a shell hit the driver's compartment.

Deakin and I jumped out and found Lucas had been killed outright. The Mark IIIs were approaching. The car was burning. Deakin and I ran for it.

As soon as the Mark IIIs saw us running, the leading tanks opened up with their light machine-guns. We'd still got a chance, because they were over six hundred yards away. Deakin was ahead of me when he fell. I fell down beside him and turned him over. The bullet had gone through his heart. He was dead. As I ran on, I caught sight of a small wadi to my right. I was sobbing for breath. I never thought I'd reach it. Then I felt a searing pain in my left arm and knew I'd been hit. At last I got there and flung myself over the edge and slithered down into the soft sand and lay there, too weak to move, waiting for them to come and take me.

But they never came. Perhaps they hadn't time to stop even one tank for the sake of taking one more prisoner. Perhaps they thought they'd hit me when I fell down beside Deakin. At any rate they never came.

As soon as I'd got my breath, I scrambled into some camel-grass and concealed myself as best I could. Then I examined my wound. At that moment it didn't look very serious, though it was painful. The bullet had ripped open the top of my forearm. The gash was bleeding, but it was only a surface wound. I bound it up with my field-surface dressing.

Somehow I had broken my watch. But I think it was only half an hour after I'd reached my wadi that the sandstorm reached its height. The south wind was now sweeping up the sand into a thick cloud which covered the desert like a cloak. I was panting for breath in the sultry heat while I made my plan.

Rommel's attack was moving north and east. We were withdrawing eastward. Therefore if I moved to the north or to the east I would risk running into enemy troops. My only chance was to go south and hope I would be able to skirt round to the east when I had got out of the battle area. Perhaps my choice was wrong. Perhaps it would have been better to make for the coast. Anyhow, once I'd made my decision, I stuck to it.

There was only one snag. Although I'd got a compass, I'd got no food and, far worse, no water. I knew that they'd have set fire to the armoured car. My only hope was to find a stray tin. One often did find odd tins of food or water in a battle area.

Though the storm was still raging when night came, I decided to begin plodding south. I tied a handkerchief over my mouth and nose and started walking. I hoped to find Deakin's body and the armoured car, but in the thick darkness of sand and night it was impossible. I held my compass in front of me and moved slowly south.

Towards dawn the storm lifted, and the sun shone clearly across the desert. I still forced myself to walk on, hoping to find food or water.

Presently I saw something black, lying in the sand ahead of me. As I got near I saw it was a jerry-can. I rushed up to it, but it was empty.

In the next clump of thick camel-grass I lay down and tried to sleep, but my arm was throbbing and I was terribly thirsty. The sun rose inexorably hotter and hotter. I covered my head and forced myself not to think of water and all cool things— mountains, streams, glaciers, water-meadows, ice clinking in misty glasses.

Though I dozed a little, I kept waking to find the sun still beating down on me.

At last it began to set.

When it was cooler, I began walking again. I think that by then I was so weak and parched I no longer feared capture. I stumbled through the first hours of that night until I decided to lie down for a short rest. And like a fool I fell asleep.

When I awoke, the sun was already hot. My wound was throbbing horribly, and my thirst was anguish. For a time I lay hopelessly in pain. But I knew that I must move to find water soon, because I was certain that I could not endure the scorching heat of another day.

Slowly I got up and began walking forward, step after step, across the burning desert stretching infinitely before me. No longer now did I look round for fear of being spotted by the enemy. Frantically, at every moment, I scanned the horizon for a speck that might reveal a human who could give me water—a human, friend or foe.

My arm was now stiff, and there was a fierce burning pain under my armpit. As the sun rose higher in the sky I began to panic. Wild thoughts shot through my mind. Perhaps I should go north rather than south? Perhaps I was heading for a vast empty space?

I tried to make myself think calmly, but I was sick and dizzy.

Then to the west I saw what in the shimmering heat looked like a hut on the horizon. I stumbled towards it. For a moment my fear left me. But as I approached I saw it was a derelict Crusader tank. There was still a chance it might have water. I reached it, only to find it was completely gutted. I crawled underneath the tank into the shade. Even lying there the sweat was pouring down me. After an hour or so I forced myself to move. It was about four in the afternoon, and my only hope was to spot or be spotted by some human being.

I walked on and on until I fell to the ground. I can hardly remember that night because I was already delirious. But I can remember waking up for a while and seeing the cursed sun shining once again, and seeing my arm red and swollen. And I can remember lying down again, because I was too weak to move. And I can remember preparing myself for death.

It was there, stretched in the sand like a dusty doll, that they found me.

I was by then unconscious. I have only vague memories of being carried lying on a litter, and then waking in a tent. During the hours of delirium which followed I can remember only one thing clearly—the face of a girl who seemed to be looking after me. It was a lovely face, and a kind face, and the eyes were dark and beautiful. But there was something wrong with it. Not until the second day did I realise what it was. On her chin and cheeks were faint tattoo-marks. I was revolted and turned away.

The girl must have thought that I was in pain, for she pressed a cold cloth on to my forehead, and when I did not move and she thought I was asleep, she began softly stroking my hand.

Gradually I realised where I was.

Some men from a Bedouin tribe had found me and taken

me to their tents. I was lying in the Sheikh's tent. The girl was his daughter. Her name was Mabrouka, which means 'blessed'.

I knew then only a few words of kitchen Arabic. I write 'then'. But in fact it was barely three months ago, though it seems three years, and what I have written now in a few lines took me then in my weakness several hours to discover.

My wound had turned septic, and although it was cool in the tent I was sweating badly. The Bedouin had medicine which they said would make me well. I comforted myself by thinking that before the discovery of penicillin not every man died who had a septic wound. For three days I could not move, and all that time it was Mabrouka who nursed me.

Often Sheikh Salem, Mabrouka's father, would order her away and sit himself by my side. But soon she would return, and he would leave unwillingly. I sensed that for all his kindness he was afraid. I thought then that he was afraid of the penalty for sheltering me. His tents would have been razed to the ground and his men perhaps hanged or shot. I know now the true reason. He had seen further than either of us . . .

One morning I told Salem that I felt strong enough to wander round the camp.

'Yes,' he said, 'you are healing now, praise to God.'

It was pleasant to walk about and to greet in the open such people as Salem's young brother Khalil, who had visited me in the tent. Yet I soon tired, and went back to lie down.

That evening it was Salem who brought me my food.

'Where is Mabrouka?' I asked, without thinking.

'Now you are better, it is not fitting that she should be near you,' he replied. 'She is young and unmarried. She has taken her things to the women in another tent. It would be well if you did not meet again.'

'But you don't understand,' I said.

'I do indeed,' he replied, and left.

Now this is going to be difficult to explain. But I must try to make it clear—for the sake of the future. At that moment I wasn't in love with Mabrouka. I didn't even want her. Yet I missed her greatly. There had been something soothing in her presence. We had laughed together over little things. And I knew she was fond of me.

Late one afternoon, a week later, I had taken a stroll for a short way outside the camp. This was now quite safe to do, for I was wearing Bedouin clothes, and there were no troops about. I was still weak, but it was a joy to be able to walk again.

The sun was close to the horizon when I wandered back towards the black tents. My thoughts were far away—I was thinking of the lawns of Fanshawe—when I saw Mabrouka in the distance. I called out to her. For an instant I was afraid she was going to run away, but she turned slowly towards me.

'Mabrouka,' I said, 'I am glad to see you. I wanted to thank you for all your kindness to me.'

'It was nothing.'

'It was much.'

'No.'

She would not look at me.

'Mabrouka,' I said, 'don't be frightened of me. I'll do nothing to harm you, I promise. But I enjoy being with you and seeing you. Please let us meet when we can.'

'It is impossible,' she said softly.

'Mabrouka, look at me. Do you think I would harm you? Look at me.'

'No!' she cried passionately. 'You are good. I know. But you do not understand.'

'Let us meet here when we can at this hour—if only for a few minutes.'

'Very well,' she said. 'But now leave me, please, leave me.'

After that we managed to meet almost every evening to exchange a few words before returning to the camp by different ways. And slowly I grew stronger. And though I put all thoughts of possessing her away from my conscious mind, I couldn't control my dreams, which began to be filled with the vision of her dark eyes and red lips and slender body.

Then every day I made myself walk further about the camp in order to strengthen my body for the long, difficult journey back to our lines. By now we had heard from other Bedouin that the English had been beaten back to Mersa Matruh—some said as far as Alexandria. I tried to get fit quickly, so that I could leave the camp as soon as possible, for it was becoming harder every day to be so close to her, and yet so far. I guessed now that she would yield to me. But I knew that the penalty for her might be death.

I began to walk in the opposite direction so that we should not meet. For three days I did not see her. On the fourth evening I took a far longer walk than usual. I had probably been over-straining myself to get well, for on the way back I felt so weak that I had to lie down. It was at least an hour after sunset when I approached the camp. The night was dark, but I had taken a back-bearing and I could see the little fires twinkling ahead.

Suddenly she rushed up to me out of the darkness.

'I thought you were captured. I thought you were killed,' she cried, and flung herself sobbing like a child into my arms.

Then I knew that I loved her, and I knew that she loved me. We were alone together. Nothing else mattered—neither the past nor the future. We were alone, and we loved each other. That was how it began.

Whoever reads this, whether it be Rupert or Bill, or any friend of mine, please try to understand that it is for the sake of Mabrouka's future that I have put this down. You will probably be reading this, if it ever reaches you, on a placid lawn in England. You'll think I was mad, or just infatuated for the moment. But it wasn't so. We loved each other—perhaps more intensely because only our hearts and bodies could join: there were too many barriers between our minds. And you must realise that I cared about the danger as much as she—if not more, because she loved blindly. But I knew that I must leave, for as the days changed into weeks my wound was healing and I was getting fit. I tried to live only for the present. But I was tortured by the future and by my unwilling deceit of Salem. I'd begun to like him very much.

I must also ask you as you read this to remember that we were living in the desert. How much lies behind that simple word! It means now to me openness of mind and heart. It means a feeling that one is very close to things our senses are still too blunt to see. And as the days passed by I felt that I was slowly changing. It was as if I'd been short-sighted and could now see to a wider range of vision. I can't explain it better than that. What's more, I felt a great sense of freedom.

Then two things happened. A Bedouin arrived at the camp with the news that Rommel had captured Alexandria and was advancing to Cairo. And two days later, to my dismay, Mabrouka confessed to me that she was pregnant. The first meant that there was no need for me to leave the black tents— or so I tried to persuade myself, for if Rommel was about to overrun all Egypt there was no point in travelling eastward. The second meant that in any case I could not leave before telling Sheikh Salem my decision about Mabrouka. For I knew only one thing could save her.

———◆◆◆◆———

In spite of Mabrouka's entreaties I tackled Salem that evening.

It was the most difficult think I'd ever done. I told him very slowly and gently that I loved his daughter and that she loved me. And then I told him that I wanted to marry her. His expression never changed.

'That is impossible,' he said. 'You are not of our people. You are not of our faith. It is completely impossible.'

'Does it matter that I am not of your people?'

'You will soon be leaving us. You will not return.'

'If I am spared, I will return.'

'You could not live with us.'

'I would take her away to live with my people.'

'Perhaps she would not go.'

'Ask her then.'

'Because you are not of our faith.'

'I went to our churches in England from habit,' I replied. 'I never believed in all they taught. But I believe that Christ was a great and good man. You believe he was a prophet. I believe there is something greater than we can see, which is in this desert and in the moon and in the sky and in our hearts. I call that God. I believe in that God called by whatever name.'

'It is impossible. Leave us as soon as you are strong enough to reach the coast. There you may find a boat which will take you back to your people.'

Then I knew that I must tell him.

'There is one reason why I must marry Mabrouka before I leave,' I said slowly.

He looked at me for a moment without moving.

Then he stood up so violently that I thought that he would try to kill me. He was still trembling when he spoke.

'We saved your life. This is how you have treated us.'

'I do not ask your forgiveness for me but for Mabrouka,' I said. 'For myself I can only ask this. Let me take her as my wife. When the time comes for me to leave I promise that if I get through alive I will return. But before I leave here I shall make a will, which as a soldier I can do, so that if I die Mabrouka and her child will be provided for.'

'What is your money to us? You have betrayed us. You have betrayed our friendship for you.'

'I am prepared to do all I can to make amends.'

'There is nothing you can do now but go. There is a man from our family who will take her now as his wife to avoid the shame.'

'No,' I said. 'No. Rather than that I would take her with me through all the dangers. I love her. And she loves me. You can kill us both, but you will not part us in that way.'

'That is all that can be done,' he was saying when Mabrouka ran into the tent and flung herself weeping at his feet.

'Do that,' she cried, 'and I will kill myself as certainly as I am your daughter. Do you not love me? Do you want to strike my happiness from my hands? I love him. I love him more than life. And if I cannot bear his child and own him as father I will kill myself.'

'Child, child, quiet, be quiet,' he said.

But her sobs threw more violent.

Then I saw his hand, in spite of himself, moving to stroke her head, and I knew that we had won.

So I took Mabrouka as my wife. And for the last three weeks I have known greater joy than I thought existed in this world.

I've been very happy—even though I have not been able to live completely in the present, for I've not been able to forget that the day would come when I must leave her.

<hr />

Three days ago a Bedouin who visited our camp told us that Rommel had been halted at El Alamein. The Eighth Army is still fighting. I am now perfectly fit. My wound has healed. I would never forgive myself if I remained here now. Ever since I heard that Rommel's forces had been held I have felt guilty for staying here so long.

Salem's brother Khalil will be my guide for the first stage of the journey. I can never repay these people what I owe them. They have saved my life. They have accepted me first as a friend and finally as one of them.

I have nothing I can give them even as a token of my gratefulness. Mabrouka has my signet ring and my broken wristwatch. My only other possession is my compass, and that I shall need. With the greatest difficulty I have managed to persuade Salem to accept a promissory note for £20. I would have liked to have made it far, far more.

'If ever we are in need, we shall use it,' Salem said.

--------◆◆◆◆--------

When I have finished writing this I shall tear out the pages and give them to Mabrouka to hide with her things—in case the camp is ever searched by the enemy.

I can't give details of my journey, but it will be hard, and I know there is a chance I won't get through. I am going in Bedouin clothes, so I can claim no protection as a soldier. I may be shot.

I leave to-morrow.

As I am writing these words, I can hear Mabrouka crying in the other tent. It is terrible to hear her. But if I stayed, pure guilt would ruin my happiness and perhaps destroy my love.

My conscience is clear. To-night I have made a will providing for Mabrouka—or for my child should Mabrouka die.

I'm not being morbid when I say that I doubt if I shall get through. I just have a hunch about it—as I did about the patrol.

So let's suppose I die and Mabrouka gets the money. Then what?

I would like my child to be brought up in England. Even if the war lasts another four years my child will still be young enough to adapt to the new surroundings without much difficulty.

But Mabrouka? How strange and frightening she would find England. And yet I hate to think of her parted from her child, because I suppose she would see me in that child.

I cannot find a solution.

But one thing I ask you—you, Rupert, or you, Bill, or any of my friends who are alive. Please do your best for the happiness of them both. Please look after them. Bill would do it better than you, Rupert, because, bless you, Bill is younger and less conventional. He may be able to discover a solution whereby she comes to England sometimes, or the child goes to see her. I'm lucky to have enough money for that to be possible.

And yet, even as I write these words, doubt sets in. Why do I want my child to be brought up in England? Because I love England and believe in all that England still has to give to the world. Because I like to think of my child walking across the lawns of Fanshawe. Because my heart is still in Fanshawe. But those are selfish reasons. Part of me now reasons differently. In spite of all the hardship and squalor of their lives, these people, I'm sure of it, are closer to happiness than we are—perhaps because they are at once closer to real and unreal things. Mightn't it be better to leave the child in this wide freedom? I don't know.

It is late, and I must get up early. I know that my final requests, if I don't get through, should be clear and definite. But still I don't know. So I shall leave the decision to you.

Sorry. But there it is. Things may be changed by the time you get this. You may see it clearer than I do. You must decide.

Mabrouka is still crying. There are only a few hours left now. I must go to her and try to make each minute last a year.

I may get through. Perhaps one day I will read these papers in peace and security. I doubt it.

I'm not sorry for myself, but for Mabrouka. She will never be able to understand why I must leave her. I pray that in time she will forget the grief of our parting and remember only our happiness together.

So far as I'm concerned, I reckon I'm lucky. I wasn't brilliant.

I was conventional. I'd never have got outside my rut if I hadn't been jolted out of it.

I've known much happiness. I've left, so I hope, a part of me —for what that's worth—behind in the world.

My conscience is clear. I leave in peace.

DAVID HOLLAND.

IV

I read David's diary once again. Then I lit my pipe and lay on my back in the sand, thinking.

I had thought that I knew David. But the person who emerged from the diary was almost a stranger to me. Even its style surprised me—though I recalled that he had never written me a letter. I supposed that his narrow escape from death and his three months in the Bedouin tents had changed him. That and his love for Mabrouka. I don't think he had ever been in love before.

Yet, though he had changed, the essential remained. The 'directness' was still there. There was no deflection in his response to all that had happened. There was the same quixotic approach to life. Also his trust in me had not altered. They were his legacy to me—those words asking me to look after Mabrouka and his child. He had left the final decision to me, and I must now make it, for I was convinced for the first time that David was dead. Neither he nor Khalil had survived the journey.

I had refused to believe that David had been killed because I had such a strong hunch that he was alive. And in a way my hunch had been right, for David still lived—in his son.

I thought next about Salem and his daughter and his grandson. Why, when I first spoke of David, did Salem's attitude change to supicion? David had taken Mabrouka as his wife. There could be no shame. Why, then, had he become hostile? It could only be because he was afraid that I would take the child away from them.

Why, then, had Mabrouka given me the diary?

Either from loyalty to David or because she wanted me to know that she and her child had a legacy. Which?

I knew enough law to realise that it was doubtful whether

David's title would pass to his son. (It was an amusing thought that the half-naked little Bedouin I'd seen hopping across the camp might be a Baronet.) But one thing was certain—David had made a soldier's will that night. If that will was still in existence it would be valid. Mabrouka would inherit what he had left her. David had suggested it was sufficient not only to pay for his child's education in England, but also for her to live in England or to travel to and fro.

Before I returned to their camp I was determined to try to find the answer to four questions.

First, did Sheikh Salem want his daughter or her son to go to England? The answer was certainly, no. Secondly, did Mabrouka want to accompany her son to England? I doubted it. Thirdly, did she want him to go? I was uncertain. Lastly, and most important, for the ultimate decision was mine, did I want David's son—I did not even know his name—to be brought up in England? Yes. Certainly, yes.

I remembered David's words: 'Even if the war lasts another four years my child will still be young enough to adapt.' The boy was still easily young enough. David had said that he wanted his child taken to England, and then had been doubtful —probably because he had been thinking of Mabrouka. The difficulty could be solved somehow. The important thing was to get hold of the will and then remove the child into civilised surroundings.

My mind was made up. I still, however, did not know how I would be received when I returned to Salem's camp. I decided to write Baring a short note in case there was trouble.

I shouted to Ali, who was lying asleep five hundred yards away. He came up to me sulkily.

'Ali,' I said, 'it's now mid-day. I'm walking back to the camp. You have food and water and bedding. I am leaving you here. You will not move from this spot. If I have not returned by mid-day to-morrow, you will go straight back to El Adem and give this note to Khawage Baring. Do you understand?'

'But why should I not come with you to the camp?'

'Because I must go alone.'

I repeated my orders and left him more confused and sulky than ever.

When I reached the camp I walked straight to Salem's tent. The loud barking of the dogs had forewarned him of a visitor and he was standing outside, watching me approach without surprise. He replied to my greeting, but did not invite me into his tent.

'I have come alone, and I want to speak with you alone,' I said.

'You can speak. There is no one to hear us.'

'I have read the diary of my friend David. I know that he married your daughter. I know that the child I saw was his son. I know that you have got the will he made giving money to your daughter before he started on his journey with your brother. I want to do what is best for all of you. I come as a friend, not as an enemy.'

'You wish to do what is best for all of us?'

'Yes.'

'Then you will go now and forget you ever came here.'

'You will not even listen to what I have to say?'

He looked at me in silence. Then he turned round towards the tent.

'*Tfaddol*,' he said. 'Enter.'

We sat down alone beside the fire.

'May I ask you a question which may hurt you?' I began.

'Speak.'

'Your brother never returned?'

'No.'

'What do you think happened?'

He looked out dreamily across the desert.

'How can we tell?' he said. 'It was a long journey. Perhaps they were shot. Perhaps they died of thirst. Who can tell save God?'

'It was noble of your brother to go with him.'

'He was our friend.'

'Then why would you not speak of him?'

'Because we knew you would want to take the child Daoud away from us. That we cannot accept. The child belongs to Mabrouka. He is all that is dearest to her in the world.'

'Could she not come too?'

'And leave her own people and the man who is now her husband and go to live in a strange land? No. Never.'

'The child could come back to her sometimes.'

'If he left us now the boy Daoud would belong to your people. He would wear your clothes and take on the clothes of your mind and your belief. He could not return to us.'

'Why not? Are we so far apart?'

'As far as the stars from the sand.'

In the silence after his words I offered him a cigarette, but as usual he refused.

'May I see David's will?' I asked.

'Certainly. But you may not keep it.'

He rose and walked into the other half of the tent. Through the curtain of black cloth dividing us I could hear the sound of a box being unlocked and opened. He returned with a page torn from an army notebook. It was neatly folded as the promissory note for twenty pounds had been. I opened it and read it carefully.

There was no hitch, no ambiguity.

David had left Mabrouka, or his child, should Mabrouka die in childbirth, ten thousand pounds.

I handed the paper back to Salem.

'The other page you had like this,' I said, 'brought you twenty pounds. If I sent this to London, it will bring Mabrouka ten thousand.'

He was silent.

'Do you realise what that could mean for Daoud, your grandson? What future is there for him here? He will lead the same life day after day in this desert until he dies. But with this money he could go to England as his father intended. He could go to school and to a university. And he would be free to take up whatever profession he chose. The whole world would lie before him.'

'Would he be happier and better than if he stayed here?'

'Certainly.'

'You from the West are very sure that you have much to offer us,' the Sheikh said quietly. 'You think we are ignorant and simple. You have cleverness and skill and wealth. But where has it brought you? Are you any closer to happiness or to God than we? Have you any more freedom? You say the world would lie at his feet. We say that the world is a poison which poisons the soul of man gradually.'

I can't remember what I said in reply, nor all the various phases of our argument. But at last I realised that I was making no progress against the mound of his prejudice. I played my next card.

'The money belongs by law to Mabrouka,' I said. 'If she wishes to accept it, would you object? If she wishes to send Daoud to England, would you try to prevent it?'

'It is her money and her child. I would not interfere.'

'May I see Mabrouka?'

'I will bring her to you.'

A few minutes later Salem returned, and Mabrouka followed him shyly into the tent.

Bedouin girls age quickly. But even now as I watched Mabrouka across the fire I could understand why David loved her. Her limbs and body were still wonderfully slender, and her broad forehead and large brown eyes and delicate lips made her look at once innocent and appealing. There was something very sweet and graceful about her as she sat beside her father, glancing at me timidly.

I explained to her that David had asked me in his diary to help her and her son. I told her that he had left her a large sum of money. I begged her to let me make arrangements for Daoud at least to go to England.

'If you do not wish to come,' I said, 'we must arrange for you to meet Daoud whenever possible.'

Then once again I explained to Mabrouka all the advantages of sending him to England. I told her that David had asked me to advise her and that I advised she should let her son go. When I had finished she turned to her father. I could see that the mention of David's name had moved her.

'I know little of his people or his country,' she said. 'I know only what he told me when he was with me. I cannot say yes or no. You, father, must decide.'

Even as she spoke, the tears filled her eyes.

'I, too, know little, my child,' her father said softly.

'You must decide,' she repeated.

Suddenly she began sobbing and ran out of the tent.

Salem threw some camel-grass on to the fire and watched the flames leap up before he spoke.

'When you came I did not trust you,' he said. 'I trust you now. I know you are not thinking of your own benefit. You must believe that I am not thinking of mine. I want to think over what you have said. You have told me you must return north to-morrow. It is now an hour before sunset. If you will return here soon after the sun has set I will let you know my decision.'

'Where can I find Daoud? I would like to be with him,' I said.

'He is out with the flocks. I will show you where you can find him. But I must tell you that he believes Mabrouka's second husband is his father. It is better so. You must promise me you will not speak to him of your friend.'

'I promise.'

The Sheikh showed me where the flocks were cropping, and I left him.

———◀•••▶———

As I wondered slowly from the camp I supposed that Salem was trying to understand what I had said, to perceive the reasons for my arguments, to discover what philosophy lay behind them. And I determined that I, too, must try to appreciate the background of his attitude.

The nomad's way of life demands toughness of mind and body. To glean existence from the barren desert, to take advantage of the scanty grazing where rains have fallen, requires as much freedom of movement as a ship on the seas, and as much decision.

The Bedouin in their sea of sand have remained aloof from the invasions by force and by thought which have surged across the world since the days of Mohammed. Sometimes they have become involved and perished. But the survivors have withdrawn into the remoteness of the desert and preserved intact their way of life. And therein lies the clue.

The Galilean peasants were protected from disturbance by the power of the Roman empire. Their society was simple and gracious, fortunately ignorant of the complicated power-mechanism which protected it. In their ignorance of the outside world, in their intelligence and concern with God, the Galileans resembled the Bedouin. They sprang from the same stock.

It is no coincidence that two great religions came from the stillness and simplicity of the desert. It is no coincidence that they found roots amongst people protected from the turmoils of the world, the one by the power of an empire, the other by an ocean of sand. And perhaps, I thought to myself, in as much as they have remained largely thus protected—even though their ocean is no longer impassable—perhaps the Bedouin have preserved their religion more purely. Then, from the back of my mind came a phrase which I remembered from Gibbon, of all people: 'The slaves of domestic tyranny may vainly exult in their national independence. But the Arab is personally free.'

I found Daoud looking after a dozen goats. He was very shy when I went up to him, so I sat down and began playing with sticks in the sand, and presently he joined me. He had Mabrouka's forehead and lips, but his nose and firm chin and very blue eyes were David's. Sometimes the resemblance between the two was so great that I could imagine it was David dressed up as a Bedouin child. There was the same look of impudence, the same smile, the same vitality. He was radiant with health. And as we began playing our game with sticks I noticed that he was alert and intelligent. I was entranced by him, and he seemed to like me.

There was so much that I longed to say to him. 'How would you like to go to England?' I wanted to say. 'How would you like me to be your guardian?' All kinds of stupid words came into my mind. But we talked about his goats and the camels, and soon it was time for him to drive back his little flock.

I had noticed that he was fascinated by my cigarette lighter, and when we reached the camp I gave it to him. He played with it for a moment and then handed it back to me.

'No,' I said. 'It's a present.'

His eyes opened wide as I handed it to him.

'For me?' he asked.

48

'Yes. To keep.'

'Thank you, thank you,' he said, suddenly becoming shy again. Then he turned away and drove his goats towards his mother's tent, clutching the lighter in his hand.

The sun had set and a bitterly cold wind was blowing as I walked towards Salem's tent. He was alone.

'Welcome,' he said. 'Sit down there close to the fire.'

Though he had drawn his robe tight round him, he was shivering.

'Food is ready,' he said. 'That will warm us.'

We did not speak until we had eaten and were sipping tea.

'We are grateful to you, Mabrouka and I,' he said in his clear, deep voice. 'You have come a long way to see us.'

'I am glad I came.'

'You are now our friend. Yet we cannot understand you, or you us.'

'If Daoud came to England, yet returned here when possible, he could understand us both.'

'If he had known wealth and comfort, would he understand the way we live? If he had been taught your ideas day after day, would he understand ours? No. He would despise us. He would see that our life was bare. He would not see what lies behind it. For only living here as we do can a man perceive what is hidden.'

'Did David despise you?'

'Does not your guide Ali despise us?'

'Aren't you willing to take the risk?'

'It is not my happiness which is at stake.'

'How can you tell what happiness and freedom of mind Daoud might find with us?'

'I cannot be sure. Whatever my decision I should always fear I was mistaken.'

'Then you have not decided?'

Salem produced the neatly-folded page from the army note-book and looked at it.

'I should always doubt my decision if I did not believe in God,' he said. 'But I know that if the child stays here he will be close to God.'

Then with a gesture so slow and unhurried that I did not at first see what he was about to do, he took the page and dropped it into the middle of the fire. Instinctively I stretched forward to save it, but he grasped my arm, and before I could shake myself free the page was burnt.

'Do you realise what you've done?' I cried. 'You've destroyed his chance of freedom.'

He turned his face away from me and moved towards the opening of the tent.

The wind which had swept across a thousand miles of desert was blowing hard against us. For a while he stayed still with the wind lashing round him.

'There is our freedom,' he said.

As I left their camp soon after dawn the next morning to rejoin Ali, I saw Daoud walking beside his goats in the rising sun.

The 1946 Ms

To-day is May 15th, 1946, the second anniversary of Pointer's dictatorship. I am sitting in the kitchen of a little cottage in Sussex, and at this moment I can see three birds pecking away at the seed I've put on the garden table outside this room. They will give me warning of any visitor.

I have got a full block of writing paper, and as I finish each page I shall place it in the airtight steel box I've fitted under the flagstones in this kitchen, so that even if they come for me before I've finished, at least part of my story will be safe. I don't think they will find the hiding place. I've left some other papers in the recess behind the mantelpiece where they are certain to look in order to make them think they've found all that I've hidden. It's a gamble, of course. They may take up every flagstone. Perhaps no one will ever take up that flagstone, and this page will remain in its steel box long after mankind has played out its sad history. So be it. But I am writing this to please myself, to keep my mind from thinking of the future, and I am writing this as a last confession. Also, if I can complete my story I shall feel relieved of my burden of responsibility to posterity. How pompous that sounds! And really it is rather stupid of me to feel that way. I am no historian, and as a writer I'm in the beginner's class. There must be many other people who are writing secret accounts of these last three years. I've tried to persuade myself that I needn't write this; but I am in rather a unique position, because I am the only person (apart from two of his close supporters whose accounts are certain to be biased) who saw the very beginning of Pointer's struggle to power. I was present that night after the battle of Midan when he decided to become Dictator of Britain. I saw the fatal germ sown in his mind. If only I had known then . . .

But I must tell my story in correct sequence.

I was born in a house in Rutland Gate on June 3rd, 1916, during an air raid on London. Four days later my mother was notified that my father had been killed fighting in France. His older partner had been running his firm in the City, which had prospered during the first year of the war, so my mother was left with enough money to send me to a good school and later to Cambridge, where I read Law, had a grand time, and made several good friends. I was called to the Bar early in 1938.

After the Munich Conference I was afraid that war was inevitable so I signed up with the Inns of Court Regiment as a trooper. I had loathed parades and camp in my school O.T.C., and had resigned before taking Certificate A. I dreaded the war, and I dreaded being called up.

I was living with my mother in the old family house in Rutland Gate. A few months after father's death, mother had begun writing a novel to distract her mind from her misery and loneliness. The novel was a strange mixture of bitterness and sentimentality. Within three months *Walking Alone* had sold 40,000 copies and mother had set out on her triumphant literary career. The success of her novels brought mother into a new world. She was attractive and fashionable. She could afford to entertain well, and soon her drawing-room in Rutland Gate could contain the pick of London's social lions.

Two days after war was declared I was called up. For the next six months I was a trooper in the R.A.C. O.C.T.U. Life was tough and healthy. Off parade and sometimes on parade we had great fun. The first day on parade we appeared in the tunics and forage caps which had been hastily issued to us in London. Neither the tunics nor the forage caps fitted us, and we had forgotten how to hold a rifle. We looked like the refugees from General Franco's army. The last day on parade, when the inspecting General congratulated us on our turn-out, we felt proud and happy. As I stood rigidly to attention I suddenly remembered Richard Wright, the young lawyer in a soft black suit and hat. I had changed my skin.

I joined a yeomanry regiment which was training in the North of England. I knew two of the officers before I joined; but for the first four months I felt shy and uncomfortable. Gradually I came to be friends with the men in my troop and later with my fellow officers. It was not until after our first battle that I realised just what splendid officers and men they were. There can be no happier command than that of a troop leader; his responsibility is definite. Eighteen men and three tanks are in his keeping; he is responsible to his senior officer for the efficiency and welfare of these men; they are his children, they belong to him and to no one else.

———◆◆◆◆◆———

Just now the birds flew away from the bird table. But it was only a hawk swooping past. The interruption has made me think about what I have written so far. I am afraid it is plain, and not much to the point, but I thought that I should write some report of my life before the Dictatorship because I want to show that I am and always have been sane and normal. A report by a lunatic is properly disregarded; history written by a hysterical neurotic is suspect. Therefore I must prove that I was sane and am still sane. Yet even as a plain report of my early life I realise I must have left out some quite important facts. However, what I have written will at least show that I was no infant prodigy, no bespectacled genius, no half-wit concealed in the west-wing of a manor, no Bloomsbury exotic.

———◆◆◆◆◆———

It was after the famous battle of Midan that I first met General Pointer. His career before the war had not been particularly remarkable. As a cadet at the R.M.C., Sandhurst, in 1919, he won the Sword of Honour. He was commissioned in 1920 and joined the Pultan Lancers, then stationed in India. In 1926 he was mentioned in dispatches for gallantry on the North West Frontier. In 1930 he went to the Staff College where, I've been told, he did not do well. Shortly before the war he was given command of the 'Beech' Armoured Brigade, then unformed and untrained. In one year he had created the finest armoured brigade in the country. His energy was great, and he managed to inspire his officers and men with loyalty and devotion to himself. His Brigade sign was a pointer and his men became known as 'Pointer's Boys' long before they left for France. Pointer's superior officers laughed at his brigade sign and at his enthusiasm, but they recognised that he was a good soldier, and they stopped laughing after his superb performance in France. In that grim battle he lost two-thirds of his men, but he saved the corps he was protecting, and he won glory for his men and a fine reputation for himself. On his return from France he was awarded a D.S.O. and given the command of an armoured division.

When his division joined us two weeks before the battle of Midan it already was known to be highly trained and competent.

Half an hour before first light on the day of that famous battle, the tanks of our regiment moved out of close leaguer. We were to advance at 06.30 hours. Every detail had been arranged; we sat in our tanks and watched the minute hands on our synchronised watches creep slowly towards the half-past mark as the dawn came softly across the hills and the tank engines spluttered in the cold, still air. At last at a signal from our Colonel the tanks surged forwards, leaving long clouds of dust in their wake. Our division was to attack the left flank, while Pointer's division pinned down the enemy's main armoured concentration in the centre.

Army manœuvres and battles are always made to seem simple and orderly after they have finished. When the turmoil of the battle has subsided, the commanding officers taking part, intelligence officers, press reporters and historians all conspire to produce a lucid account to please the War Office and posterity. But during the battle chaos reigns. From Hannibal to Pointer no General has been able to see or know how clearly all that was occurring on the field of battle. The chaos of the battle of Midan has been tidied up to make a clear-cut story in which Pointer's performance appears as the logical result of the Commander-in-Chief's plan. But we who were there know differently.

Our regiment made contact with the new German panzer division on the Midan plain early in the morning. The ground was flat with no hull down positions for us or Jerry, and the great escarpment to the south gave us little room in which to manœuvre. It was a battle tank for tank, in which, from the start, we were outnumbered and outranged by the new German gun. Those were the days before the appearance of the British and American heavy tanks which were perhaps responsible for our victory in the battle of Europe.

By mid-day my regiment had beaten the first wave of fifty German tanks, but we had lost forty tanks ourselves, and my tank and John May's were the only two tanks still firing in my squadron. I was running out of ammunition and the Jerries were still advancing. It couldn't be long now. I knew they'd got my range because the inside fittings of the tank were banging in on us from the force of the impact of German armour-piercing shells on the steel plates of our tank outside. The whole tank shook each time a shell hit us. I handed my flask round to my crew.

Suddenly a great explosion burst in my ears. The tank rocked, and we heard the ominous clatter of metal we knew so well. Our track had been shot away. Then over the wireless, which had gone dead for a while, I heard Dick, my squadron leader's voice, saying 'Withdraw now, withdraw.' But we couldn't move because our track had been shot away. Then the tank shuddered again as another shell hit us. I heard a small cry. I peered down but it was difficult to see at first because the tank was full of smoke. The shell had hit the gun mounting and disabled the gun. My wireless operator had been hit. A nasty looking splinter had pierced his forearm The rest of us were unhurt. I bound a bandage tight above his elbow joint to prevent bleeding, then I said down the Tannoy intercommunication: 'I'm going to count up to three and when I say "three" we bale out.' I heard my voice counting 'one, two, three,' and in a moment we were all sheltering behind the tank from the storm of machine-gun bullets. But another wave of German tanks was slowly advancing towards us. Presently they must get us. Bill's arm had started to bleed again. I handed Ken, my driver, some maps and security documents to destroy. As I tightened the bandage I looked round for any possible means of escape. The ground was quite flat. I looked again at the enemy and was amazed to see their tanks had halted. Then I saw why. To the east a great mass of tanks were charging down on the enemy in arrowhead formation. They were advancing straight into the wind, and vast clouds of dust churned up by their tracks made it impossible to count their numbers or to identify their units; the leading tank alone could be seen clearly as it surged towards the enemy's thickest concentration of tanks. It was a Crusader tank with a long red pennant streaming from its wireless aerial which had not been lowered. The tank made a conspicuous target for the German gunners; shells were bursting all round it. I found myself holding my breath in dread of the moment when it must certainly be hit. The tank streamed onwards, leading the great wedge of tanks behind it. I felt, somehow, as if that leading tank was drawing the wedge forward by its volition alone, and that if the leading tank were hit the whole wedge would stop. I could see another spot of red above the turret now as the tank approached. Then I recognised the divisional sign. It was Pointer's Division. The spot of red above the turret was Pointer's cap. The General was leading his division into action against the enemy. His tanks never stopped to fire though now they were within 600 yards of the enemy. At 500 yards, as if by command, they opened fire simultaneously. They swept onwards, fire spitting from every gun. The nearest German tanks tried to wheel round and so offered a broadside target; those further back hesitated then also wheeled round, but our tanks were surging down on them, and it was too late; our tanks were now among them dealing out death from their quick-traversing turrets. I found myself cheering from excitement.

Pointer never lost control of his tanks for a moment. He led them straight through the German tank positions, then wheeled west and rallied them towards the setting sun. He wanted to gather his tank force before darkness fell. His support group were advancing to hold the battlefield his tanks had won. His tanks were approaching us and we waved and cheered at them. He must have seen us because he altered his course and made straight towards us. His tank stopped by my derelict tank. 'Jump on, all of you.' 'Thank you, sir,' was all I could think of saying. We scrambled on the back, and his tank surged away towards the convenient site he had chosen for his leaguer. Presently he turned round to me and said, 'Was yours the lone tank firing on my left?'

'Yes, sir.'

'Good show. Get your crew fixed up in B echelon and then join me for some food.'

'Thank you, sir.' I'd have died gladly for him at that moment.

After we had arrived in leaguer, I got Bill comfortably ensconced in an ambulance. Ken and Hutch, my driver and gunner, found a cushy berth and good food at the back of a three-tonner. We had lost our tank and all our kit. We did not know how many of our friends might not be dead or wounded, but a wave of happiness filled our minds as we realised that we were for the present at least alive and safe.

Pointer had been criticised for his insistence on maximum comfort during a campaign, so I knew I would get a good feed. All the same, I was surprised that he had had a mess-tent erected in close leaguer. I walked in a bit shyly I admit, because I thought that perhaps Pointer might not be there, and I'd have to explain what I was doing walking into the Divisional Officers' Mess. The first thing I saw was a wooden trestle table covered with glasses and all kinds of bottles. Then Pointer noticed me.

'Ah, here's our lone tank fighter. Come in. Whiskey-soda? Wade, bring this officer a whiskey-soda. Don't even know your name.'

'Wright, sir.' He turned to his B.G.S.

'Tony, this is Mr. Wright. He carried on a lone action by himself on our left flank this afternoon. Look after him, will you, and see he is driven back to-morrow to what's left of his regiment?' He turned away to read some reports which had just come in. Almost every word that was spoken that evening is clearly printed in my mind, partly, I suppose, because of my excitement at meeting him, partly because my memory is like that: I forget a name as soon as I hear it, but I can always remember a conversation almost word for word. The B.G.S. told us that the reserve division was pursuing the withdrawing enemy forces.

As I sipped my whiskey-soda I could stare at Pointer as much as I liked. He was sitting at the head of the long trestle table which it seemed served both as dining and conference table, for the staff now began to sit down; and maps, reports and bottles were passed round. Pointer's thick fair hair was beginning to turn grey at the temples; but with his well-trimmed moustache and piercing blue eyes, he looked far younger than several of his staff. His broad shoulders, narrow waist and straight back made him look the perfect General of cheap fiction. Then as I watched him while he read the incoming reports, I realised with a shock that there was something wrong about him. It was like admiring a perfect reproduction of the Mona Lisa, and suddenly discovering a wart on the nose. But with Pointer the flaw was not obvious. There he sat with his red tabs and fresh complexion, the ideal fiction General; but I was watching his hands. They were slender like a woman's hands, the fingers were long and shapely; his nails were perfectly manicured and an unnatural pearly-pink in colour. The fingers of his right hand were softly caressing the back of his left hand in a way which made me shudder. There was something horrible and feline about it. I looked at his hair again. The long wavy strands were carefully brushed back with a neat parting. He must have combed his hair after the battle. In the Spartan tradition perhaps, but there was nothing about him to suggest clean, hard living and loving. He was too sleek and feline. That was it. He didn't look the perfect fiction General. He just missed it. He looked like a successful ham-actor playing the part of a General. At that moment he looked up quickly, saw me staring at him, and smiled, looking right into my eyes. His smile was kindly and I smiled back. His eyes were piercing into me, holding my gaze steadily. It was with an effort of will that I lowered my gaze.

I decided that my imagination had tricked me.

'Another whiskey-soda for Mr. Wright, Wade.'

'Thank you, sir,' I said.

The orderlies began to lay the white tin plates for dinner. I sat down two places away from him, in obedience to a wave of his hand. I was glad when we began to eat because I was very hungry. The Divisional Intelligence Officer, who sat next to me, kept asking me questions about the day's battle, so that it was not until the end of the meal, when port was being passed round and when most of the staff and his A.D.C. had left, that I managed to hear what Pointer was saying. A signal had just been handed to him. 'To-morrow we go into Corps reserve,' he said.

'Gentlemen, I would like to thank you for your co-operation.' He raised his glass with a graceful gesture and drank.

Instantly Tony sprang up. 'To the General.' We rose to our feet and drained our glasses. I watched Pointer. He was flushed with excitement and wine. He stood up.

'Let us drink to final victory,' he said. As we drank he smiled at me again. I think we had all reached that pitch of nervous exhaustion when you cease to feel tired any more. Further toasts were drunk in Pointer's honour. There were only four of his cronies left now, so I rose from the table to leave, thinking they would want to be alone, but Pointer signed to me to sit down again. Perhaps they thought I didn't count.

'Yes, Jack, it was a great charge you led,' Tony said. 'Our children will read all about it in the history books.'

Pointer hesitated, drained his glass, and then said deliberately, 'I wonder if history books will say I should have continued the advance?'

'What? Batted straight on all through the night?' said Tony. 'Exactly.'

'Your reserves would never have got through to you, your tank crews had been fighting all day, your regiments were disorganised. It would have been disastrous.'

'I think so, but will G.H.Q.?'

'What do you mean, Jack? G.H.Q. are delighted with you.'

'They are delighted now because at noon to-day, before I led in my attack, they expected defeat. To-night they are pleased by contrast. Yet by to-morrow they will have grown used to the victory and will ask why I didn't follow it up.'

'But Gerald's division are chasing them hard.'

'Yes. But it took time to bring them up out of reserve. Precious minutes were wasted.'

'You obeyed orders.'

'To-day I gave orders to myself. You know that as well as I do. I reported that I could advance and I was told to advance. I reported that I was rallying to move into leaguer and I was told to rally and to move into this leaguer, while Gerald chased them.'

I felt embarrassed by this conversation between very senior officers, but I didn't see how I could leave without drawing Pointer's attention to my presence.

'Anyhow, why should you care what H.Q. thinks?'

'Tony, you're a splendid staff officer, but you don't see the big picture.'

Tony was about to reply but noticed my presence and checked himself. He drank deeply, then he said in a rather thick voice: 'Well, Jack, I know one thing. Every man in this division, who saw you lead that attack, will for ever give you complete loyalty.' He turned round to me, 'That's true, isn't it?'

'Indeed it is, sir,' I said, looking at Pointer, whose eyes seemed to be glittering strangely in the light of the oil lamps. I felt this was the moment for me to leave, so I rose to my feet.

'Sit down a moment,' said Pointer. 'Do you mean what you said? That those men would give me complete loyalty?'

'Yes, sir,' I said. 'They'd follow you now wherever you went.'

'Of course they would,' Tony said thickly, 'they'd follow you anywhere. How does the saying go? "In sickness, in health, in life or in death or something, in war and in peace." No, that's wrong. They wouldn't follow you in peace. By God, but I think they would even then. By God, but I bet they would follow you even in peace time. Yes, if the thing was done the right way, and it COULD be done the right way. Can't you see General Pointer's triumphal march down the Mall? That would make the wretched politicians sit up. Then we could get something done in England. Jack, that's what you must be, you must be . . .'

'Tony,' Pointer said commandingly. He had stood up, and was breathing quickly. 'We've all had enough to drink tonight. We've got a hard day in front of us. Tony, go round to the A.C.V., find out what's doing, then come back and report to me in my tent.' I thought Pointer was going to leave but he sat down again. Tony walked out quickly.

————◆◆◆◆————

I thanked Pointer for my food and drink, said good night and walked out into the cold night air. I had meant to borrow some blankets earlier in the evening, and now, as I walked round looking for some hollow to shelter in from the bitter wind, I cursed myself for having forgotten. Luckily I had my British Warm with me, yet it would still mean a cold night. I could have woken up a lorry crew but I had not the heart to spoil their sleep because of my stupidity. The wind seemed to be increasing in intensity, and after wandering round for some time, I grew so tired that I lay down by the nearest bivouac which protected me from the wind. I wrapped my coat round me, dug my feet into the sand and prepared for a rough night. Then I heard a voice from inside the bivouac say: 'What did the politicians do after the last war? Sweet nothing. They just piddled round in small circles.' It was Tony's voice. Then another voice began speaking coldly and without emphasis. At first I couldn't think who might be speaking. Then I realised that it was the Intelligence Officer, who had asked me so many questions during dinner.

'May I speak now, sir? Reproduction of speech by wireless and gramophone has changed politics. To-day it is the orator who appeals to the lowest common instinct in his audience who triumphs. The popular press might unseat the orator, but in a democracy it is divided. Moreover, the press has so perverted prose and logic that in print only a flashy appeal to cheap sentiment can affect the multitude. The demagogue persuades the people to elect him. He gains power. But what is that power? It is conditional upon the constant approval of the masses over a period of time. Imagine our successful demagogue to have only a little honesty and for once to intend some really beneficial measure for the government of the masses. The medicine which does you good frequently tastes bad. If his beneficial measure offends the taste of the press and platform duped masses, then, if he insists on that measure, must he lose power? In a democracy, yes, he must. And the next demagogue with a pleasing syrup will take his place, although in the long run that syrup may harm the masses. But they like the taste of the pleasing syrup so—supposing that syrup is pacifism and disarmament—England goes down the drain.'

'What we need is men of action in power,' said Tony.

'Yes, sir, of course. But what happened to our men of action after the last war? They counted themselves lucky to get jobs as shop-walkers. And who had the administrative power? The safely entrenched Civil Servants, the clever boys in reserved occupations, the boys who never fired a bullet in anger, the sods who sat comfortably in Whitehall writing neat memoranda on their particular topics, while men of ideals, men of guts, got killed in the mud. And in between the two wars the Civil Servants wielded a more enduring power than our demagogues. When Democrat Number One's government fell and Democrat Number Two took over, our Civil Servants didn't change. Governments may rise and fall, but Civil Servants alone endure in all their pompous permanency. Safety first is their motto. Appeasement their pastime, procedure their pet. They would no nothing in a great matter rather than perform a little wrong. The accumulated power of the black-coated brigade is enormous. Correct, smug little men in Whitehall, who have never voyaged beyond Brighton, cheap fiction, tea-time music and a watery catholicism control the lives of millions of men and women in distant lands.'

Tony's voice broke in. 'I think you're too harsh on the red tape brigade. After all they are only the machine of government. Behind them are forces who really rule—irresponsible Money, Careerist politicians.'

The Intelligence Officer replied 'Very well, include them too. I am not denouncing a class but a whole regime. You know the thing I mean—the people who ran England for twenty shoddy years, men without a sense of greatness, of adventure, of empire—not men at all.'

'Sometimes they export the black-coated species who, when he finds himself transported to a foreign soil, quickly seeks his home manure and soon surrounds himself with an artificial reproduction of that petty piece of England he has grubbed in all his life. Yes, that is THEIR idea of empire, nothing of Clive or Rhodes about those fellows. Instead, with them, golf clubs, cosy teas and pretty dances spring into life on Eastern soil. And our clerk insulated by his social life thinks to understand the mentality of a foreign people by dining with a few rich merchants; and chaos results. You have Singapores. Have we then no men of action in our colonies and mandates, our embassies and legations? Yes we have. But their every action is checked and controlled by London. They cannot get to know the people of the land they inhabit because by day they are chained to their office by papers from Whitehall, and by night they must lead the correct social existence.'

The passionate voice stopped and there was silence, then in a different tone the speaker resumed, 'I'm sorry, sir, I've spoken a lot. But you have been good enough to listen to me so far. Please hear me to the end. We have surrendered our rights, our heritage and our administrative Government to a bureaucracy which began as our servant, but is becoming our permanent master. The policy of government is determined by demagogues who are themselves controlled by the ignorant duped masses. Nobody does the RIGHT thing but only the POPULAR thing. England is only struggling through this war because a dictatorship is beginning to exist in England today; but the politicians and bureaucrats still hamper our war effort. And once the great pressure of war is removed, England will revert to party squabbles and official inefficiency. Unless, sir, one man who commanded great respect and great power welds England into one single party.' He paused for a moment, then he said: 'With no opposition party or press to hamper his action.'

Another silence fell. I was appalled by the I.O.'s crude rehash of Fascism, but most of all I was worried because some of the things he said were almost true. I could not leave now for fear of being discovered, so I waited in suspense.

'You mean dictatorship,' said Tony.

'A rose by any other name. Because dictatorship was bloody in Russia, and is beastly in Germany and putrid in Italy, that's no reason why it shouldn't be peaceful and decent in England. But it could only begin peacefully if it began by a complete political victory.'

For the first time Pointer spoke. 'And a complete political victory could be won only by a man who had large military force in his control and was prepared to use that force ruthlessly. Well, gentlemen, we will discuss this matter again. Neither of you chatter, so I can trust your security. Goodnight to you.' As they began to move out of the bivvy I ran away into the night.

When I rejoined my regiment the following day I discovered that since they had only three tanks left, they were on their way back towards railhead to be re-equipped with fresh men and tanks. During these delicious days of leisure, while we were being re-equipped, I had time to think about all I had heard that night in Pointer's leaguer. The bare facts as I found them were these: Pointer was an ambitious General with something wrong about him; Tony worshipped him; the Intelligence Officer was a dangerous careerist looking around for a clear star to hitch his waggon. Pointer was a rising man; only sudden death could prevent him reaching great military power. During the drunken evening after Pointer's splendid tank charge, Tony and the I.O. had suggested he should become Dictator of Britain; Pointer had listened to the suggestion. That was as far as I could get; and now that I was immersed in regimental life again, it seemed to amount to very little. As I inspected new tanks and men's kits, the whole of that evening seemed remote and unreal. I couldn't believe that Pointer seriously considered becoming Dictator of Britain. Even if he did try, obviously he would fail and be imprisoned. For a time I wondered whether I should repeat what I'd overheard; but Pointer would deny it or laugh his way out of it; and who would believe me?

Once re-equipped our regiment was sent to another theatre of war; and I tried to forget Pointer and his staff. But still, when I was tired or depressed, that evening haunted me with a strange fear. I was reminded of that evening again when I was summoned to the Orderly Room by my Colonel, who told me that Pointer himself had recommended me for a Military Cross.

I can only write this by day when the birds are singing. By night I have no warning. The night is my worst time. I try to sleep; but then I think; perhaps you've only three more nights left. Think of the books you've never read and now may never read. Don't waste hours with sleep when you have so few hours left. But after all, with any luck, I've got at least three more nights before they come for me.

I was hit in the head by a piece of shrapnel early in June, 1943, and a few months later I was invalided home. It was lovely to join my family again. I spent two grand weeks in London, and was then sent to a hospital in the country for a second operation on my head.

After a time I was allowed to read, and I followed the war news as best I could. I realised that the war in Europe would finish quite soon. The incessant bombardment of Germany had seriously affected civilian morale; the combined British and American armies, under Pointer's command, were closing in on an exhausted enemy. Pointer's name by this time was as famous in America as in England. It soon became obvious to me that he must have detailed a clever publicity agent. He was always photographed doing the popular things: handing his whiskey flask to a wounded soldier, patting the heads of refugee children, sitting down to a meal with a group of Tommies, pinning medals on American soldiers. Fine legends were fabricated round his name; in disguise he had driven far behind the German lines during a reconnaissance; he ate troopers' rations and only drank alcohol when available to his men (this last I knew to be untrue); he had defied the Prime Minister and got away with it. There is no point in elaborating the tissues of falsehoods which bolstered up his splendid fame. It is enough to say that by the end of 1943 he was an allied hero.

In Europe the end came quickly. In a superb combination of military, naval and air force power, Pointer swept into Germany and our victory was total, definite and complete. Pointer's great military machine was timed to combine with a mass advance of the Russian armies from the East. In the squabble over the future government of Germany Pointer took no part. Promptly after the collapse of the German armies he returned home. His fame was universal—and there were still the Japs to beat.

But I am writing a personal, not a general, history and I must limit myself to the limits of this writing block. The whole craft of writing a history like this lies in the process of selection. You must know what to reject and what to insert. It's no good my writing down facts which can be found in a newspaper.

My second operation had not been successful so I was

invalided from the army with a little medal to wear in my buttonhole. Since the doctors said I must live quietly in the country my mother took a cottage in Sussex overlooking Ashdown Forest. (It is in this cottage that I am writing to-day.) Mother had an important job in London, so she could only spend an occasional week-end in the cottage. The war provided mother with excitement and an opportunity to use her great talent for organisation. Her friends told me that her energy was splendid; she could work hard all day at the Ministry and appear radiant and witty at an evening party.

I was not lonely in the cottage. Every day I read the papers carefully, and if some of mother's friends came to a meal over the week-end I would gather all the information I could from them. Though the War in the East continued, many of the vast forces roused to defeat the Germans were to be demobilised gradually, in accordance with the plan of demobilising men as jobs for them were vacant. This reassured me; for it ruled out the possibility of any coup d'etat. Pointer himself received no command in the Pacific, either through the jealousy or suspicion of the government. The popular press began to build him up as a wronged man—especially as the war in the East did not go particularly well. I had resisted the temptation to tell any of my friends what I had heard outside Pointer's tent, partly because I thought it would be injurious to the general war effort, partly because I still could neither believe that Pointer's intention was to seize power, nor that such a *coup d'état* was remotely possible. The present government had won the war against the Germans; most of its members were liked and respected, though their failure to finish off the Japs and also to settle the strikes, which were now spreading, was resented.

I came down to breakfast one Sunday to discover from the papers that there had been a modification in the plan of demobilisation. Twelve of Pointer's oldest units were to be demobilised immediately. They were to march through the streets of London in a triumphal march led by Pointer. I remembered his words: 'A complete political victory could only be won by a man who had large military force in his control and was prepared to use that force ruthlessly.' I looked out of the window and watched the birds playing on that table which I am watching now. I decided that the hour had sounded when I must repeat what I'd heard outside Pointer's tent. But who was the right man to approach? Certainly a member of the government. I went through the list of my mother's influential friends. Hadn't she said that Murdoch had dined at her table at the Savoy? Murdoch was Home Secretary. After breakfast I asked her about Murdoch.

'Yes, he's only recently appointed Home Secretary as a reward for his long services as a Civil Servant. I rather think him a bit pompous but quite intelligent. He told me he never travelled without a copy of *Walking Alone*, which I thought was sweetly touching of him.'

'Hasn't he got a house near here?'

'Yes, it's that house on the left just after you pass Edenstoke.'

'He'd be there to-day?'

'Yes. He's always there on Sunday.'

'Could we drive over for a glass of sherry before lunch to-day? We've just got enough petrol.'

'I can't drive over because Rebecca is arriving at any moment. You can go if you want to. But why this sudden interest in celebrities?'

'There's something I must tell him.'

'How exciting. What is it?'

'I'll tell you this evening, Mother. Can you give him a ring to say I'm coming?'

'Of course I can, darling. Shall I say you'll be coming at twelve if that is convenient to him?'

'Yes, please do.'

Just before I left Mother said:

'You won't be too serious with him, will you? These Cabinet Ministers have to be serious all the week; there's nothing they hate more than having to be serious out of school. But I'm sure he'll be interested to hear of your campaigning experiences.'

———◆•••◆———

As I drove down the quiet leafy lanes which led to Edenstoke, once again I doubted whether the horror that I dreaded could ever happen; yet I must repeat my story. I did not fear the possible consequences. I was almost certain that Murdoch would hear me to the end. After all he was a friend of my mother's.

Murdoch lived in a Victorian Gothic mansion. A showy drive led to an impressive porch. I pulled the bell, and at length a portly butler appeared and ushered me immediately into his presence. Murdoch was a small, skinny little man with dull blue eyes and a bald head. On attaining success he had adopted art as a spare-time hobby. Now he was wearing a dark blue tweed suit and a pale blue tie. He tried to balance the lack of distinction in his person by a grand manner.

'So you are Julia Wright's son. I'm delighted to meet you. My congratulations on your medal. Now will you take a glass of sherry, wine or bitter beer?'

'Sherry, please, sir.'

'Now would you prefer a dry sherry or a sweet sherry? I have a fine Amontillado you might perhaps choose to taste.'

'Thank you, sir.'

After we had settled down he said: 'Now your Mother tells me you have some piece of information to impart to me. As you probably appreciate, we have more sources of information than the public guesses, and I can tell you in confidence that there are few things in my department's province which happen in Britain to-day that we don't know about immediately. Nevertheless, I have always made it a rule, however busy I may be, and the last few months have been strenuous months for us, as you can imagine, yet my rule has always been to listen in person to informal information from persons who are, well, you know what I mean, persons of some consequence.'

I told him as clearly and as briefly as I could about the conversation I'd heard outside Pointer's tent.

When I had finished he stayed silent for a moment, then he stood up.

'It was a grim battle at Midan.'

I waited for him to explain what he meant.

'Pointer must have been hard put to it at times. You know he dined with me at my club when he was last in England on leave. I can remember him telling me, in confidence, of course, that during that tropical campaign the loyalty of his staff at times had been positively embarrassing. I can well imagine it. And your little story serves excellently to illustrate the intensity of his staff's devotion.' He glanced at his watch.

'I advise you to write down your little story. It will make interesting reading in your memoirs. Certainly I have been most interested by listening to it and I am delighted you came to visit me.' He walked towards the door.

'But, sir, I can't have made myself clear. I think that Pointer is going to try to become Dictator of Britain.'

He turned round slowly and stared at me.

'My good young man, you can't know what you're saying. I tell you I know Pointer. He dined with me at my club when he was last in England. He's a friend of mine. Not everybody likes him, as you know, but we all admire him. He's devoted his life and energy to the defeat of Fascism. He's the last person in the world to bring Fascism to Britain. In fact, I will let you in on a secret—the Cabinet have decided to offer him a post so that he can help us in the work of national reconstruction. He has accepted that offer, and it will be made public to-morrow. I think that will settle the foolish nonsense that the popular press have been spouting,' he added with satisfaction.

'I think he will scheme to become dictator.'

'My dear fellow, I really can't help what you think. I've told you the facts. And now if you will excuse me, I have some work which I must finish before lunch.'

'But please listen to me, sir. . . .'

'Aren't you being just a little, shall we say, importunate? You've won a decoration which makes me all the more surprised that you should be guilty of such gross disloyalty to the General under whom you served. But, of course, your mother told me. You've been seriously wounded. Doubtless it will take you some time to recover from the shock. Well, Mr. Wright, thank you for coming to see me.' He glanced at his watch.

'Sir, do you want to see England ruled by a dictator?'

'You are becoming impertinent. Impertinence will not help you. I should advise you to temper your speech and to improve your manners if you do not wish to meet severe trouble.' He rang the bell. The butler came in. 'Will you see Mr. Wright to his car?' He turned his back on me to look through the window. I could see his hands twitching behind his back.

<hr>

I drove home slowly. I remembered what Tony had said: 'The accumulated power of the black-coated brigade is enormous. Correct, smug little men in Whitehall who have never voyaged beyond Brighton, cheap fiction, tea-time music and a watery catholicism control the lives of millions. They are the all-powerful machine for those other vaguer, vaster, irresponsible forces. . . .' Murdoch himself was the complete case for Tony. It was his attitude that was the truth behind Tony's tirade which might make his attack against democracy dangerous.

Mother met me at the door: 'Richard, what have you been doing? Murdoch has just rung me up and he's terribly upset. He says you've made dangerous allegations which you can't substantiate, allegations against General Pointer of all people. Darling, you must be careful what you say to a man like Murdoch. I had no idea you would do such a thing or I'd never have let you go. You were never like this before.'

'Where's Rebecca?'

'Upstairs titivating before lunch. Now, Richard, promise me you won't be difficult while she's here.'

'Mother, I've not wanted to trouble you before to-day, so I've kept quiet. But to-night, after Rebecca has gone, you must listen to me.'

That night, when I'd finished telling Mother my story, she said: 'Darling, aren't you taking it all rather too seriously? Of course a man like General Pointer doesn't want to lose his power now the war is over. Why should he? The politicians made a pretty good mess of things after the last war. I'm sure General Pointer couldn't do any worse than they did even if he did get into power.'

'But it would be a dictatorship.'

'Of course it wouldn't, darling. This is England. Not Italy or Germany. We're free. We wouldn't stand for a dictatorship, not for one minute. But I think it would be an excellent thing to have a Prime Minister with far-reaching powers. Only think what he could do. Finish off this long, dragging, far-away war. End all these strikes, settle the whole business of demobilisation, get England on her feet again.'

I saw that it was hopeless to argue.

Later she said: 'By the way, dear, I suppose Pointer would remember who you were if he heard your name?'

'I doubt it.'

'But he'd remember giving you dinner.'

'He might. Why?'

'If he's back in time he's almost certain to be dining at Nancy's house on Friday. I'm really looking forward to meeting him.'

That night I could not sleep for my head was aching badly. I kept thinking about Pointer's return to England. What could I do? Who would believe me? The trouble was my wretched health. I looked ill and had at that time a slight stammer. People would think I was unbalanced. As I lay staring at the ceiling I tried to assess calmly the chances of a dictatorship in England. Of course it wouldn't be called a dictatorship, 'a rose by any other name'. And therein lay the danger. The people of Britain were for the most part ignorant of the laws which made certain their freedom. Many of those laws had been suspended at the outbreak of war, and they had not noticed—partly because they were all on the same side as the government. The government wanted to beat Hitler and so did they. The people and the government were pulling together and in the same direction. It was only at rare moments, when the pull was in opposite directions, that the people could be made to take interest in the fabric of their freedom. If Pointer could obtain a majority in Parliament and muzzle the opposition press, he could remove the freedom of the people before their very eyes because only a few of them would know what was being taken away from them. We breathe air every day, but we are not conscious of that air. We in Britain had breathed the air of freedom for so long that we had become forgetful of it; and it would not be until after Pointer had cut off the air supply that we would notice that the atmosphere was becoming fetid so that we could no longer breathe.

My head was aching terribly, and I felt dazed with pain. Vague tunes and phrases were creeping round and round in my head: We don't know what our freedom is, so Pointer's going to take it away, take it away.

I woke to find my mother by my bed. She told me that I was feverish so she had sent for the doctor from the local hospital, who was looking after me. He gave me a shot of morphine. As he left the room with Mother I thought I heard him advise another operation. I felt dazed and hopeless.

That afternoon I was operated on for the third time. I was unconscious for a fortnight. The operation was a drastic one, but it was successful, and my head has given me little trouble since, apart from occasional headaches.

I can remember vividly the morning I regained consciousness. I had been dreaming that I was in a scout car behind enemy lines, and I was trying desperately hard to get back to base. There was a lane to the west. I charged down it, dreading the shots which would mean I'd been spotted. Then I saw a tank charging down the lane after me. I drove flat out. Now I was approaching a narrow bridge, and as I approached the bridge became more and more narrow until suddenly my scout car merged into my bed and I awoke in hospital.

I was not allowed to read, and my mother was in London so it was from my hospital nurse I discovered the events of the last two weeks. The coal strike was spreading and now threatened to become general. Pointer had been offered and had accepted Cabinet rank. His name was on everybody's lips. He had declined the post of War Minister, and to everyone's surprise became Home Secretary. Murdoch stepped up to the peerage and the ornamental office of Lord Privy Seal. Pointer had begun business with a big sweep of the West End haunts, which netted the leaders of the notorious airport robberies gang. Now as strikes mounted in fury, the public looked increasingly towards him as the man who gets things done. Pointer himself said nothing, but he was due to break his silence that very evening at six o'clock—on the wireless.

'So you will be able to hear the General speak himself,' my nurse said brightly.

'Are you sure the ward wireless is working?'

'I am certain it is. Would you like it on now?'

'No. Not until 6 o'clock.'

The minutes dragged by slowly until at last the moment

came. The nurse switched on the set just as Big Ben was striking. The bell's deep throbbing note sounded out into the evening air as it had sounded for so many years, and, to-night especially, the bell meant permanency and security. The news began sensationally. The Cabinet had resigned early that afternoon, but already a new one was installed. The Prime Minister had gone and several of his colleagues. The new national leader in this hour of emergency was—Lord Murdoch. There was a gasp throughout the ward at the announcement. It seemed as though the stars in their course had conspired to deal the next stroke. 'General Pointer remains as Home Secretary.' Something like a cheer rose up from the ward. 'Thank God there's ONE man there anyway,' said my neighbour, an unhappy, worried little fellow, who ran a chain of cinemas in the outer suburbs.

Then Pointer began to speak. The whole ward was silent.

His calm, steady voice inspired confidence; his measured phrases made from simple words seemed in effect to say: 'Trust me. I know exactly what to do and I'm doing it.' He spoke slowly and deliberately. The official report of his speech is still in my wallet. I shall pin it on to this sheet of paper so that you can judge the speech for yourself.

———◆◆◆◆———

'Although I am speaking to all the peoples of Britain, it is the relatives of the men who fought in the armies of Europe that I wish most of all to address. Though this is the first time I have spoken to you, there is no need for introductions. You know me and I know you, or, if I do not know you, I know your sons and husbands. We have fought together through hardship and bloodshed for five bitter years. But from those years one great good has arisen. We have forged the bonds of comradeship which will last far into the years to come.

'A part of that noble army, which it was my honour to command, has now returned to this country to be demobilised. The rest will return to England when the eastern war is settled—and that I assure you will come more quickly than you think. A steady and controlled flow of men will stream back into civvy street. But the number of jobs available depends upon trade, and trade depends largely upon confidence and security. To-day, because of the strikes throughout this country, neither confidence nor security exist. I must make it clear to you that unless confidence and security can be restored, trade will continue to suffer. Unless, in fact, these strikes stop, it will be impossible to demobilise our armies now in Europe. Those brave lads, your sons and husbands and sweethearts, who have struggled as valiantly to win this war, will be defrauded from their just reward because we in Britain cannot manage matters better here at home.

'I am certain that you will agree with me that we must therefore take every step possible to restore security in this country. I should not be your friend if I concealed from you the gravity of the present situation. Every day, strikes, disturbance, even riots, are spreading like a scourge through this our country. Local authorities, despite their heroic efforts are losing control in various districts. If that lack of control were to become general, why then, there would be nothing to prevent anarchy, bloodshed, and perhaps civil war.

'It is in these circumstances that the government has asked me to restore order and security. It is in these circumstances —because I feel it my duty to the men who served in my armies in Europe, and because I am convinced I will succeed—that I have accepted this serious responsibility.

'The situation is becoming more dangerous with every hour that passes by. Only resolute command can restore control, and this the new government are determined to exercise. My steps may seem drastic to you, but I must ask you to believe that they are necessary. If we act, as it may appear, with haste, it is only so that we can return to normal life again more swiftly. I have been forced to declare a state of martial law. As from 6 o'clock this evening every citizen in this country will be subject to martial law. There is no cause for alarm. My purpose is to suppress irresponsible and dangerous agitators, not interfere with peaceful and law-abiding citizens. You may rest safely in your houses to-night. There will be no disturbance.

'I realise only too well the rumours and alarms which will begin to be spread directly I have finished speaking. And it is to prevent the spread of such rumours and alarms that I have been forced to take two actions. Even now, while I am speaking, arrangements are being made for the mass publication throughout the country of an official news sheet. In addition wireless news will be broadcast every two hours. These two methods for keeping you informed should prove sufficient. For the present at least there will be no other newspapers published. In the present circumstances it is obviously advisable that there should be one sound fountainhead for news, rather than a hundred unreliable and irresponsible sources which would ferment alarm and perhaps riot. Agitators and rumour mongers will be immediately arrested.

'I shall speak to you again at six o'clock to-morrow evening. I hope that I shall have some progress to report. But before I end I must tell you of one more step I have taken. Strikes are preventing the production and distribution of various essential commodities. We cannot let our people starve while good lies round the corner. The mills must be manned, the trains and lorries driven. At such a moment we cannot afford the luxury of allowing a man to pick and choose his occupation. The National Service Acts of the late war in Europe will be revived and every fit man called up for duty within the next few days. Every man must work where he is wanted. Or he must take the consequences.

'But time is short. Many things still remain to be done. I wish I had the time to explain to you all in full detail the reasons for my actions. Parliament, of course, will hear it all to-morrow.

'To-night dark, menacing clouds make all things dismal. Yet, believe me, one day these clouds will vanish, and the sun will shine clear and bright again over this land we love so much. But until then I ask for your devotion to your duty, your courage, and your trust in me.

'Keep calm, sleep sound and safe to-night, go back to your work to-morrow. And may God help us in our struggle to bring back peace to this our troubled land.'

I lay in my hospital bed staring at the ceiling. If Pointer succeeded freedom was gone; freedom of speech, freedom of the press, freedom of employment, Parliament would remain just as long as Parliament approved of Pointer. But it was impossible he could succeed. He had gone too far too quickly. The people of Britain, the gentle, tolerant people of Britain, would for once be incensed by this rape of their freedom. They would arise in their anger and destroy Pointer and all his power. It could only be a question of hours before the wireless would announce his overthrow.

But the days passed by, and the wireless still sounded Pointer's praise. In the House of Commons he made a clever and convincing defence. The government majority was firm though the Labour benches bitterly assailed the Ministers. Meanwhile the strikes went on and thousands of men were jailed in the north. In Wales riots broke out and were violently quelled.

Slowly like a poison the horrible thought crept into my mind: Pointer had succeeded. Britain was no longer free. But what had happened? Why was there no general revolt?

It was only six months later that I learnt how nearly Pointer had been overthrown.

Looking back on it all now, the events seem similar to those for the last three thousand years in any country where a master stroke has been dealt. Pointer moved with speed and determination. As the troubles increased they seemed to justify the arbitrary steps which had provoked them. Before the week was out Pointer struck again. On the Sunday a vast protest demonstration was to be held all over the country and such was the turmoil that it was freely stated that Parliament would overthrow the government at a just moment on Monday. On Saturday evening Pointer moved. He lopped the heads off the popular movement by mass arrests throughout the country. By dawn the prisons were full, and the best possible leaders of resistance were in captivity. A purged and bewildered Parliament met only to adjourn itself. The prison camps used for Germans during the war proved insufficient. Further prison camps were built. Labour camps were built in convenient industrial centres. Then came the first revolution, flaring out of London's Dockland. Though mistimed and badly coordinated, it nearly succeeded. The Freedom Troops, as they were called, reached Whitehall before they were finally dispersed.

The second revolution, two months later, was a more serious affair because it was backed by considerable private help from the Dominions and the U.S.A. For three days it looked as if Pointer must be defeated, but against a trained armed force we were bound to be defeated in the end. Our casualties were, of course, suppressed. I'm afraid they must have been considerable. I say ours, because, although I was still an invalid and was no good in the actual fights, I joined the Freedom Troops and was helping them as best I could.

⬥•••⬥

Gradually Pointer's régime settled into power. It was the old, old story. Outside the camps, people could be divided into three groups: a minority who supported Pointer's régime by conviction or by interest, the majority who disliked his régime but who found resistance impossible and acceptance more comfortable, and those who, realising that open resistance was impossible, had gone underground to work for Pointer's downfall.

This last class is now composed of several organisations of which the S.F.T. or Secret Freedom Troops is, I think, the largest. We work in constant danger of arrest; and arrest for us means death. You may get caught one day, however careful you are. And I don't blame Burgess, my chief, even though he didn't manage to destroy all his papers. It was that one paper he left which has landed me in the cart. That's why they may come for me any moment now; but they will hesitate, of course, because of my mother.

The very first time they met, which was at Nancy's dinner party, Mother scored a success with Pointer. Soon they were friends. It was Mother's worried voice on the telephone which told me that the authorities had discovered I was a member of the S.F.T. I hope my arrest will end her friendship with Pointer. I know Pointer too well to dream that her friendship could prevent my arrest. Of course, Mother hinted on the telephone that if I promised to be a good boy something might be arranged, but at last I think I convinced her that for me there could be no surrender.

Last night I could not sleep again. I kept thinking about my arrest and what they might do to me before I was shot. The real thing is never so terrible as imagination paints it and I tried to make my mind concentrate on what I would write this morning. I tried to think why all this misery had come to Britain. And now I must write down my thoughts quickly, because this may be my last morning. I wish I had peace to weave my reasons into one clear argument for freedom. Perhaps when I have finished writing, from the threads of my reasons, one simple pattern may appear.

The Arabs say 'The world is a poison which poisons the soul of man gradually.'

During the Hitler elections in Germany, radio gramophones installed in all the large railway stations played records which said incessantly 'Vote for Hitler. Vote for Hitler. Vote for Hitler.'

Before the war, experts were invited to attend the trade show of a short film which played for only fifteen minutes. As the experts walked out at the end of the film, one said to a friend, 'I can't think why my mind has suddenly gone dirty, but throughout that film I kept thinking of a short, smutty word.'

His friend looked surprised. 'And it begins with F?'

'Yes.'

'That's very odd. I kept thinking of that word, too.'

They then discovered that five others of the experts attending that innocent trade show had thought of the same word. Later it was discovered that the man who cut the film had amused himself by writing that word across the join of the film. Now, in order to obtain the effect of continuity, each film photo flashes across the screen at a great speed. I can't remember what fraction of a second each photo takes to pass across the screen, but I know that it flashes past at a speed which makes it impossible for the eye to read consciously any word written on one photograph. The conscious mind cannot accept it, but the unconscious mind can. That surely is the secret of all advertisements. You see an advertisement for Hambort's Laxative Pills disfiguring the countryside. Consciously your only reaction is to resent the blot on pleasant country, yet your subconscious mind has registered the message of that advertisement; and later, when you need a laxative, you go to a chemist's shop and ask for Hambort's Pills. That is the secret of the record which played in the railway stations, 'Vote for Hitler. Vote for Hitler.'

The conscious minds of many might be offended by it, but their subconscious registered and obeyed. Psychologists say that we are conditioned by our environments. We may not notice ourselves being changed by our surroundings, but that change is proceeding.

Arabs say, 'The world is a poison which poisons the soul of man gradually.' Why? Because they think that the instrument of everyday life is playing a record which says in effect: 'Vote for evil. Vote for evil. Vote for evil.' The film of existence gradually poisons the mind. We begin life simple and clean. Our lusts and longings and ideals are fresh and strong. We may even in our youth determine to make the world a better place to live in. But though we cannot hear it the record is always playing in our ears as we mix with worldlings and bitter people. The film is always flashing past on the screen as we lead a comfortable life. The effect is strongest when we are complacent or begin to stretch out for power, or when we are tired, disillusioned or defeated. And our mind is gradually poisoned. We in our turn become mean and petty and cynical. Only a strong faith constantly renewed can drown the record's message to the subconscious.

What was done in Britain before the war to inspire the nation with a strong faith?

Politicians appeased first the comfortable classes who wanted safety first, then they appeased foreign aggressors. The Church, while continuing in effect to condone exploitation, money grabbing and greed in Britain, at one period looked favourably upon a movement pledged to international pacifism. Business amorality flourished while the Word of Christ distorted from subservience to temporal powers was sicklied over smug congregations on Sundays. The war saved our country from slow death. The war demanded a spiritual revival. The great masses of our people yearned for a faith. But what happened? Politicians curtailed liberty, suppressed information, spread the red tentacles of bureaucracy, forbade broadcasts on the very subjects bound to raise the people's spirit, refused to reveal our aims in fighting the war.

The Church provided brave padres, political bishops, anæmic broadcasts. Internal dispute and long concern with sectarian differences, dogma, schism and temporal matters had weakened the Church so that there was no united strength to voice the Word of Christ from pulpit, wireless, stage and screen.

Always the men serving their country were treated like fools to be humoured so that they could fight. Sometimes I wondered whether the powers were frightened to give our men a glimpse of a better world. Our men were not encouraged to think about plans for after the war. Many did not know the reason why they fought. The food for their minds came from two sources: the press and the wireless. The press provided popular magazines with indifferent dirty jokes, naked girls and trivial stories. The wireless produced crooners, monotonous jazz, second-rate comedians, tea-time music, and patronising talks. All this was designed to appease what the authorities imagined to be the lowest common factor amongst those serving their country. The men thirsted for better things.

They wanted wine, they were given flat lemonade.

For ten years before the last war was declared, a great war of creeds had been raging in Europe sometimes openly, sometimes underground. Our men were fighting against a strong creed. Our politicians and our Church provided them with no moral armament to defeat that creed. We were fighting against evil things in Germany, but that same evil existed on our own side and in ourselves, and quite soon it became clear that the war on the Home Front would be the most bitter. Those great masses of men and women who were on the side of freedom and equality needed more than brute force to defeat the creed of brute force; they needed a burning faith in freedom and equality. That faith never came. Our moral armament was inferior to that of the enemy, both at home and abroad. The result is now plain for posterity to see. The bodies of two mighty nations, Germany and Japan, lie crippled at our feet; we have crushed their bones and consumed their flesh; but their evil has triumphed, because today Pointer is Dictator of

Britain, the creed of brute force flourishes, and for us the record plays a tune to poison the soul.

————◆•••◆————

I believe that we lost the struggle against evil because of the great price that we set on material things. Both political parties concentrated on material interests to the exclusion of mind and spirit. It is hard to have a soul on an empty stomach, so the slum child has small chance of finding beauty and truth. Then let us give the people good food, clear air and decent houses, before we expect spiritual development. Filth, squalor and disease crab the spirit. Since body and mind are one, a sick body may cause a sick mind. Therefore we should cure the body of our country by removing slums and malnutrition. But that is only the beginning. Our comfortable suburban dwellers have long enjoyed good food, clean air and decent houses, yet their minds and their souls are sick. The politicians who shouted for better living conditions seemed to ignore that the spirit is more important than the flesh.

This concentration on the body of the country produced and increased that vast bureaucracy which has now spread tentacles into every home. It was imagined that control by the government was bound to be better than control by the individual. But if the machinery and personnel of government control be of a poor quality, then to change from private ownership to government ownership is only to change from one evil to another. We should have improved the quality of the machinery and personnel of government before attempting nationalisation of large concerns; for government control as we have seen it in Britain, though sometimes more efficient, removes the human touch one stage further away. The miner's welfare is determined by an official in Whitehall who does not understand the miner. A farmer's pig in Cumberland, a child's tooth in Dorset, are controlled from London. A vast gulf divides the governed from the governors. Yet one set of politicians cried for further nationalisation without analysing the tyranny of petty bureaucracy and another set blindly supported the monstrous growth of great monopolies which was creeping over Britain, and which has now served Pointer's purpose so well. The men of the Left proclaimed that nation-alisation meant economic liberty for the worker. The men of the Right prated about individualism and meant by it merely Big Business. By their concentration on the body of the country, the Right, Left and Centre were gradually moving towards that destruction of individual freedom which is now complete.

The telephone bell is ringing.

It was Mother.

'Darling, I've got the most wonderful news. I'm so happy I can hardly think what I'm saying. Listen. Can you hear me, darling? It's all right. Nothing's going to happen to you. You're safe. Do you hear? You're safe. Oh, darling, I am so relieved. You can't imagine what misery I've been through. But I must tell you what's happened. I saw my friend—you know who I mean—last night and he told me the news. They are coming for you at ten o'clock this evening, but it doesn't mean anything. They'll take you to London and you'll go before the court to-morrow morning. He's fixed the whole thing. It's so wonderful of him. At the court there'll be that doctor who looked after you in hospital. He's going to certify that your head wound has unbalanced you. Yes, that was the word he used. And then you'll be let off. And then, darling, and then, you'll be free. Oh, it's so wonderful to think of. You can leave England as he suggests that very day and get away from it all. I was sure you won't want to stay in England after what's happened. Oh, yes, and I was to tell you this. Be careful to support what the doctor says when you are questioned. I mean you'll have to say that there are long periods when you go blank and can't remember afterwards what you've said or done. You will do that, won't you, darling? Richard. Hullo? Richard? Operator, operator.'

I put down the receiver, and Mother's voice was chopped into silence. I have disconnected the telephone to stop it ring-ing. The time is eight-thirty and I suppose I shall never hear her voice again. I wish now that I had said goodbye.

Well, I haven't long now to finish this story. I have just

lit a cigarette, and my hand is perfectly steady. I'd like to put that on record. I hope I'm steady when I make my last stand.

The sun is setting behind the forest, and the village in the valley is slowly being covered with mist.

Oh, God, thank you for giving me strength to resist this last temptation. Please help me in these next few hours, and do not let me whimper.

I am all alone with the sky, but I am only one of many. All over the world thousands of men and women are fighting the same battle all alone in their wilderness. Perhaps one day they will find a way to join together, so that the lone voice crying in the wilderness shall wake to find himself shouting in a crowd.

The sun is setting now, and all the sky is crimson. Please let peace come to my heart as I look for the last time at this great frontispiece of heaven, this lovely sky. But yet I still must be sad for all the sacrifice and love which are wasted in this existence we call life. And as I watch the sky grow dark I must wonder. Will mankind for ever grope in darkness, or will the sun rise one morning on a better world?

I must put this sheet of paper away now.

Testament: Cairo 1898

The padre always stops by my bunk on his rounds. The sick bay of the ship is crammed. But they've given me a top bunk near to the ventilation pipe, so at least I can breathe, and I'm well out of the way of the rest of them. Before I left Cairo I managed to scrounge a notebook with enough pages to finish this last letter of mine.

My next of kin will probably be my sister Maude. In any case, whoever he or she may be who comes to open this packet, and begins to read these pages I've written, will be very shocked, I'm sure of it. But it's hypocrisy that keeps the world from knowing the truth about hundreds more people than you'd ever guess about. Anyhow I hope some people will understand.

The padre says the M.O. can't fathom me out. He says that I don't seem to fight against my illness. He says that all I'll do is scribble in this book. He always refers to me now as the scribe. But I don't care now. They can call me what they like. All I *want* to do is to get it written down. I'll leave this book with the rest of my junk.

I'll begin from the moment when I fell sick after the march up country on the way to fight the Dervishes in the Spring of 1898. I collapsed with a bad pain in my chest. I was invalided back down the Nile. I was coughing up blood.

The Military Hospital in Cairo was overcrowded and under-staffed. Those who were strong enough to move had to lend a hand in helping the orderlies look after those who were really sick. My bed was at the end of the ward next to the wall. I was glad of this, because I felt so wretched that I just didn't want to talk to anyone.

I couldn't move, but when there was no orderly about and I wanted help of some kind, the boy in the next bed to me was always eager to give a hand. He was only a couple of years younger than me. He'd joined up in the army partly because he was fed up with life at home and partly because he'd been taken in by the glorious accounts of military life which still appear in newspapers and magazines in England. Within a fortnight of landing in Egypt he'd come down with a bad go of dysentery which had nearly killed him. He was better now. But the disease had left him weak and painfully thin.

Gradually I found out a bit about his home life. His name was Ted Mason, and he was sixteen years old. His family came from near Bath. He had a quiet voice with a pleasant Somerset accent, which immediately attracted me. His father worked as a railway porter at Bath station. His mother was a strict member of the Evangelical Society. The atmosphere of piety in their small cottage had become so wearisome to him that he'd decided to get away at any price. The army seemed the easiest possibility of escape.

Ted had very fair hair. A thick lock of it slanted down over his forehead. He kept pushing it back with his left hand. His features were very delicate. I could see that his skin was as soft as a girl's. With his large blue eyes and slightly girlish appearance I reckoned that he was going to have a rough time of it in the Army.

When I began to get stronger, Ted scrounged an old draughts-board from the ward next door and we began to play chequers together. Ted didn't play very well because he'd start by being over-cautious. Then he'd make some rash move which would give me the advantage. He was a good loser but, even so, I let him win half the time because I enjoyed the look of happiness on his face when he'd beaten me. When I'd first arrived at the hospital his cheeks had been somehow sunken into his face, but as the days passed he began to get better and his face started to fill out. The flesh now seemed to glow on his limbs.

One afternoon I'd won three games of draughts in a row. Suddenly I saw a move I could make which would let Ted win a game. I made the move. I expected Ted to take advantage of it, but his hands remained still. I looked up at him as he sat by the side of my bed. From the expression on his face you'd think I'd done something to hurt or offend him.

'You did that on purpose,' he said. 'You made that move so I'd win.'

'Rot,' I answered.

'You did, all the same,' Ted said. His Somerset burr had become more pronounced—as it always did when he was excited. 'Can't you see that I enjoy playing draughts with you—whether I win or lose? And that's because you're my friend,' he said.

As I gazed at him he smiled. His lips were rather full. His teeth were very white and straight. As he smiled the lock of fair hair had fallen over his forehead. I had a sudden desire to raise my hand and push the lock back into place Then as I looked at the slenderness of him and the softness of his skin I suddenly felt a pain of longing so strong that for a moment I couldn't breathe. I wanted to seize the boy there and then and hold him in my arms. I couldn't speak. I realised that Ted was now watching me with concern.

'Are you all right?' Ted asked. 'You've gone quite white.'

I tried to laugh. 'I'm fine,' I said. 'In fact I'm so much better, I hope they'll let me out of this place in a fortnight's time.'

'That's good,' Ted said. 'I reckon I'll be due for release about then, so we could go to the Sick-leave Camp together.'

There was such eagerness in his voice that I glanced up at him. But he gazed back at me quite innocently.

———◆◆◆———

Later that evening I tried to draw Ted out about his love-life—if any—down in Somerset. Immediately he became oddly bashful. Soon I detected that he was thoroughly embarrassed. This gave me hope, because obviously if he'd had a girl behind a haystack he wouldn't keep quiet about the fact. Presently, in a low voice so that the man in the next-door bed couldn't hear, he told me there was a girl he'd met one afternoon at some local fair. He told me her name was Mary and she was seventeen years old. But though he'd written to her he hadn't had any letter from her since he left England.

Quite frankly, I thought he'd made the story up. However, I hid my impatience to find out the truth. I now had only a fortnight to wait.

My plans for taking out Ted alone as soon as we reached the Sick-leave Camp were at first mucked up by the man in the bed on the other side of Ted. His name was George Wheeler. He was a trooper in a lancer regiment. He was in the hospital because he'd broken a leg in a fall from his horse when he was on exercises. He was a hefty-looking bloke of about thirty, with small inquisitive eyes, and thick lips which, for some reason, he kept licking with his tongue. His face was flabby and of a sickly greenish tinge. Yet he gave the impression of immense strength. Though his looks were against him, George was very popular in the ward because he had a tremendous fund of thoroughly dirty stories which he loved to tell. Some of them were really funny. I noticed that Ted laughed at them as loudly as the rest of us. For all his ugliness, George had a way with him, and as soon as his leg made it possible for him to hobble about the ward I saw that he spent most of his time between our two beds. He seemed equally fond of both of us. In a husky voice, flatteringly pitched into a tone of confidence, he'd tell us of his sexual adventures in the back streets of the Cairo Medina. He told us there was a child-brothel which he'd twice visited.

'It's strictly out of bounds,' he said. 'I expect it's even illegal among the Gippos. But the boss of the place is careful to keep on the right side of the police. He buys the kids from families who are starving. The little bints are quite something, I can promise you. Some of them haven't even been broken in.'

I glanced up at Ted's face whilst he was listening to this story. His eyes were shining with excitement.

'Couldn't the three of us go one evening?' Ted asked. 'When we get to the Sick-leave Camp?'

George's tongue slid over his upper lip. 'You bet we could,' he said. 'That is, unless our friend here has any objection.'

I'd been with a bint when I first came out to Cairo. I'd enjoyed it all right at the time and, it seemed, so had the bint. She'd begged me to come back—and that was even before I'd paid her off. I'd enjoyed the love-making for the moment. But afterwards it had left me with a sad feeling of dissatisfaction, only partly caused by my fear that I might have caught something.

'I've no objection,' I said. 'But let's make sure we find some girls who haven't got the clap.'

———◆••◆———

Discipline at the Sick-leave Camp was severe, but there weren't enough N.C.O.s to enforce the rules which the Colonel in charge had posted on the main notice board. At night it was well known that if you tipped the sentry on the gate you could get out. So, five days after we'd arrived at the camp, Ted, George and I—with George leading—were walking cautiously along the narrow alleys of the Medina. We stopped outside a door which, although its paint had flaked off in patches, had the look of being very solid. There was a bell-handle to the right of the door. George pulled it three times. We waited for a while. In the silence, we could hear footsteps coming down stairs. A slat in the door was pulled back and an eye peered out at us. Then the slat was snapped shut and the door was opened. We walked into a dimly lit small hallway. The whitewashed walls were streaked with damp. The whole place reeked of decay and cheap scent.

Once my eyes had got used to the faint light, I could make out the man who had opened the door for us. He was slim, with a narrow face and a dark skin. With his hooked nose and narrow eyes he looked more Turkish than Arab. He wore baggy white pantaloons and gold slippers. His tunic was fastened at the neck. It was made of silk embroidered with silver. Stuck into the belt around his waist was a silver-handled whip which hung loosely at his side like a snake.

He seemed pleased to see Ted and me. But when he recognised George, he scowled and began to jabber at him in Arabic. I only knew a few words of the lingo. However, George had told us that he'd picked up quite a bit of the language during the time he'd been in Egypt, and he answered back the brothel-keeper with confidence. I could see the man glancing towards Ted and me from time to time. Then he shrugged his shoulders and led us up the stone stairs. We entered a long room with a cushion-covered divan running the whole length of one side of it. Immediately George sat himself down on the divan and motioned for Ted and me to sit down beside him. The man now spoke a few more words to George in Arabic.

'He wants to know what we'd like to drink,' George explained. 'If you take my advice you'll stick to beer. The whiskey here is doctored muck—as I've got good reason to know.'

'When are we going to see the bints?' Ted asked, after we'd ordered three bottles of beer.

George laughed. 'Hark at the infant,' he said, leering towards me. 'He can't even wait five minutes for it.'

'What were you arguing about with the brothel-keeper?' I asked George.

For an instant George looked embarrassed. 'Last time I was here there was a bit of a row because he claimed I'd hurt one of the girls,' he answered. 'But I soon put him right on that. I explained that she was only screaming and carrying on so as to get more money out of me.'

'Why does the man carry a whip?' I asked.

George guffawed. 'He's got a regular little school to look after here,' he explained. 'Sometimes he has to use the whip to keep discipline.'

At that moment, the door opened and about a dozen girls began to file in. They were all of them naked.

'Now we'll have the parade,' George said.

But I'd hardly heard his words for I was staring at the girls in dismay. They were indeed children. Some of them couldn't have been more than twelve—if that. The girls now lined up against the wall opposite us and stood facing us in silence. The brothel-keeper shuffled in with our three bottles of beer.

'Who's going to chose first?' George asked. 'I think little Ted should. After all, he's the youngest, and I bet it's his first go.'

I glanced towards Ted. I thought that he might be nervous. But as he drank his beer his gaze was fixed on the girls.

'That suits me,' he said, and took another gulp of his drink.

'Then which one is it to be?' George asked.

Ted pointed to a girl of about fourteen. Her breasts were large and rounded and her waist was very narrow. Her skin was lighter in colour than the rest of them.

'You've chosen well,' George said. 'I've had my eye on that girl for quite a while. She's light-skinned and blue-eyed because she's a Circassian from Northern Syria. Circassian girls are in great demand in Eygpt. I expect you'll find she's good at her job.'

'Your turn next,' George said, turning to me.

But as I'd looked at the children, I'd already made up my mind I wasn't going to have any one of them. Yet if I refused now, both George and Ted might well guess my secret. I pointed to a dark-skinned girl who looked older and more brazen than the rest.

'I'll take *her*,' I said.

George finished his bottle of beer, belched, stood up, and lumbered over to the line of girls. He walked along the line, touching their breasts as he moved past them, and stopped in front of a small girl. She was very tiny and very thin. She couldn't have been more than thirteen. Her tawny skin glistened in the lamplight. She looked up at George in fear. George put a large red hand around her neck and drew her towards him.

'I'll have this one,' he said gruffly.

The brothel-keeper held out his hand.

'We pay him in advance,' George said. 'You can give your girl what present you like at the end of it.'

We produced the tariff in piastres. The brothel-keeper tucked the money away in the breast pocket of his tunic. He snapped out some words of command to the three girls, opened the door and led the way for us up the stairs on to the second floor. We walked into a large dormitory which was divided into cubicles by partitions. Even before we had left the downstairs room, with its long divan, the girls left behind had clustered together and had begun chattering as if they were on a school-treat.

The brothel-keeper opened the door of the far cubicle. George and his little girl went into it. I heard the sound of the key being turned in the lock. The man's hand was now fixed on the whip at his side. He motioned to the dark-skinned girl I had chosen to go into the next cubicle. I followed her in, and I also locked the door. I heard Ted and his Circassian girl enter the cubicle next door. I heard the lock turn. Then I heard the brothel-keeper shuffle out of the room.

'*Ismak ey?*' I asked my girl, using the few words of Arabic I'd picked up.

'*Ageleye,*' she answered.

'*Enti quyaisis,*' I said to her. 'You're very sweet.'

When she smiled I saw a glitter of gold teeth; so obviously she hadn't been destitute all her life. Slowly I began to take off my clothes. I still hadn't made up my mind if I would have her or not.

From George's cubicle next door I heard a clatter as the belt from his trousers fell to the ground. The partitions dividing the room into cubicles did not reach the ceiling, so every sound carried. An instant later I heard the rustle of the mattress on the floor. Then, I heard a little gasp of pain from the child. A few moments later the mattress rustled again. The partitions were so thin that I could even hear George's heavy breathing. Then there was a sudden scream of pain from the little girl.

'*La!*' she cried out. '*La—Min fadlak. Min fadlak*'.

Her words ended in a muffled kind of moan, and I guessed that George had put a hand over her mouth.

I was naked now, but I felt sick and disgusted. If I'd been a perfectly normal person, I suppose I might have burst open the lock in the cubicle next door and stopped the cruel scene that was probably taking place. But I had Ted to think of. I didn't want to risk a fight with George then and there. The Egyptian police might be called and we'd all be put on a charge —if only for being out of bounds.

From Ted's cubicle, on the other side of me, there came not a sound. Meanwhile my dark-skinned girl, Ageleye, was lying on the bed, looking up at me enquiringly. I sat down on the bed beside her, I stroked her cheek and tried to make it clear to her that I didn't want to make love that night. But even as I spoke her soft hand was sliding between my legs. Then she put her other arm around my neck and pulled my head towards her. Her tongue pressed against my lips, gently and caressingly until I opened my mouth, and her tongue plunged between my lips. Then her tongue began turning in my mouth in a very slow, rhythmic way, while her hands between my thighs never stopped their delicate movements. When she realised that I was excited, she lay on her back and almost pulled me down into her—and all the time she wriggled with that same slow rhythm. Soon it was all over. We lay back panting, entwined in each other's warm limbs.

As we lay, I could hear the girl in George's cubicle crying softly. I could hear George dressing himself. I heard him unlock his door and walk out of the dormitory. He had not spoken a word to the little girl.

From the cubicle on the other side there still came not a sound. I longed to know what was going on. As if she had guessed my thoughts, Ageleye gave me a smile like a mischievous child. She got up from the bed and walked towards the partition which divided me from the scene I fancied watching. On our side the partition was covered by an old striped blanket. Carefully Ageleye drew the blanket aside. In the partition was a small crack. She looked through it and shook her head. She beckoned me to come and look through the gap in the partition. Stealthily on my bare feet, I walked up to the gap. I put my eye to it and peered through.

The Circassian girl was lying flat on her back on the mattress. Her legs were parted in the usual position. Ted was kneeling between her legs desperately trying to arouse himself. It was obvious from the girl's bored expression that nothing had happened. It was also obvious from the sweat on Ted's face, from his look of despair, and from his limpness, that nothing ever would happen. For the first time I saw his body completely naked, and mixed with my fierce desire for him was now a kind of pity.

Then I realised that I was hooked. I knew that I was in love with him.

━━━◆◆◆◆━━━

When we got back to the Sick-leave Camp that evening, Ted and I said good night to George whose tent was on the nearside of the camp. I was glad to be away from him. His bragging descriptions of what he'd done to the girl in his cubicle almost made me retch. Ted and I walked stealthily back towards the big hospital tent in which our beds were side by side. We were silent. I couldn't think of anything to say, and I suppose Ted was still feeling ashamed because he hadn't been able to have his girl.

'Did you have a good time?' Ted asked me after a while.

'Yes,' I answered. 'Fine.'

'My girl was terrific,' Ted said. 'I really let her have it good and proper.'

I was silent once again. Then I had an idea. 'If we can get out to-morrow night by dropping the guard some *baksheesh*, why don't we go for a sail on the Nile? We can hire a *felucca* for a few piastres. With the full moon it ought to be tremendous,' I said.

'Should we take George too?' Ted suggested.

'No,' I said. 'To tell you the truth—I'm getting a bit browned off with George and his dirty stories. Let's go—just the two of us.'

'That's all right with me,' Ted answered.

———————◆◆◆◆◆————————

We hired the *felucca* easily enough. The crew consisted of an old man and a boy. The old man held the rudder while the boy—he looked about fourteen—hauled up the triangular sail. There was hardly a breath of wind. The Nile was so smooth it might have been made of steel. It reflected, in occasional rivulets, the full moon which hung in the sky above us and seemed so low it might have been a lantern in a courtyard.

At first Ted and I sat in the stern with the old man who reminded me of some figure in a stained glass window. He had a thin, wizened, dried-up face. His *galabieh* which fell from his shoulders to his grimy feet made him look a bit like an Old Testament prophet. Once we had reached the middle of the Nile a cool breeze sprang up. Presently I saw Ted give a little shiver. This was the moment I'd been waiting for.

I passed him the bottle of *arak* I'd bought for the occasion. He passed it back to me, and I had a swig. It was real fire-water. Then I offered the bottle to the old man, but he shook his head. I took another long gulp from the bottle myself. I looked towards the old man. For an instant his cunning bleary eyes flickered between the two of us. Ted didn't understand the meaning of the expression on the old man's face. But I did, so next time he glanced towards me I gave him a very slight wink. You don't have to talk much to the Arabs. Somehow they seem to guess what you're thinking in a flash. The old man got up and shuffled towards the arched section of canvas which covered almost the whole length of the boat, and served as a cabin of sorts. He unfastened a canvas flap and drew it back. A small oil lamp was burning in the cabin. There was a bunk on either side of it.

'*Tfaddal*,' the old man said, 'Enter.'

I smiled at Ted and went into the cabin. It stank of paraffin and *hashish*. Ted followed me in and sat on the bunk opposite me.

'What's all this about?' Ted asked.

'I don't know,' I lied. 'Perhaps it's because he's a Moslem and doesn't like to see us drink. Anyhow, at least it's warm in here.'

While I spoke, the old man pulled across the flap of the awning and closed it. On a small wooden box I saw there were two glasses and a water jug. I poured *arak* into both glasses. I filled them to the brim with water. I handed a glass to Ted. I raised my own glass.

'Here's to our friendship,' I said.

'I'll drink to that,' Ted answered. He took a great gulp of *arak* and choked a little.

I produced a tin of cigarettes and we lit up.

'What did you think of your bint last night?' I asked.

'She was all right,' Ted answered.

'Was it the first time?' I asked him.

Ted took a sip of his drink. 'Yes,' he said.

'You've never been with a girl before?' I asked.

'Not like that,' Ted replied.

I looked at him as he sat on the bunk opposite me, with the glass of *arak* in his hand. It was warm now in the cabin, and he'd undone the top two buttons of his shirt. Even by the light of the oil lamp I could see the softness of his skin. I was almost certain, now, that soon that slender body would be naked in my arms. At that moment I was sure he felt the same about me as I did about him. While he gazed at me, in the light of the smoky lamp, he looked like a boy of fourteen.

'When you were at school,' I said, 'there must have been some other boy you were really keen on.'

Ted gave a little laugh. 'Yes, there was—to tell you the truth,' he said. 'But how did you guess?'

'Did you do anything together?' I asked, ignoring his question.

'Only schoolboy stuff,' Ted answered.

'And since then?' I asked.

'Nothing,' Ted said. 'I've never had the chance—until last night, that is.'

For a while we were both silent. I could hear the ripples of water lapping against the side of the boat. I filled up both our glasses.

'It's close in here,' I said, and I unbuttoned my shirt. 'Do you ever miss that boy?' I asked.

Through the murk of the cabin I could see Ted gazing at me. 'What boy?' he asked.

'The boy at school you were keen on,' I answered.

'No,' Ted answered. 'Why should I?'

'On the boat coming out here,' I said, 'didn't anyone try anything with you?'

'One did,' Ted answered. 'But he's not likely to try that again in a hurry.'

Outside I heard the old man shout out something. I heard the creak of the sail.

'Drink up,' I said to Ted.

'What's the hurry?' he asked, and stretched himself out on his bunk.

'Come on,' I said. 'Let's drink up. I think we're turning back.'

Ted laughed. 'Do you want to make me drunk?' he asked.

I was glad he'd laughed. I wanted our first moment of love-making to be something happy—something neither of us would regret. For that's the way it should be, without any fear and without any guilt.

'Of course I want to make you drunk,' I answered. 'I want to get you as keen for it as you were last night.'

'You don't want to go back to that place, do you?' Ted asked.

'No,' I said. 'There's no need to.'

I could see that Ted was staring at me in a bewildered kind of way. But surely he must have understood by now.

'There's no need to,' I repeated.

Then I leaned over to the oil lamp and blew it out. The moonlight outside came in through small slits in the canvas. Within a few seconds my eyes had got used to the half-darkness. I could see that Ted was still stretched out on his bunk. I moved over to him. I leaned down and put my right hand on his shoulder. He didn't move. With my left hand I began to unfasten the remaining buttons of his shirt. Ted still didn't move. I slid my hand under his shirt, I felt the warm skin of his shoulders. He was still lying on his bunk without making a single movement. I took my hands out of his shirt and un-fastened his belt. I could hear that he had begun to breathe quickly. Gently I slid his trousers down from his narrow thighs. Then I lowered myself down on to the bunk beside him and pressed his warm body against mine. I began to kiss the skin of his cheeks and his smooth forehead—and then, very gently, his lips—the lips on which my eyes had fixed so many times. I moved my right hand down to his groin. Suddenly, with a violent heave of his body, he pushed me away from him and struggled up from the bunk. Rapidly he tugged his trousers up around his waist and buttoned his shirt. At first I thought that he had drunk too much *arak* and was going to be sick. Then I felt the thud of his fist striking wildly against my jaw. I shot out a hand to hold him off me. Sweeping over me, I felt a rage of disappointment and bitterness so terrible that I think I could have killed him.

'Don't you dare hit me,' I said to him quietly. Then I gave him a violent push that sent him reeling back on to his bunk.

I managed to find the bottle of *arak*. I gulped the rest of it down neat. As I stood there with the *arak* burning in my throat his words stabbed out of the darkness at me like some Dervish dagger.

'You rotten bastard,' he said. 'You dirty fucking bugger. You're filth. That's all you are, filth. George warned me that you were a rotten bloody nance. But I wouldn't believe him.'

'Get out,' I said. 'Get out before I kill you.'

'Don't worry,' he said. 'I wouldn't stay in this stinking hole with you for a minute longer.'

He tugged at his clothes to make sure they were in order and hurled himself towards the entrance through which we'd come. He snatched and clawed frantically at the flap of canvas. Then he managed to get it open. He stumbled out on to the deck. I fell back on to my bunk and sat, with my head in my hands, retching violently. I felt bitter and angry and desperately disappointed.

When I came out of the cabin, Ted was sitting on a sack beside the old man. He wouldn't even look at me. I clambered forward. The breeze was steady. In the prow the boy was crouched beside a coil of rope. I sat down in the only space there was—which was beside him. The boy glanced at me and smiled. I turned away from him because I didn't want him to see my wretchedness. The *felucca* was gliding smoothly along the dark river. The lights from the houses on the banks were reflected in it as if it were a mirror. I took out my tin of cigarettes and handed it to the boy. He smiled again and took one eagerly. We lit our cigarettes. We smoked in silence.

Presently I began to look at the boy. He was light-skinned and slight in build. When he stood up to adjust the sail-ropes his movements beneath his *galabieh* were firm and graceful. He came back and sat down beside me. I noticed that his head was set very delicately on his shoulders. There was a smooth hollow of flesh below his neck where it joined his chest. Once again, the boy turned and smiled. This time I gazed steadily at him. His eyes were very dark and wide-set. Perhaps it was the long lashes which made his gaze look so gentle. But there was now something soft and yielding in his expression. The *felucca* moved along the river in silence. The boy threw away his cigarette. For an instant he was motionless, still watching my eyes as if he expected an order. Then he stretched out his hand and took hold of mine. His hand seemed to burn my skin. I didn't move, neither did I withdraw my hand; I suppose I was still thinking about Ted. Then, very gently, the boy drew my hand down to his ankle and pulled it gently up his leg beneath his *galabieh* until it reached his thighs. His skin was smoother than any I had ever touched. He was no longer smiling. He was staring at me solemnly. Then he pulled my hand and placed it over his groin. I could feel the tautness of him throbbing against the palm of my hand.

We were approaching the landing stage. I moved my hand away from him.

'*Gib felus,*' he said. 'Give *baksheesh* to the old man. Then I can come with you.'

I walked back aft. My heart was pounding. I wanted the boy, if only because I felt that somehow he could make me forget about Ted. But I was afraid of some trap.

When we tied up, Ted thrust his half-share of our expenses into my hand without a word and walked off. I paid the old man. Then I added a large tip. I was all right for money because I had almost all my army back-pay. For an instant the old man looked surprised. Then the boy came up to him and spoke hurriedly in Arabic. The old man gave me a vicious leer, so I could guess what the boy had told him. But I didn't mind. The boy helped me on to the landing-stage. The old man gave us a wave of his hand and we walked off. By that time I really didn't care what happened.

'*Mush bayid,*' the boy told me. 'It's not far.'

I followed him along a series of narrow alleys which twisted like serpents. I wondered if I was heading into some carefully planned ambush, but there was something about the boy's presence and the way he looked up at me now and then which made me feel that he liked me.

'What's your name?' I asked him.

'Talaat,' he replied

'Talaat, where are we going?' I asked him.

'To the *hammam,*' he answered. 'The man there is my friend.'

Then I remembered hearing that Cairo was dotted with these Turkish Baths—some of them quite large buildings, some of them where desires of almost any kind could be satisfied. Presently we turned left into a very narrow alley. A faint light was shining at the end of it. By its glow I could see a large building. There was no way out of the alley as the end of it was stopped up by this huge house. Once again I wondered if this was the moment when they would try to rob me. Then we walked up to a newly-painted door. Talaat pulled the bell vigorously several times.

'This is the *hammam* of my friend,' he told me.

Talaat spoke partly in Arabic and partly in English which I suppose he'd picked up from various tourists who'd hired the *felucca*. Presently, the usual slat in the door was pulled back and an eye peered out at us. Talaat spoke quickly in Arabic. There was a sound of bolts being pulled back. The door was opened. We walked in and the door was quickly closed behind us. My first impression was of an overwhelmingly warm dampness which seemed to fill the whole anteroom in which we were standing. Then I observed the man who'd opened the door to us. He was immensely fat. The old expression 'as broad as he was long' might almost have been applied to him. His flabby cheeks quivered as he smiled at little Talaat. Then he bowed to me.

'*Tfaddal, ya Effendi*,' he said.

'Give him some money now,' Talaat said.

'How much?' I asked.

'Show me your money,' Talaat ordered.

I handed out a few piastre notes. Talaat took three of them and gave them to the fat man who seemed satisfied. He now opened two doors which led into a vast, circular, dimly-lit room surrounded by cubicles. The rush of heat was like the blast of a furnace. For an instant I couldn't breathe. I started to cough. Talaat noticed this and laughed. The fat man was holding a key with a number written on it. He gave the key to Talaat. On a stone slab at the end of the room I could see about twelve naked men lying flat and almost motionless. Some of them were being massaged by younger boys. Others were asleep, wound up in cotton sheets. Talaat walked to a cubicle on the left and opened the door with the key. I followed him into the small room. The cubicle was lit by a small oil lamp. In it were a wide canvas-covered bunk, a small wooden stool, and three wooden pegs stuck into the streaming wall. I was wearing the half-military hospital uniform. Talaat took off my jacket, hung it on one of the pegs, and gestured to me to take off all my clothes. Then he went out, shutting the door behind him.

Once I'd stripped I found I began to sweat less. I lay on the bunk, wondering. Then the door opened and Talaat reappeared. He was carrying a bowl of hot water, a cake of soap and a scrubbing brush. Over his arm were two towels. He put the bowl down on the stool. Then he slipped off his *galabieh* and for the first time I saw him naked. His body was even more graceful and lovely than I'd imagined. For an instant he stood there with his hands resting on his lean buttocks watching me. His body was hairless. His gleaming skin was firm and smooth. As he stood there, motionless, the shape of his body was so clear and the limbs were so polished that in that dim light he might have been a bronze statue.

Suddenly, he grinned and with his surprisingly strong arms turned me on to my stomach. Very gently, he began to scrub my back. I tried to lie still but I was quivering with excitement. When he had finished he turned me so that I was facing him. He dipped his hands into the hot water and rubbed them with soap. Then he began washing me. He started with the hair of my head, then my neck. Soon he was washing my shoulders and next my chest, till, at last, his small hands reached the stiffness of my groin. Talaat's hands were gentle and soft and expert. When he saw that I could bear the tension no longer, he stopped and lay down beside me. Then I turned round and drew him towards me and pulled him on to me as if he were a glove. As I began to move he turned his neck round and his lips joined themselves to mine.

A few minutes later we were lying warm and sweating, clasped in each other's arms. I knew it was getting late. I knew I would have trouble getting back into the Sick-leave Camp, I didn't care. I was happier than I'd ever been in my life. For once I wanted nothing in the world more than what I held firmly pressed against me in that small fetid cubicle.

After a while his right arm began to stroke me, and soon we were making love again. But this time his movements were different and more intimate. I had a feeling that he was giving himself to me in a way he had never done with a man before. When we had finished, he kissed me on the lips and signed to me to put on my clothes.

'*Bokra—essaa kam*? What time to-morrow?' he asked.

I thought quickly. If I went out before tea I could be there at six.

'Towards sunset,' I told him, and he nodded.

———◆◆◆◆———

On the way back from the *hammam* he made me memorise the streets so that I could find it again.

I was afraid that when I got back to the Camp Ted might have been a fool and told everyone that I'd tried it on with him. But as soon as I got into the ward I was greeted as cheerfully as usual. I realised that Ted had had the sense to keep quiet.

———◆◆◆◆———

The following day I arrived at the *hammam* soon after six. The fat man answered the door and grinned at me. He jerked his head towards the main Turkish bath.

'Your friend is there already,' he said.

He gave me a spare key and pointed to the cubicle. I unlocked the door. Talaat was lying asleep on the bunk, curled up like a child. As soon as I came in, he sprang up and flung his arms around me. He almost tore off my clothes. Within a few minutes we were making love again.

Perhaps love gives us some extra insight. Though Talaat's love-making was as exciting as ever, I felt there was something worrying him. Later, as we lay in each other's arms, I tried to find out about him. He was called Talaat because he was the third born of the family, and *talaata* means three in Arabic. His mother was a Syrian, his father was Egyptian. They lived in Kantara. They were desperately poor, with eleven children. They'd sold Talaat to the old man with the *felucca* for a few hundred piastres. Talaat was virtually the man's slave. He'd come to the *hammam* to meet me without the old man's permission. If the old man had no customers that day there would be no trouble, for he was in the cabin smoking *hashish*. But if customers came he would be angry.

As Talaat spoke, an idea came into my mind. But it was so fantastic that I instantly dismissed it. However, the thought of the old man's anger disturbed me. So I gave Talaat the present of money I'd brought him and eventually persuaded him to accept it.

'*Bokra*,' I asked. 'To-morrow?'

Talaat nodded. 'Do not fear,' he said. 'I will be here.'

As I walked back to the Sick-leave Camp I realised that like an idiot I had forgotten that at four o'clock the following day there was to be a sick parade, which always took ages. I was now afraid I'd arrive late for our meeting.

That afternoon, in the hot sunshine, we stood outside the Medical Officer's tent. By persuasion, and by a little cunning, I'd managed to be sixth in the queue. When I got into the tent the Chief Medical Officer asked me to strip. He examined me all over for crabs or lice or venereal disease. Then he glanced at my medical chart. He took out his stethoscope and made me take deep breaths in and out. He listened to my chest and to my back longer than he'd ever done before. When he'd finished he looked grim. 'You won't do,' he said. 'We can't treat you here. You'll have to be invalided home.'

Hurriedly he wrote out a chit. 'Give this to the Camp Adjutant,' he said. 'He'll make the necessary arrangements.'

———◆◆◆———

I decided I'd delay handing in the chit till the following day. I now realised that my plan might work. At any rate, I was set on trying it. I unlocked the tin box I kept under my palliasse. I took out a quarter of the money in it. I began to walk down towards the Medina, to the *hammam*. Perhaps it was what the Medical Officer had told me, or perhaps it was because I was hurrying—I don't know—but the pain in my chest which had been hurting me on and off during the last month now started to cause me real distress. I reached the *hammam* at about half past six. As usual the fat man opened the door to me.

'Your little friend is there,' he said to me. But for some reason he looked upset.

I hurried to the cubicle. Talaat was lying naked and flat on his back. But I noticed that he'd tucked his *galabieh* beneath him. He smiled and stretched out his arms when I came in, but he didn't get up from the bed. I bent down and kissed him. He drew my mouth to his lips. For a while we kissed each other.

Then Talaat pointed to the three wooden hooks. I stripped off my clothes and hung them up. I lay down beside him on the bunk. I kissed his head, his forehead, his eyes and his lips, while my hand slid down his slender body. Suddenly I felt a desire so intense that I couldn't wait any longer. I pulled him on to his side. At that moment I gaped in horror. From the calves of his legs right up to his buttocks and back until they reached his shoulders ran the thin red lines of a whip. In places the flesh was cut and blood was oozing out. Now I knew why he was lying on his galabieh—he didn't want to stain the bunk.

'Who did it?' I asked. Even as I put the question I knew the answer.

'My Master,' the boy replied. 'The old man. He missed three people who wanted to go out in the *felucca*, because I wasn't there to hoist the sail. When he is angry my Master is *wahad shaitan*—a cruel devil.' Talaat tried to smile. 'I can still make love to you,' he said, 'but in a different way.'

I shook my head. I still lay beside him, stroking his cheek, while I told him my plan. Presently I asked him if he would agree to it. I told him I was going to be invalided back to England in a big ship. I told him I would get an army pension. I told him that with bribery I was almost sure I could get him on board in the steerage. I explained that I'd learnt carpentry at the school I'd been sent to, I was clever with my hands. With the little capital I'd got, I believed we could set up together in a carpentry shop.

I went to my trouser-pocket, I took out the money I'd drawn from my box, I gave it to him.

'I don't want you to go back to that *felucca* ever again,' I said. 'Can you find a room somewhere in the town?'

The boy looked at the notes and nodded.

'Can we trust the fat man who owns this *hammam*?' I asked him.

'*Aiwa*,' the boy said. 'Certainly. Very much.'

'So at least we can meet here every evening.'

'*Na'am*,' he replied. 'Surely.'

'Would you like to come to England with me?' I asked.

For an instant the boy pressed his lips against my shoulder. '*Aiwa*,' he said. '*Ana ahebak ketir*. I love you very much.'

'I will tell you when my ship's due to sail and what you must do.' I told him.

Talaat took my head and pressed it against his chest.

'You are now my Master,' he said. 'I do whatever you order me to do.'

———❖———

Of course it was a great idea. But like most ideas that have seemed great to me in my life I soon realised that it wasn't going to be as simple as all that. I remembered that on the way out, when we'd stopped at Malta to collect some supplies, there had been two gangways—one for the passengers and the other for the troops and crew. Each gangway had two guards mounted on it. Those of the crew who'd been allowed ashore had been issued with special passes which they had to present when they came back on board. The ship on which I was due to be invalided back had come from Bombay. It was manned by Lascars. My great hope was to get hold of some Lascar and to bribe him to give up his boarding pass so that Talaat could use it to get on to the ship. On the journey from Cairo to Port Said I would be on the troop-train, so I'd have to arrange for Talaat to get to the harbour separately. I'd also have to arrange some meeting place.

All of this, in due course, I managed to organise. But even on the train I began to have doubts. I knew that I could be wonderfully happy with Talaat. But I wondered how he'd take to life in England. As I've said, he spoke very little English. He'd be in a strange land without any friends except me.

Talaat and I met in Port Said in a café close to the station. I told him to wait for me there while I went in search of some Lascar to bribe. Then my troubles began. The first was that only a handful of Lascars had been allowed ashore. None of the ones I approached—when at last, in a mixture of English and bad Arabic, I'd made them understand what I wanted— was willing to be landed in Egypt without any papers or hope of support. They were all paid a puny wage. But at least their jobs were safe, and on board they had free food and lodging. I walked down to look at the ship. I'd only got another hour before I was due to embark. Two gangplanks had been let down. There was a guard mounted on each of them—examining the boarding pass of each passenger or sailor. Suddenly I realised that my idea had been useless. I went back to the café. I sat down beside Talaat. By now I'd only got half an hour left. It took me every minute of that to explain the only sensible plan I could now think of. I told him that I'd go back to England where—the doctors had told me—I was certain to be invalided out of the army.

I'd be a civilian. I'd be free to move as I pleased. As soon as I was fit, I'd get a job as a steward on a ship sailing to Egypt.

I gave Talaat half of the money I'd got left. I told him he must get himself apprenticed as a carpenter to some reliable Egyptian. He must leave his address with the fat man at the Turkish bath. Then, finally, I promised that I'd be back within six months.

Talaat listened to me solemnly.

'Do you promise?' he asked me after a pause. 'Do you promise in the name of Allah you will come back to me?'

'I swear it,' I answered.

Talaat looked keenly into my eyes. Slowly he nodded his head.

'Yes,' he said—almost to himself. 'I trust you. I know that, if you can, you will come back to me.' Then, for a moment, he paused. '*Ana ahebak ketir awi*,' he said. 'I love you very much. I will think of you every hour of every day.'

When I saw the tears in his eyes, I felt a sudden surge of powerlessness as I remembered that I was only an unimportant little trooper—with not much money left. If I'd been rich or if I'd been an officer I'm sure that I could have got that boy on board as my servant. But, as things stood, there was nothing I could do beyond keeping my promise to him and coming back to Egypt to live with him.

I wanted to hold Talaat close to me and to kiss him when I said goodbye. But the café was crowded. Already people were staring at the two of us. I think Talaat was also aware of this. After I'd paid the bill, he pressed my hand under the stained table cloth. Then he got up from his chair.

Half Marks

I stayed late at the hotel where I'd been dining with some friends, and on my way out I stopped at the porter's desk.

'Any chance of you getting me a taxi?'

'Not at this time of night, sir. Your best chance is to see if you can pick one up outside. There's a gentleman waiting there for one now.'

'Thanks. Good night.'

I pushed through the heavy revolving doors into the gloom of the London black-out, which had not then been lifted. It was raining hard, so I decided to wait under the cover of the hotel's awning. I took out a cigarette.

By the flare of my lighter I saw that the other man was standing near me. As I put away my lighter he switched on his torch and turned the light straight on my face. Then he switched off the light.

'Aren't you Ronald Craig?' he said in a thick voice.

'Yes.'

'One of the fellows I was dining with pointed you out to me in the restaurant. My name's Robertson. I used to know your sister quite well. Which way are you going?'

'Battersea.'

'Good. I live in Cheyne Row. We can share a cab.'

'If we can get one,' I said.

'My dear chap, there's going to be no trouble about that. No trouble at all.' He spoke slowly and sometimes stumbled over a word. 'I've got one of the hall-boys out scouring the streets.' I could imagine rather than see the expansive gesture that went with this information.

'I thought the hall-porter said . . .'

'Yes, yes. But they know me here. And they know it pays to treat me properly. The hall-boy will be sweating his insides out to get me a cab—I can tell you that. Because he knows that if he brings one quickly he'll get a fat tip and if he keeps me waiting about he'll get no tip at all.'

I could hear him fumbling for his cigarette case. The flare of his lighter illuminated for a moment a fleshy, middle-aged face above a white silk scarf.

'I told you so,' he said triumphantly. 'Here he comes.' And he shone his torch on a taxi moving slowly towards us through the pelting rain. The hall-boy was standing on the running-board. His tight uniform was drenched and clung closely to his very thin body.

'Here we are, Mr. Robertson.' His teeth were chattering, but he tried to sound pleasant.

'In you get, Craig.'

He stepped in after me and sat down heavily. First he shone his torch on the hall-boy who stood shivering by the open door of the cab, then he focused his torch on the gold watch strapped round his thick hairy wrist.

'You kept me waiting five minutes,' he said to the boy. 'Only a shilling for you to-night.'

'Very good, Captain Robertson. To Cheyne Row, sir?'

'You don't mind dropping me first, do you?'

'Not at all,' I said. 'It's on my way.'

The boy gave the driver the address, then he turned to Robertson.

'Good night, sir.'

'Good night, my lad.'

The driver pulled back his shutter.

'You'll have to pay extra fare.'

'That's all right,' Robertson said in the contented voice of one who has dined really well, and leaned back comfortably. He smelt of cigar smoke and expensive hair wash.

'Wretched nuisance, this taxi shortage. Makes dining out at night an appalling business. Not that it's worth dining out anywhere these days. My club's gone to pot and, of course, restaurants are completely impossible.'

'I think restaurants are quite good, considering,' I said.

'That's because, as I could see just now, you are young. You don't know yet what really good food is like, so you can't judge its importance. I tell you there are few greater pleasures

in life than a really good meal—with good wine, of course.'
He paused, breathing heavily.

'I do enjoy a good meal now and then,' I said for want of a
better answer. This seemed to annoy him.

'Yet there are other things you enjoy just as much, I suppose.
That's the trouble with your generation. Lack of taste. Not
only for food. Take pictures, for instance. What do you care
for really good pictures?'

'Oh, quite a bit.'

'Well, you may, but most of your contemporaries don't. Not
that I wasn't the same at your age—full of high ideals about a
better world, but with no proper understanding of civilisation.
When I got back to England after the last war I gradually
discovered two things: first, that all this business about a better
world was poppycock. Second, that I was uncivilised.'

He stopped and once again began fumbling for his lighter. I
turned towards him, and this time as he lit his cigarette I had
a good chance to look at him. His face was creased and paunchy
and flushed. His eyes were bloodshot; his breath reeked of
brandy.

'I tell you I discovered I was uncivilised,' he repeated defiantly, as if I had contradicted him. 'So I settled down to teach
myself a few things about how to live. I'd been left the house in
Cheyne Row, which helped a bit, and I settled down to lead a
civilised life. . . .'

He went on talking as the taxi slithered its way through the
rain towards Chelsea; and gradually a picture of his house
formed in my mind. From the dark cold of the taxi I saw the
comfortable bachelor establishment with expensive plumbing
in three bathrooms, with Guardis and Canalettos on the panelled
walls of his dining-room. I saw the imitation coal fire glowing
discreetly in his richly-carpeted sitting-room. And I saw the
pattern of his life between the two wars.

He was called by his man-servant at eight, with tea and biscuits. Breakfast was laid in the sitting-room, because it was
easier to warm than the dining-room and faced south. He
arrived at his office at about ten o'clock and dealt with the
affairs of the small firm he owned, until one o'clock, when he
lunched at his club.

After he had finished his brandy and cigar, he took a taxi

back to the City, where he stayed until teatime, when he returned to his club for a rubber of bridge. At six he went home to Cheyne Row, and friends might be dropping in for a cocktail. He was proud of his cook, and enjoyed giving small dinner parties.

After dinner there was more bridge, and so, after a couple more whiskies and soda, to bed.

Naturally there were deviations in the placid routine. There was Ascot, for instance, and the fourth of June. Sometimes, he hinted slyly, there was a girl who lived in a mews off Berkeley Square.

What's more, he liked nature at the right time and at the right place: grouse were to be shot in Scotland in September; the sun shone at Cannes in May; snow lay at St. Moritz in December.

And I mustn't suppose that he was getting soft. Hardly a week-end passed without his getting in two rounds of golf, though nowadays the lack of caddies, of course, was rather a bore. Come to that, lots of things were difficult to get in wartime, but you could always get them if you knew how, and had the cash . . . and so on.

He went on talking. But I was not listening any longer to the actual words he said. I was listening, I cannot quite explain how, to the deadness which was in him. His solid form moved comfortably over the face of the earth, drawing in rich sustenance from various pastures. But the spirit inside him was stone dead.

I had stopped listening, but from the tone of his voice, I knew he was asking me a question.

'Excuse me,' I said apologetically.

'I was asking you whether you went to many shows in London?'

'No, not many.'

'I saw a splendid show the other evening. Excellent tune in it. How did it go? Oh yes, I know! "I'm going to get lit up when the lights go up in London." Amusing idea. I know I got absolutely lit up last time when the old war was finished. We all did, you know. Ah, that war was different. Leave in the old days really was something to look forward to. I knew your sister quite well, you know. Heavens, *what* a charming person. I suppose you hardly remember her?'

I lied. 'Hardly at all,' I said.

'She was a glorious creature. All of us in the brigade were head over heels in love with her. I can remember the moment I first met her—the very moment. It was a dance in Belgrave Square. . . .'

He began telling me the story of their first meeting, and I stared out at the dark wet road ahead. I did not need to be reminded of my sister. I was eleven when she died, and can remember her well. I lied to him because I did not want to share my memories with him.

But as he told his story about the dance at Belgrave Square, and as the taxi slid forward slowly in the rain and darkness, I began to think once again of that particular evening which I now realise is for ever impressed on my memory.

I can remember almost every word spoken that evening, though I do not remember the date. I think it must have been in the autumn of 1915. My sister had promised me that if I was quick over my bath she would tell me a fairy story before I went to bed.

I was in my dressing-gown, curled up in an armchair near the fire in the sitting-room downstairs, listening to what the fairy princess said to the prince.

'Had the fairy princess got brown hair like you?'

'Yes, Ronald, she had.'

'And did she live in London?'

'Yes. She lived in London.'

The clock struck seven.

'Now, Ronald, it's time for bed.'

'Oh, no, Mary! Please not. I don't know what the fairy prince looked like yet.'

The front door bell rang.

'May I go and answer the door?'

'No, Vera will go.'

I listened impatiently to Vera's heavy steps plodding up from the basement. I do not know why I was so excited.

'Who do you think it is, Mary?'

'I don't know. Perhaps someone for Mummy.'

'But Mummy is out this evening.'

I heard Vera open the front door and a man's voice say:

'Is Miss Mary at home?'

My sister sprang up and moved quickly to the door.

'Stephen!'

He walked into the room.

'Mary, I was so afraid you'd be out!'

'You're not going back?'

'Yes.'

'But your wound's hardly had time to heal.'

'I'm all right now. Besides, they need officers out there, you know.'

For a moment there was silence. I was glad he hadn't noticed me curled up in the armchair because I could stare at him as long as I liked. I'd seen officers often before, but never one like him. He was tall and slender, and his eyes were a deep blue, and his hair was curly and golden.

'Mummy will be terribly sorry to have missed you.'

'I didn't know your mother was out. Ought I to go?'

'No, stay, Stephen.'

Then he noticed me.

'Hullo! This your brother?'

'Yes. Ronald, get up and say "how do you do!" '

'How do you do?' he said. 'Don't be shy, old man. How old are you?'

'I'm nine.'

'Won't you sit down?' my sister said.

He sat down in the armchair by the fire, and I stood beside him.

'Come along. That's right.' And he lifted me on to his knees. I snuggled up against him and he put his arms round me. I remember all that. I felt he was my friend, and I began to stroke the gold hairs on the back of his hands. I was absorbed in looking at him and his uniform. I can remember that there were long moments when both of them were silent.

'When do you go back?'

'To-morrow.' I could feel his voice vibrating as he spoke.

'As soon as that?'

'Are you sorry?'

'You know I am.'

There was more silence. Then a barrel-organ began playing in the street outside.

'What's that tune, Mary?' I asked. It was he who answered, and he looked steadily at my sister.

' "If you were the only girl in the world," ' he said.

'What's that pretty ribbon on your chest?'

'That is the Military Cross,' my sister said at once.

'But there's no cross.'

'No. Ronald, that's the name of the medal, not the ribbon.'

'Have you been brave?'

'No! I've just been one of the lucky ones, that's all.' He was not looking at me, he was looking at my sister. I suppose he was grateful to me for giving him a chance to talk indirectly to her.

'Have you killed a German?'

'Yes, I have. Several Germans.'

'Are the Germans very wicked?'

'Not very much more wicked than other men. But they are stupid, like sheep, and their leader is wicked. He wants to rule the world, all of it.'

'But he won't, will he?'

'No, he won't, because we are going to beat the Germans.'

'And then we'll rule the world?'

'Nobody will rule the world.' His voice trembled, and I wriggled round to look at his face. He was not looking at my sister now. He was staring straight ahead at nothing in particular. And as he spoke, his eyes shone and his face was radiant with love and kindness.

'Nobody will rule the world. After we have beaten the Germans, the people of every country will be free to choose their own leaders and the people of every country will work to make this world a better place.'

At that moment his whole being was transfused with a strange light so that I felt he didn't belong to our small sitting-room; he didn't belong to the everyday world that Mary and Mummy and I lived in. He belonged to the world of stories and dreams.

And then I remembered why I felt I knew his face so well; for with his golden hair and his deep blue eyes he looked like Saint George in my picture-book. He was the knight in shining armour, the knight of chivalry and honour. And I loved him with all my heart.

Vera came in.

'Now, Master Ronald. Bedtime.'

'Oh, Vera, please let me stay.'

'It's high time you were in bed.' I tried not to cry as I was led away.

'You'll soon see him again, I'm sure,' Vera said.

She was wrong. He left for France the next day, and my sister had died from Spanish influenza before he came back to England. So I never saw him again.

But in my mind he had remained the emblem of all that was chivalrous and beautiful and romantic. And as I stared out of the taxi window I wondered what had become of him. I couldn't remember his surname. Perhaps Robertson, if he wasn't too fuddled, might recollect it

But the taxi had stopped in Cheyne Row.

'Just hold my torch for a moment while I pay my share, will you?' he said, and clambered out heavily. He handed the driver a note and stood swaying slightly as he waited for his change.

'Do you remember a captain in the Brigade of Guards with the christian name of Stephen? He was a great friend of my sister's in the last war.'

He giggled. It was a foolish giggle.

'His other name was Robertson,' he said.

'Do you mean you're Stephen Robertson?' I said, and probably I sounded as shocked as I felt.

'Who the hell do you think I am? If it hadn't been for that influenza epidemic I'd probably be your brother-in-law.'

I stared with horror at his puffy face. The picture in the nursery-book came into my mind. I switched off the torch.

'Good night to you,' he said. 'Drop in for a drink one evening. I'd be delighted.'

I handed him back his torch.

'Thanks,' I said. 'Good night'

As the taxi swung round I saw Saint George fumbling with his latch-key.

The Girl in Number Seven

Tangier has changed.

When I first went there a dozen years ago the city bristled with smugglers, gigolos, forgers, 'confidence-men', spies, gun-runners, dope-peddlers and sex-fiends. Today the place is almost respectable.

As soon as Morocco gained her independence all the brothels were closed, the international police force was disbanded, and the whole town was 'purged'. The residents were only just recovering from this shock, when the Sultan took away the town's Royal Charter, abolished its special status as an international zone, and reduced Tangier into the same position as any other Moroccan city.

The effect has been immediate. Fifty banks have closed. Three hundred firms have left. Scores of residents have packed their bags and vanished. The smugglers' fast cabin-cruisers have slid away from their moorings. Hundreds of flats and villas are empty. And the whole atmosphere of Tangier has altered.

I can remember—twelve years ago—an evening in the Parade Bar, run by a tough young American, when a well-known Italian gangster, who had been Capone's right-hand man, knocked out a notorious smuggler and had to retire through the door marked GENTS because the force of the blow had broken the harness of his shoulder-holster. The Parade is still run by the same American. He is no less tough, but he has grown far more amiable, and the bar now has the breezy, wholesome charm of a country club in Virginia.

The well-paid spies and gigolos, the bogus Barons and self-styled Colonels, the smart 'kept' women and their keepers, the more affluent crooks and financiers, all used to gather in Dean's Bar, presided over by the famous Dean in person, mixing a dry martini with the air of a member of the Borgia family preparing a loving-cup. Dean is dead, and his Bar has become quite cosy.

Tangier has changed.

I went to lunch at a villa that ten years ago was famous for its Bacchanalian orgies. Within those brightly-painted walls naked film stars had washed themselves in milk and almost obliterated themselves in champagne. But when the smart Moorish butler showed me into the drawing-room, what did I find? My host and his elderly secretary at work on a tapestry. There were the two of them, surrounded by ormolu clocks and horsehair armchairs, tatting away, dipping their needles in and out between sips of sherry. And their conversation was so prim and discreet that I might as well have had lunch in Tunbridge Wells.

That night I dined with an American banker who was interested to back a film story of mine that happened to be set in Morocco. As the headlights of my car shone up the turning on the mountain road that led to the villa, an impressive iron gate was opened by a Moorish servant and I drove up a long avenue of eucalyptus trees and stopped outside the white washed front of a single-storeyed house with two pillars forming a porch.

As soon as I was shown into the gilt-and-white drawing-room, my heart sank. Planted like overgrown shrubs on either side of the fireplace were Sir Edgar and Lady Dakin. I had met them at Dean's Bar. They were extremely staid and very dull.

Then I saw the other guest talking to my hostess, and my depression lifted.

The other guest was Claude.

As soon as I saw Claude I realised that Tangier might have changed, but Claude had remained unaltered. The town might have grown respectable—but not Claude. One glance was enough to tell me that he had in no way reformed. The stained tweed jacket, the threadbare grey flannel trousers, the whisky glass held defiantly close to his knobbly neck, the slight list to starboard, the red-rimmed, peering eyes, the unshaven chin—it was all there. Claude had survived the purge.

Claude was a journalist who had lived in Tangier for thirty years at least. He earned the money to buy his drink and support his girl friends by working as a 'stringer' for a London paper. He got no fixed salary; he was paid according to the amount of the material that he sent in that was used. When his drink bill reached such heights that credit was denied him, or when his young mistress threatened to leave him, Claude had been known to invent a sensational news story to raise some ready cash. On one occasion he invented a revolution in Tetuan and ran it for eight whole days. Claude won himself a whole crate of whiskey and a strip-tease artiste before it was discovered that not one shot had been fired in anger in Tetuan or anywhere near it.

Claude was sacked. But there are many British newspapers, and editors retire or die. And Claude always managed to find *some* paper to write for. And with the passing of the years he had become one of Tangier's institutions, a familiar landmark. And there he stood, gaunt and haggard as ever, inclined at his usual angle, like an untouched monument in a blitzed city.

As we greeted each other I wondered why Dexter Brent had invited him. For my quiet-spoken, grey-haired, middle-aged host was obviously the most conventional and fastidious type of American. Perhaps Claude was a friend of Brent's pretty wife, Maria. I had not met her before. She was very graceful and beautifully dressed in a plain black gown that obviously came from a Paris house. She spoke English with the trace of a foreign accent. She was about thirty-five years old and looked Italian with her pale olive skin and large dark eyes. But as I watched, Claude turned to her and made some remark, and she answered him politely but coldly and turned away to talk to Lady Dakin. One thing was certain. Maria Brent was no friend of Claude's.

A Moorish butler in a grey livery and a white turban and white gloves came in and announced that dinner was ready. Claude gulped down his drink so quickly that he nearly choked, and we walked across a marble hall into the dining-room.

Sir Edgar Dakin and I sat on either side of Maria Brent. Lady Dakin sat on Dexter Brent's right, and Claude lowered himself unsteadily into the chair on his left.

As soon as we had sat down, Brent smiled apologetically at Lady Dakin and turned to Claude.

'Before I forget it,' he said in his quiet, controlled voice with its faint Southern accent, 'there's a favour I'd like to ask you.'

'And what's that?' Claude asked, taking a long draught from the glass of wine the butler had poured out for him.

'Well, my bank has decided to start a charity fund to help orphan children in Tangier, and I want your help in launching our appeal.'

Then I understood why Claude had been invited. Brent wanted free publicity.

'There's a fund started already,' Claude said.

'My bank has decided to start a fund of its own,' Brent said.

'To get in with the Moroccan government or to get yourself publicity or both?' Claude asked.

Brent was annoyed.

'To help the children you see begging in the streets,' he said.

'I see,' Claude said, and was silent.

There was an awkward pause.

I turned to my hostess.

'Have you been out here long?' I asked—to break the silence.

Maria Brent turned to me in surprise. Her wide eyes gazed at me in reproach, as if I had insulted her.

'But I am Moroccan,' she said.

I happened to be looking at Claude at that moment. He smiled at me mischievously and raised his glass as if to drink a toast to my embarrassment.

'Maria's family are one of the oldest in Mogador,' Brent said smoothly. 'Her grandparents built the Jamaïl Hotel.'

Claude gave me a broad wink. I decided he had had far too much to drink. Sir Edgar and Dexter Brent then began a long conversation about the cost of building in Morocco that lasted throughout the sole and the steak. Now and again I noticed that Claude would gaze—almost furtively—at his hostess, and once, I was almost certain, he gave her one of his oversize winks. But if Maria Brent saw his wink or his covert glances she gave no sign of recognition, no flicker of a response. Her eyes moved serenely and confidently round the glittering Sheraton table while she talked pleasantly to Sir Edgar and to me in turn. Her conversation was polished, and she was obviously well read.

Meanwhile, Claude was drinking steadily, and his host was

growing impatient with him. I began to be afraid that a row was imminent.

The explosion came when we joined Maria and Lady Dakin for coffee after drinking some sour port and excellent brandy.

The conversation had turned to the latest Rabat scandal. A young secretary from the British Embassy had been caught in an illicit brothel when the police had raided it. His career was in danger.

When Dexter Brent spoke, for the first time there was a trace of emotion in his voice.

'The young man deserves to be sacked,' he announced firmly.

'Nonsense,' said Claude.

'He was in a position of trust and he betrayed it.'

'Pure poppycock,' said Claude. 'Besides, the girl wasn't even under age.'

'What's that got to do with it?'

'If the girl had only been twelve there *might* be some point in blaming the poor man.'

'I don't think this is the kind of conversation to conduct in mixed company,' Brent said stiffly.

'In some of the States in your country,' Claude said in a slow drawl, 'you can *marry* a girl at the age of twelve. Don't you discuss *that* in mixed company?'

'That's different.'

'Why? Are girls made any different in America?'

As Claude leaned forward defiantly, his elbow brushed against a Lalique ashtray on the table beside him and it fell onto the parquet floor and broke into small fragments.

'Sorry,' said Claude. 'I'll buy you a dozen more to-morrow.'

He looked over his shoulder and spoke as if to an invisible secretary.

'Jenkins,' he said, 'remind me to make an appointment with my glass-blower to-morrow.'

Claude stretched out his hand for the tumbler of whiskey beside him.

'Don't you think you've had enough to drink?' Brent asked coldly.

'Yes, I do,' Claude said surprisingly quickly. 'And I think I should now retire to my deliciously downy couch to sleep. I've a deliciously downy companion waiting for me there.

She's an old hag of sixteen. So you could propose to her inside or outside the good old State of Tennessee. Ta for the grub. Good night all. When I'm gone, do *try* to keep the conversation clean.'

Claude rose unsteadily from his chair and then fell back again.

'My head is in the clouds,' he said. 'But my feet are of clay.'

I walked across the room and helped him up.

'I've got a car outside,' I said. 'I can give you a lift home if you like.'

'That would be very kind of you,' Brent said.

'That would be very kind of you,' Claude said, trying to imitate Brent's Southern accent.

I thanked the Brents for dinner and said good night to the Dakins and steered Claude out of the room.

'Coffee,' Claude said. 'Must have some coffee.'

'I thought you wanted to go home?'

'Coffee first. Downy couch afterwards,' he said.

So we drove to a café in the Place de France and sat indoors because it was cold outside.

'Did I behave badly?' Claude asked.

'Yes,' I said.

'Really badly?'

'Monstrously badly.'

'Good,' said Claude. 'Serves her right. She wouldn't even catch my eye. Not even when I winked at her.'

'You knew Maria Brent before tonight?'

'Knew!' Claude laughed. 'Yes. I knew her.'

As he sat at the marble-topped table, he was listing so far to starboard that I was afraid he would fall over. He peered at me through his red-rimmed eyes.

'Would you be surprised to learn that my past had been not altogether blameless?' he asked.

'No,' I said.

'I thought not,' Claude said with a sigh.

For a while he stared down at his coffee in silence. Then he said: 'Would you be very kind and order us both a brandy?'

'Certainly.'

Claude remained silent until the brandies arrived. Then he raised his head and winked at me and nodded several times.

'Do you know how much you'll have to pay in France for those brandies?' he asked. 'The equivalent of five shillings. Twenty years ago in this town you could get blind drunk for two and sixpence. Those were the days! Of course the trouble was I hadn't always got two and sixpence. And that was where the Belgian banker came in. The old stoat.'

I felt I was losing track of the conversation.

'The Belgian banker?' I asked.

'Yes. The Belgian banker. You see, in 1937 the bank at home wouldn't let me have any more money. I was overdrawn, that's why. But it put me in a terrible fix. No girls and no liquor. So I went round to Dean's Bar to see if I could borrow some money from some of the English colony. And there I met the Belgian banker. Michelet—that was the name of the old stoat. He'd just come out to Tangier to start up a new branch here. That sounds funny to-day when everything's closing down. But in those days banks were sprouting up overnight like mushrooms, and Michelet wanted to cash in on it . . .

'Well, I got into conversation with him at the bar, and presently this Michelet—he was a beefy-looking man of about fifty—began asking me if I knew where he could find some local colour. Was there a native quarter, he wanted to know . . .

'Well, as soon as any tourist starts talking about local colour and native quarters you can be quite certain what they want. Sex. So I made a few inquiries and found out that this red-faced, paunchy old Michelet was keen on young girls. Now, as it so happened, I knew the very place to take him—because I'd spent my last few pesetas visiting the place myself.

'You see, there was a girl there I was mad about. The house was run by a huge fat Spanish woman who stood no nonsense from her clients or from the Moorish girls who worked for her. She was an amusing old reprobate, and I used to drop in for a chat with her, and she'd show me her newest recruits. And that's how I met little Aïsha.

'Aïsha was fifteen years old at the time. As you know, a Moroccan girl of fifteen is as grown up as an English girl of seventeen or eighteen. And Aïsha was the most beautiful girl I've ever known. Even now, I can remember the shape of her shoulders and the curve of her breasts and her slender legs and the softness of her skin—and above all, the innocence of her smile, as she lay, stretched out on the shabby divan-bed, staring up at me, without a trace of guile.

'But when I got home that night I found I'd lost my wallet. I had paid off the fat Spanish woman before going upstairs so there could only be one culprit. Aïsha. Innocent-looking little Aïsha.

'Early the next morning I went back to the bordello and battered on the door. After a time, the door was opened by the Spanish woman.

' "Back already?" she asked crossly.

' "Yes," I said. "Where's Aïsha?"

' "Asleep in bed. You know the room. It's number seven."

'I went upstairs. The door to number seven wasn't locked. I walked in. Aïsha was asleep. She was curled up like a child, with her cheek resting on her arm. She looked so innocent that I decided I must have been wrong. Perhaps I had lost my money on the way home. Then I saw the corner of my wallet protruding from under the striped linen pillow.

'As I watched, Aïsha woke up and saw me standing by the door. Then she saw the edge of the wallet sticking out, and her arm moved like a flash to conceal it. When she realised from my face that it was too late, she sat up in bed and grinned at me without a trace of shame. So I put her on my knees and gave her a good spanking. But she laughed and wriggled so much that I gave up. And she looked so attractive—all flushed and panting for breath—that we made love again. And this time I let her keep my wallet. After all, there wasn't much left in it.'

Claude paused and sipped his brandy.

'So when the Belgian banker—that lobster-faced Michelet—began talking about the native quarter, I decided to take him to the fat old Spanish woman's house. I wasn't going to let him see Aïsha. Not on your life. But there was a girl there called Lalla who I could fix him up with—while I paid a visit to Aïsha.

'So first I borrowed ten pounds off him, and then I took him down to the Zocco Chico and along the winding narrow alleys and dark passageways that led to the brothel. And then the fat old Spanish woman went and ruined everything—everything.

'Before you could say "Mammon" she had spotted that the

Belgian was rich and eager—a perfect customer, in fact. So the mercenary old hag immediately produced her star turn, Aïsha—my darling little Aïsha from room number seven. And that was how it all began.'

Claude stared mournfully into his brandy glass. I ordered another round.

'How all *what* began?' I asked.

'Aïsha's great career,' said Claude.

'I don't understand.'

'Well, the Belgian went mad about her. He came back the next night and the next. He was there every night for a week. Then he decided he couldn't bear the thought of anyone else having a look in—me in particular, of course. So he paid off the Spanish woman and removed Aïsha to a flat on the Marshan.

'That lasted for six weeks. But then the nasty old Belgian found out that I was visiting Aïsha during banking hours, so he decided to take her away from Tangier altogether.

'Aïsha was only fifteen, remember, and the only language she spoke was a Moroccan dialect of Arabic mixed with a few rude words of Spanish and French. But by now Michelet was besotted about her, so he sent her to a private school for foreign children near Paris and had her taught French and English and history and literature and deportment—the lot. Think of my darling little Aïsha, swotting away at arithmetic, when she could have been having a good time with me! What a waste of time! But she had ambition, had little Aïsha, and she worked hard, and she was quick to learn—as the Spanish woman had discovered.

'When Aïsha was seventeen, the Belgian took her away from school and introduced her to the fringes of Paris society.

'With her looks and her charm and her high spirits and vitality, Aïsha was a smash hit. Men fell for her like ninepins. Suddenly the paunch-bellied, red-jowled old Michelet realised he was in danger of losing his little treasure for good and all. There was now only one thing he could do to keep her. And he did it. He married her. And there you have the story of this evening in a nutshell.'

Claude popped a lump of sugar into his brandy and sucked it gloomily.

'What's Aïsha got to do with this evening?' I asked.

'Aïsha was our hostess,' said Claude.

I stared at him with obvious disbelief.

'But our hostess was called Maria,' I said.

'Aïsha changed her name to Maria when she was converted to Catholicism in her French school,' Claude said. 'Surely you guessed that.'

'But you said that the man who married her was a Belgian banker called Michelet.'

'And so he was,' said Claude. 'He died two years ago. And Aïsha—or Maria, as she now prefers to be called—married Dexter Brent, the solidly prosperous American banker. You see, by then she'd got used to sleeping in financial circles.'

'Do you mean to say that the elegant woman at the head of the table this evening who prattled away about Pope and Proust was the girl whose bottom you smacked in a brothel?' I asked.

'Yes,' Claude said. 'She was the girl.'

He gulped down his brandy.

'Tangier has changed,' Claude said.

Then, slowly and awkwardly by pressing on the table he levered himself to his feet.

'Tangier has changed,' he repeated.

Then he winked at me and shook his head.

'And so has my little Aïsha,' he added.

The Man who could Hypnotise Racehorses

The little man in the limp brown suit stared wearily at his gin and tonic. His long nose and large, heavily-fringed eyes set in a small, wizened face made him look like a very old gazelle.

'My name is Henry Birston,' he said. '*Now* perhaps you understand?'

The lorry driver looked at him across the table of the saloon bar and sipped his bitter.

'I can't rightly say that I do,' he said.

'You've never heard of Henry Birston?'

'No.'

'Birston with an "i", of course?'

'No.'

'That just goes to show,' the little man said, his long lashes flickering with annoyance. 'Allow me to tell you that three years ago I was famous. I, and I alone could fill the Albert Hall.'

'You don't say.'

'And the Palais de Danse at Blackpool.'

'Reely.'

'And Caxton Hall.'

'But what did you do?'

The little man raised his head proudly.

'I was one of the most celebrated practising hypnotists in Europe,' he said.

'Well, I never.'

'Across this table you see a victim of vulgar prejudice,' he said, waggling his thumb. 'A man forbidden to practise his own profession because of mass ignorance and superstition in high and low places. So far as I'm concerned you can have the House of Commons. *Odi profanum vulgus et arceo.*'

'You can't half talk,' the lorry driver said admiringly.

'Talk! It was more than talk. Though, of course, talk did enter into it,' the little man said, gazing reflectively at the ceiling with his large liquid eyes.

<hr />

It was at the Palladium, Bognor Regis, that my troubles started, he said. I ought to have been more careful because I'd seen the new moon through glass. But everything seemed all right. The 'House Full' notices were up outside the theatre, and that pleased me because a full house always makes the audience more prone to suggestion. It's the atmosphere, you know.

Before starting to operate my mass suggestion, I decided to call two or three volunteers on to the stage and operate on them. If an audience can see an individual completely hypnotised it's easier to work on them in the mass.

My first volunteer was a man. As soon as I saw him I knew he was going to be a pushover. He was intelligent, but not too intelligent, and though he walked on to the stage with a jaunty smile I could see that he was nervous, which meant that part of his mind, at least, believed that there was *something* in my powers.

I went to work on him in my usual way. I asked him to sit on a chair in the middle of the stage. I asked him to look straight into my eyes for a few seconds. As soon as our eyes met I dilated my pupils. I then began to talk to him firmly and loudly in a monotonous tone of voice. I told him he was beginning to feel sleepy, that his eyelids felt heavy, that he would soon feel pleasantly relaxed.

Then suddenly I produced my pencil. It's a little pencil, made of bright gold, that was given me, I may tell you, by the Maharanee of Swavah.

'Now you must look at my pencil,' I said to him soothingly, turning my dilated pupils on him.

And sure enough, his eyelids fell on their own accord. My battle was won. The rest was easy. I just had to put the ideas into his mind, that's all. First, I told him he was playing in the finals at Wimbledon.

'It's your service,' I said.

He got up from his chair, threw an imaginary ball up into the air with his left hand, raised his right arm, twisted his body and unleashed himself with a terrific smash. The audience howled with laughter. I had a rare old time with him. I had him dancing in a ballet, swimming the channel, and climbing Mount Everest. The audience were rolling about, they laughed so.

I finished with a demonstration of post-hypnotic suggestion.

I said: 'I'm going to clap my hands three times. At the third clap you'll wake up and a bee will just have stung you on the nose.'

Sure enough, at the third clap he came out of the trance. He looked round, a bit dazed. Then his hand shot to his nose.

The applause was deafening. I shook him by the hand and thanked him.

'Next volunteer, please,' I called out. 'And if it's a lady I promise to let her off lightly.'

When I saw her climbing on to the stage I should have called it off then and there. I'd only to say: 'I'm afraid you're not a suitable type, madam.' But my pride was my downfall. I let her come gawking up the steps from the stalls on to the stage, and I never stopped her.

She was one of the tallest girls I've ever seen, with shoes the size of a guardsman's. At first I thought she was a soldier dressed up, but as she came closer I saw that she was unmistakably female. She had projecting teeth and a smile that was just plain silly. There were titters when she sat down in the chair.

I began as usual by telling her to look into my eyes. At the moment our eyes met I realised she was going to be a tough proposition. She was so bloody stupid there was nothing there to hypnotise.

'Your eyelids are beginning to droop,' I said with as much conviction as I could muster. 'You're beginning to feel sleepy.'

'No, I'm not,' she said briskly.

When the audience laughed I began to get cross. I dilated my pupils to their extreme.

'You're beginning to feel happily relaxed,' I said firmly.

'Because I'm with you,' she said bashfully.

The laughter made me wild. I glared at her. 'Your eyelids are getting moist,' I said.

'Not yet,' she simpered.

I could sense that the audience was getting out of hand. I summoned up my energies for one last effort. I fixed my eyes on her, exerting all my powers. It felt as if my eyeballs were bursting. Then I produced my pencil. Immediately she closed her eyes. And I knew I had won.

I was still cross, though. So I told her the stage she was standing on was red hot. At once she began hopping from one foot to the other, screwing up her face and waving her hands. The audience rocked. She'd have dived into the orchestra pit if I hadn't stopped her.

Well, my fit of temper had passed and I began to feel sorry for the old crow. So I told her that the chair she was sitting on was a seat in a punt on the Thames. And there she sat with a soppy smile on her face dabbling her fingers into water that wasn't there, as happy as the Queen of Sheba.

Then I saw it was time to begin my mass suggestion. So I told her that on the third clap of my hands she'd wake up fresh and relaxed.

'One,' I said, 'two . . . *three*!'

And nothing happened. She was still trailing her fingers in the air and looking up at me with that soppy smile.

I clapped my hands again. No result.

'Wake up,' I said, sternly.

No result. She was still dabbling her fingers in the Thames.

I went up to her and put my arms on her shoulders. Then the awful event occurred. She leaned forward and kissed me.

I suppose it was the catcalls and laughter from the audience that made me lose my head. I shook her violently.

'Wake up!' I shouted. But she still smiled up at me dreamily.

I slapped her face. No result. I was so intent on getting her to come out of her trance that I didn't see her brother climbing on to the stage. And then it was too late. He knocked me flat, the brute.

I was out for three hours. The real trouble was that his oafish sister was out for six whole months. Nothing they could do could bring her round, and her family weren't keen for me to see her. In fact, they'd called in the police. And when she did at last wake up they wanted to prosecute.

Well, for various reasons the girl wouldn't give evidence against me. I got bound over for two years all the same. I was told that next time it happened I'd get three years in jail.

That morning when I left the court I felt I was a ruined man. The judge had said some very cruel things about me and I knew my career was finished.

As I walked up the lonely road there was a horse standing harnessed to a milk van. I noticed the horse because it reminded me of that stupid girl. I was about five yards away from the animal when it lifted its head, looked at me in a knowing kind of way, and neighed Whahaihai, like that.

Something about it made me furious. So I gave it a nasty stare and said, 'Whahaihai to you,' and walked on. I turned because I heard a clatter. Bless me if the horse hadn't sunk to the ground. I went back to look. There it was, lying on the pavement, breathing peacefully, its eyes tight shut. I pulled back the eyelids. There was no doubt. The horse was in a trance.

As I walked away it dawned on me that though I'd lost one means of making money I'd probably discovered another. So the next day I moved to Newmarket.

———◆◆◆◆◆———

I'd been round the bars for a fortnight before I met the types I needed. Call them Wing and Davies. Wing was a big hefty chap with a face like a beetroot and a limp. Davies, his crony, was on the small side with a foxy face and a scar on his cheek that he said had been caused by a horse's hoof, though I think it was more likely a razor.

At first, of course, they wouldn't believe me. So I took them to a field where there was a pony grazing. Within a couple of minutes it was sleeping like a two-year-old, which it probably was.

'That's no good to us,' said Wing.

'No good at all,' said Davies. He had a habit of repeating what Wing said that got on my nerves after a while.

'If you put a horse out cold like that,' Wing explained, 'it wouldn't run.'

'And the second favourite would become favourite,' Davies chipped in.

'Well, what do you want?' I asked.

'Couldn't you just half-hypnotise it so that it wouldn't go to sleep but would just run slow?'

That meant getting the animal into the stage known as a light trance.

'It might be possible—with practice,' I added.

'Could you be ready for the Bath races on May the 14th and 15th?'

That gave me three weeks. 'Could be,' I said.

'The favourites always win at Bath,' Davies said with a smirk.

'Mind you, I'll only fix one horse a day,' I said. 'It's apt to be tiring.'

'One horse is good enough for us,' Wing said with a hearty laugh.

'How shall we share the profits?' I asked.

———————◆◆◆◆———————

Well, I thought they were very unfair about the profits. They insisted we each had a third share. After all, I had to take the risk. They had only got to find the money and put it on the Tote. And I'd worn myself to the bone tramping round Newmarket trying to find lone horses to practise on. However, I'd got nearly perfect. There was one carthorse that wandered about in a daze for weeks after I'd dilated my pupils at him.

So on the 14th May we all three went to Bath. Now, the odds-on favourite for the four o'clock was Fontara (by Chanson—French for 'song'—out of Tara's Queen, and the second favourite was Starry Boy (by Castor out of Homing Maiden). The race was seven furlongs, which gave my efforts full time to have their effect. There were no other horses worth a jot in the race. What I had to do was to put Fontara into a light trance so he'd just canter down the course. Meanwhile Wing and Davies would back Starry Boy.

I confess I was sweating terribly under the new bowler hat

they had bought me, when we got into the members' enclosure But it was all easier than I thought. At precisely three thirty-five, Fontara, a chestnut colt was led into an open stall facing the paddock. The travelling lad and a stable boy began fussing round him, while the jockey was being weighed out. I leaned against a white rail only five yards away, watching innocently. It was while they were slipping the bit into his mouth that I caught his eye. He cocked back his ears and stared me full in the face. I took out my gold pencil as if to mark my race card. I held it up for a minute, and the trick was done. I saw him relax perceptibly. My task was over, so I walked off to the grandstand to join Wing and Davies who were very fretful, I thought. You'd have thought they'd got three thousand on instead of three hundred. When Fontara cantered slowly up to the start they became positively tetchy.

'I don't see anything wrong with him,' Wing hissed in my ear. 'The jockey's just holding him in, that's all.'

'Just you wait,' I said, trying to sound calm.

'That's what we're going to do" Davies said quite nastily.

When someone bellowed 'They're off', I started so that I nearly dropped the binoculars they'd lent me. But though my hands were trembling I could still see that one horse was already well behind.

Fontara finished in a slow canter, last by some forty lengths.

Naturally the stewards had the horse examined. But of course there wasn't a trace of dope. And naturally everyone held different theories about it. I thought the racing correspondent for the *Daily Post* put it best. 'Fontara ran as if in a trance,' he wrote. And in a trance he certainly was.

During the next fortnight our partnership went from strength to strength. Unfortunately, Wing was ambitious. He was tired of small meetings, he said. He wanted a big race, and he soon found one. He worked out that in the Gold Cup at Ascot, apart from the favourite, Snackbar (by Fairy Toast out of Moll Flanders), there were only two horses that could win. If I could be certain of fixing Snackbar he would put an ante-post bet on Stern Light and Fanciful.

You see, the advantage of his plan was this. Inasmuch as Snackbar was a red-hot favourite, we'd get good odds on the other two. Once we'd got our bets on it didn't matter what happened to Snackbar so long as he didn't win. He needn't even reach the course. Our odds were fixed. That's what an ante-post bet means, you see.

Well, like a fool I agreed to Wing's plan, and the next day he turned up in triumph.

'We've got our bets on at wonderful odds,' he said. 'For all I care now you can put Snackbar out for the season. In fact, it would be safer if you did.'

So I determined to send Snackbar into a deep trance. The trouble was I couldn't get near him. Our recent operations had convinced the racing world that there was an expert dope gang at work using some hitherto unknown drug. Favourites were now closely guarded, and it was only eight days before the race.

I was hustled off when I tried to approach him on his way to the gallops at Newmarket where he was being trained. I was positively threatened when they caught me near his loose box. I had a terrible week, getting up at five every morning for those wretched gallops, hanging about outside the training stables, being nagged at by Wing and Davies. My nerves were torn to shreds.

The race was on Thursday. On Wednesday morning I caught his left eye on the Heath, but it wasn't effective. That evening I had to tell my partners that so far I'd failed. You wouldn't have believed that two grown-up men could carry on so.

'Do you realise we've three thousand at stake?' Wing shouted.

'Three whole thousand,' Davies said, biting his nails.

'You're going to hypnotise that horse if it kills you,' Wing said.

The next morning was a nightmare. At dawn they rushed me down to the stables. Their idea was that I should operate while Snackbar was being put into the horse-box that would carry him down to Ascot. After I'd hung about for an hour a stable boy spotted me. He shouted out something, and immediately two very big men made a dash at me. I've never run so fast in my life. I was still out of breath when Wing and Davies drove up in a Daimler they'd hired for the day.

'It's too late,' Wing said. 'The horse-box is on its way. Quick. Jump in. You'll have to operate on the course.'

'What about clothes?' Davies asked as we drove flat out down the Great North Road. 'He can't get into the paddock in that suit.'

'We'll fix him up in London,' Wing said. 'Don't worry me.'

The race was at three forty-five. At twenty past three there I was in the paddock in a top hat and tails like the rest of the people. And I felt so nervous I thought I would faint. When number eight was led in I thought I'd die. Number Eight was Snackbar, and he was wearing blinkers. There was nothing for it. I had to stand directly in front of him. So I jumped over the rails and ran straight up to him. It was only then I saw he'd got a wall eye—just before the police grabbed me.

———◆◆◆———

The lorry driver finished his bitter. 'And I suppose you then turned into Greta Garbo,' he said scornfully.

The little man looked at him crossly.

'You don't believe my story?' he asked coldly.

'What do you take me for? I wasn't born yesterday,' the lorry driver snorted.

'You don't believe I'm a hypnotist?'

'If you're a hypnotist, I'm the King of Egypt. I've heard unlikely yarns before, but yours takes the cake. Takes the cake . . .' the lorry driver repeated in dazed tones as slowly he crumpled to the floor.

A very tall, stout lady walked into the bar and looked imperiously at the little man and the inert lorry driver.

'Really, Henry,' she said. 'Wake that poor man up immediately, or I'll tell my brother.'

The Boy from Beirut

There had been no time to change into uniform after the day's walk. And now as I walked back after a late dinner with some friends to the flat I shared with a friend, I was mildly hoping I would not meet the Provost Marshal, when I observed a civilian leaning over the side of the little bridge which spans the Barrada. I noticed him because for a moment I thought he was going to throw himself into the water, and it occurred to me that since the Barrada is only a few feet deep at that point he could be extricated easily. However, as I walked closer to the bridge I saw that he was looking not at the water but towards the gharry horses on the other side where drivers waited for stray fares. As I crossed the bridge he greeted me in Arabic.

'Good evening.'

'Good evening to you.'

'You speak Arabic?'

'No. Only a little.' I began to move away.

'Are you an officer?' From his black suit and tie I guessed he was an Arab waiter from the hotel.

'Yes.'

'Do you speak French?'

'Yes.'

'Why did you stop when you saw me standing on the bridge?' He spoke French with only a slight accent.

'How did you know I stopped?'

'I was listening to your footsteps.'

'I just thought of something, that's all,' I said evasively. He turned round and stared at my face.

'You're sure there was no other reason?' It was my turn to stare at him.

'What's it to do with you if there was?'

He smiled nervously. I noticed as he smiled that he was quite young—only about twenty-three or so. I had thought, perhaps from his neat dark clothes or perhaps from the little sags of flesh under his eyes, that he was older.

'Excuse me, please, if my question was indiscreet.'

'Indiscreet?' I felt I was getting out of my depth.

'Yes. There obviously was a reason.' For a moment I could think of nothing to say.

'Please tell me what it was?' he said. I checked a stupid impulse to run away and forget I had ever seen him.

'Oh, well, if you insist. I thought you were going to jump in.'

'To kill myself?'

'Yes.'

He laughed, rather pleasantly. He sounded relieved of some worry.

'You had never seen me before?'

'Never in my life.'

'And I have never seen you before in my life,' he said, smiling up at me. He was small and delicately made, more like a Bedu than a Syrian, with wide eyes and a firm mouth. But his hands twisted nervously together as he stood looking at me.

'You wonder now what my question was about,' he said, in such a friendly way that I did not like to rebuff him. Besides, I was rather intrigued.

'What was it about?'

The haunted look had vanished, and he was now almost cheerful.

'I had never seen you before, but I wanted to know if *you* had seen *me* before,' he said. 'But how could you have seen me if I did not see you?' he asked, smiling.

'In lots of ways. You might have been looking the other way, for instance.'

'In lots of ways. That's it. In lots of ways. I might have been asleep.' He seemed to relish his mystery.

'Will you have a drink?' he asked suddenly.

'I think every place is shut.'

He fished in his coat pocket and produced a half bottle of brandy.

'There's a coffee place still open where the drivers go. We can drink this there if you like.'

I hesitated. I was not dressed as an officer.

'All right.'

The dingy café was not far from the bridge. I ordered two Turkish coffees and two glasses.

'At least the coffee is on me,' I said, as he poured out the brandy. 'That's enough. Really.'

'I'll show you how to drink this stuff,' he said, and poured himself out a full tumbler.

'*Santé*.'

'*A la votre*.' He drank deeply.

'What's your name?'

'Faris.'

'How old are you?'

'Twenty-one,' he said. 'How old are you?'

'Twenty-six. Do you work in Damascus?'

'I used to. But now I work in Beirut. I have only come here to see my mother. To-morrow I shall return to Beirut.' He swallowed another gulp of brandy. His face was flushed and his fingers writhed nervously.

'Are you a Christian?'

He saw what I meant and smiled. 'Yes. But nowadays many Moslems drink.'

'I know. What is your job?'

'I work in a shop.'

'What kind of a shop?'

'I work in Beirut.'

'But what kind of a shop?'

He did not seem to hear my question. Suddenly I saw that his hands were trembling. I looked up at his face. He was staring at a gharry-driver sitting at the next table. I glanced at the driver. He was a stout, red-faced man in a tattered black coat. There was nothing frightening about him. I turned to Faris. Then I noticed he was not staring at the driver but at the whip which was leaning against the wall by the man's table.

'Faris. Faris.'

'Yes?' He turned away with an effort.

'What kind of shop do you work in?'

'Do you see that whip?' he said. He was breathing heavily.

'Yes.'

136

'Oh, it is cruel, cruel. Look out of the window. By the lamp post do you see that horse? Look at the way the haunch bones jerk out of its flesh. Look at the skeleton of its ribs. And if a fare comes the driver will lash it into a trot with that whip. He will lash it until blood comes.'

He paused for a moment, staring wildly.

'You want to know about me, don't you? Well, I'll tell you. I was born on a farm. I grew up with animals. I was the only child and I had no friends to play with. But the animals were my friends, and my parents who were good Christians taught me to be kind to them. When my father died the farm was sold and my mother brought me to Damascus. I was about twelve years old and I remember quite well I was standing one wet day on that bridge where we met, when a horse pulling a gharry slipped and fell. The driver leapt down with his whip and began slashing it. The frightened horse stumbled again and sprawled on the ground. The driver got furious and struck it horribly with his whip. I was frightened. But I could bear it no longer. I rushed to the driver and begged him to stop. I tried to snatch the whip away from him. Then he raised his whip and slashed me across the face. And while I stood dazed he slashed at my chest. I ran away crying to my mother, who told me that men were cruel to animals because no one had taught them that animals are our friends. I promised that evening I would dedicate my life to stopping cruelty to animals.'

He drank deeply and coughed. His eyes were glittering.

'As the years went by I discovered and tried to stop all kinds of cruelty to animals. In the East we treat our animals far worse, I am told, than you do. I fought against this cruelty. You have no idea how many devices men have for being cruel to beasts. There are the long raking whips of the gharry-drivers, the spiked goad for the poor little donkey, the sharp thong for the mule, the bar of nails attached to the camel's cheek so that it must follow in the caravan or the nails stick into it, and the long spurs of the riders. All these I tried to stop. I tried to prevent animals being beaten beneath their load day after day until they dropped dead. And when I got tired or despondent I would think of that horse on the Barrada bridge.

I would think of the blows raining down on its heaving flanks, and I would go on working. I met others who felt as I did in a society for preventing this cruelty, and gradually we began to make progress by teaching drivers that animals were their friends and by stopping, partially at least, the manufacture of some of the more cruel devices.'

He lowered his voice so that it came out with a curious hissing sound. His fingers never stopped writhing together as he spoke.

'A year ago my friends made me join a political youth club. Previously I hadn't been much interested in politics, but at this club I saw for the first time the importance of laws and of freedom. It was as if I had lived all my life without being able to see the stars and the moon but now could observe them for the first time. I now had a second cause, the cause of my country's liberty. I volunteered to take a part in the demonstration which was being planned. Well, I dare say you heard about it. The crowd got out of control. There were accidents and property was damaged. That night three members of our committee were arrested by the French police. I was one of them. They wanted the names of the rest.'

All his limbs were trembling now, and his eyes were staring horribly into the corner.

'I was put into a cell by myself. The door was slammed, and I was left alone until noon the next day, when a soldier came in and fastened a bandage tight round my eyes.

' "What's that for?" I asked. He said I would see in time. He told me to strip. Then I understood. I was going to be beaten. The bandage was so that I could not see who was beating me. The soldier tore the last clothes from my body when he heard footsteps approaching the door. Then I heard a click as the door opened. I heard the stamp of his feet as he sprang to attention. I heard two people, two people, walk into my cell.'

His voice had sunk to a hoarse whisper, and his hands were clenched together.

'Then I heard one of them say, *"Quelle jolie buste à fouetter!"* '

' I started. The whole timbre of his voice had changed. The accent was so perfect and vivid that for a moment I thought I recognised the voice.

'"What a nice body to beat!" he repeated. Then I heard the whistle of the whip as it screamed down on my naked body, and my flesh was seared with pain. I tried not to cry out, but the anguish was terrible as he lashed into me. Then suddenly as the fresh bars of pain pierced me and I felt the blood trickling down my sides, I thought, "This is how the poor horse feels when his flanks are slashed by the driver." My body is quivering like his. Blood is oozing from me as I have seen it from him. Then I must have lost consciousness, for when I woke up sticky with blood I was alone.

'I could recognise the voice of the man who beat me. The other man never spoke. The soldier told me it was an English officer, but I think he said that because he knew I liked the English. But I'm never sure. I'm never sure.'

He gulped down his brandy. 'If you'll excuse me. I feel rather ill. I think I should go home,' he said thickly.

We got up. He stood trembling by the table.

'After a bit they got tired of beating me about, and I was released. I returned to Damascus.' He was still staring at the whip.

'The next day I was walking along the street when I saw a driver slashing at his horse. As I ran forward to plead with him, and if that failed to wrest the whip from him by force, suddenly I thought, "That horse might be me and it isn't." And I . . .'

His voice came in hoarse gasps.

'I was glad. I was glad. Suddenly I wanted to say to the driver, "Go on. Lam into him. Slash him hard".'

He swayed a little and buried his face in his hands. Then he looked up with bloodshot eyes.

'Perhaps I'll get decent again. Perhaps one day I'll look at those starved horses on the bridge and feel as I did as a boy. It was all right then. I hated it then. I swear I did. I've come out the wrong side now, that's all. I'm just vicious. And I work in the right place.'

He began to retch, and stumbled to the door. I tried to help him.

'Leave me alone, I beseech you. Good night,' he said quickly, and rushed away.

The squalid proprietor came in to be paid for the coffee. He

School Curtains

My name is Felix Kallman. And I was appointed Secretary to our embassy in London early this year. I shall make this report in some detail because it is the last one I shall send.

I begin with excerpts from my diary which I write in English to gain fluence in this language.

━━━◆◆◆◆━━━

April 15th

I think I have solved the problem . . .

When first I took up my appointment as First Secretary to our embassy in London, one of my concerns was our young son, Antol. He is only eleven years old, and we were unwilling to leave him behind in our homeland. Nor did we wish to send him to a boarding school in England. The boy is still young. Divorced from the influence of his parents, he might well become a victim of capitalist propaganda.

So after my wife Katzi and I had taken up residence in our embassy in Kensington Palace Gardens, we made enquiries from the few other friendly embassies as to the possibility of sending Antol to a day school in London.

We learned from our comrades that there were no good day schools in London. But there is one school with some international flavour which at least does teach the children such useful subjects as arithmetic, writing and geography, and which seems to operate on no particular system of capitalist indoctrination. This school, which is run by a middle-aged couple, a Mr. and Mrs. Glover, is situated in the neighbourhood of Queen's Gate—not so far from our own embassy. The school caters for some two hundred children from the ages of seven to fourteen. And several of our comrades have sent their children there for want of any better institution.

April 16th

This afternoon my wife Katzi and I drove round in our embassy Cadillac, together with our son Antol, to make the acquaintance of the Glovers.

Mrs. Glover is a tall and well-made woman of about fifty with a lean, ascetic face and a kind smile which filled my wife with confidence. Mr. Glover is a large, red-faced man who looks as if he could enforce discipline.

My wife and I noticed a copy of the *New Statesman* lying on their study table. Evidently the Glovers are petit-bourgeois liberals and are probably intellectually harmless.

The formalities were made, the entry registration fee paid, entrance forms completed, and my wife departed together with young Antol to order the uniform which the school deems obligatory, while I returned to my work.

April 30th

This evening my son Antol came into my study to say good night to me. He looked very smart in his new green cap and blazer. (I only wish that it could have been a different colour.) Proudly he handed me a printed list of the children who are due to attend the school this summer term, which begins in five days' time.

I was gazing vaguely through the list, gratified to see that the names of several children of comrades were included, when I noticed the name 'Michael Fulton', the son, it was alleged, of a Mr. and Mrs. Arthur Fulton. The name rang a bell. I telephoned immediately to the Intelligence Service of our comrades next door and confirmed the awful truth.

The child is indeed the son of the alleged Arthur Fulton, who, as we knew without consulting our files, left our beloved country ten years previously. He was then named Arpad Fulop. This degenerate fascist managed to escape the iron hand of proletarian justice which certainly would have grasped him had he remained. Not only did he manage to escape from our country but, by devious methods, he had previously succeeded in removing from our ports his three cargo vessels and had placed his capital in Geneva, converting it astutely into Swiss francs before the necessary devaluation of our currency. Having gained himself an international position, he decided to settle down in England, purchasing a large mansion in London and an estate in the country where, after a few years, he and his wife became more and more English and finally ridiculously transformed their names from Arpad Fulop to 'Arthur Fulton' and from Ilona Fulop to 'Helen Fulton'.

Their son Misha, whom they called Michael, is a child, I have ascertained, of eleven and of uncertain temper. But for my vigilance he would be entering the Glovers' school this very term.

May 2nd

This afternoon my wife and I drove once again in our embassy Cadillac to Queen's Gate to see Mr. and Mrs. Glover. We were shown into their study, where I refused Mrs. Glover's invitation to a drink of whisky and immediately began to speak my mind about the matter in hand. I explained that it was utterly impossible for my son Antol to mix with the child of such scum as the Fultons. I revealed the fact, together with documentary proof, that their real name was Fulop and that they would, but for their furtive ingenuity, be doing useful work in a cultural-indoctrination camp, instead of bolstering up the crumbling edifice of capitalist 'democracy'. To my surprise, Mr. and Mrs. Glover seemed singularly unimpressed. Their reactions were typically bourgeois and emotional.

'But little Micky did look so sweet in his new school uniform,' said Mrs. Glover.

'We think he's got the makings of a fine lad,' said Mr. Glover, as he settled himself on the sofa with a copious whisky.

I then had to show the strength of my hand. I explained that unless they were willing to give me a guarantee that the Fulop child would not attend their school, I would be forced to withdraw Antol. Once again I thought Mrs. Glover's reaction extremely stupid.

'But we love the look of your little Antol,' she said. 'And wouldn't it be nice for two boys from the same country to be at school together? I'm sure they'll have so much to talk about.'

Coldly, and I trust with precision and determination, I explained that they would have nothing whatsoever to talk about, because I could trust my son Antol not to address one word to the son of a proclaimed and registered traitor.

Mr. Glover at this stage intervened—in a manner which I found lacking in courtesy and intelligence.

'We don't know much about politics,' he said, 'and quite honestly, Mr. Kallman, the political views of our parents are no concern of ours. If anything we welcome the chance of our children meeting those of other nations. But our business is to teach our boys the main essentials, and hope to heaven they get a scholarship to Winchester.'

The end of the meeting was equally unsatisfactory. The Glovers could not be moved from their obstinate standpoint.

'If you want to take your son Antol away,' Mr. Glover said, 'you can. There's nothing to stop you. And naturally we shall refund your fee.'

'But we do hope you won't,' said Mrs. Glover. 'Because he is such a sweet boy. I love the way he cocks his head on one side when he's talking.'

This is a habit about which I have constantly been forced to rebuke Antol. Evidently Mrs. Glover is a thoroughly stupid woman.

May 3rd

This morning in this matter of Antol events took a new turn. First, both my wife Katzi and Antol came into me to persuade me to change my mind about withdrawing the boy. This, of course, had no effect on me. Secondly, however, through the good offices of our comrades next door, I was introduced to a valuable potential agent, one Joe Swale, who has recently taken the post of chauffeur to the Fulop or Fulton family, after having been dismissed for some reason or other by his recent employer who was a bookmaker.

Joe Swale is a small, alert fellow who comes from the people and speaks unashamedly with the accent of the people of London. He has informed me that in view of a slight consideration (which will be only of fractional importance in our monthly estimate for Counter-Intelligence), he is prepared to inform me about the Fulops' movements and in particular about all things relating to the child Misha Fulop's behaviour at the school. This he will be able to do because one of his tasks will be to drive the boy to school, deposit him there, and collect him again. He also revealed the extraordinary valuable information that on learning from the school list of the fact that Antol Kallman, son of Felix Kallman, First Secretary of the embassy, had been enrolled, the Fulops immediately drove in their car (a Bentley) to the Glovers' school with the intention of making a serious protest and with the hopeless endeavour of persuading Mr. and Mrs. Glover to refuse admission to Antol.

Comrade Swale does not know what passed during their interview because he could not gain admittance into the school building. But over the microphonic system that he has fitted into the back of the glass-partitioned Bentley he was able to overhear the entire of the Fulops' conversation on their return journey to their house in Mayfair. It seems that Mr. and Mrs. Glover were as stupid and obstinate as usual, and in their political ignorance still do not appreciate the undesirability of the two children meeting.

The result of my interview with Swale has been to persuade me that no harm can come to Antol if I allow him to remain at the school, even if the Fulops do not withdraw their son Micky—as Joe Swale informs me is not likely.

May 4th

I am seriously concerned with the behaviour of my chauffeur Harrington, who was engaged by my predecessor Zaroucha Klauski because of his excellent references.

On my way to attend a meeting where an enlightened church leader was due to speak, the car stopped and Harrington complained of trouble in the carburettor. (On looking back through my diary I find that this carburettor trouble has occurred on every occasion that I have been to attend a meeting organised by the British-Soviet Friendship Society.)

When I questioned Harrington during the period of time that he took to repair the carburettor, on his views about the Dean, he replied: 'You can have him,' in a manner which I did not consider showed respect or sympathy.

Can Klauski have committed an error?

May 9th

Antol has now been four days at school and finds it very strange.

This evening, after Harrington had driven him back from

Queen's Gate, I questioned Antol about his lessons. I learned that the last lesson, which had been taken by a young master called Ponsonby, consisted in the geography of England totally irrespective of its strategical importance or industrial or even agricultural output. The lesson was only concerned with matters such as the most important town in Radnor or Somerset. The young master, it seems, did not show great knowledge of his subject and was reduced by his ignorance to such childish questions as: 'What is the northernmost part of England?'—the reply being, 'John of Groats.' 'What is the westernmost village in England?'—the reply being, 'Land's End.' Antol was confused by this because he thought (quite rightly) that Land's End must be a geographical expression of where the land should end and not the name of some very remote village.

The master, Ponsonby, it seems, digressed from the subject of Land's End to the Armada, which he claimed was 'a jolly fine British victory'.

I had to explain to Antol that the British Fleet only defeated the Spanish because of its superior armament, the resolute action of the peasantry who captured the Spanish as soon as they landed, and wind conditions which were unfavourable to the Spanish galleons.

The master Ponsonby has said that he will demonstrate a model of a galleon on the Round Pond during the boys' afternoon exercise to-morrow.

May 10th

I am most worried and annoyed. This evening Antol came back from school with his eye contused and a front tooth missing.

It appears that the master Ponsonby did indeed show such of the boys as were not engaged in football a model of a Spanish galleon which he floated on the Round Pond. When Antol perceived it was an obsolete and inefficient craft, he walked away.

Hardly had he left the group by the pond, than he was approached by the boy he calls Micky Fulton but who we know to be Misha Fulop. Antol is not clear as to precisely what words passed and as to how the conversation began. But scarcely had a few desultory remarks been exchanged when Micky (as Antol calls him) accused me (Antol's father) of being a 'cold-blooded murderer' and a 'slaughterer of priests'.

Antol at this insult, without hesitation, I am glad to say, struck the boy a violent blow. Incensed, the Fulop child retaliated and a battle ensued. Immediately a gang of boys formed a ring around the two combatants. And it was not until the master Ponsonby, encumbered as he was by his heavy wading-boots, managed to get out of the pond, that he could stem the ruffianly onslaught of the boy Micky who, although he is of the same age, is taller and weighs more than Antol.

May 11th

To-day I drove round with my wife to see the Glovers to deliver a firm protest.

I found both Mr. and Mrs. Glover extremely unco-operative. It appears that they are not altogether convinced that the fight was instigated by the Fulop boy. Mr. Glover even suggested that Antol had called Micky a 'bit of fascist scum' before Antol defended himself. Once again I repeated that unless the Fulop boy was removed, I would be forced to remove Antol. This seemed to make little impression on them and I was left in the air.

It appears that the Fulop boy has not been punished any more than my Antol, because they do not approve of corporal punishment and consider that the black mark which each boy has received together with the humiliation of being made to walk separate and alone in the middle of the homeward defile of two-by-twos which is known as a 'crocodile' has been sufficient punishment.

I discussed the matter at length with Katzi, who agrees with me that for the time being there is no advantage in removing Antol. I agree with Katzi that it might damage our embassy's prestige if we now withdrew our boy from the school and the Fulop child remained. But I am still worried.

May 13th

Comrade Joe Swale came round to see me this afternoon.

He informs me that the Fulop boy was seriously damaged in the fight. His nose was fractured, and he lost two teeth as against Antol's one. Swale further informs me that the Fulops also went round to the school the following day to make a complaint. He thinks they may be on the point of removing their son.

Excellent.

May 27th

This evening Antol came back from school with his face gravely bruised, his knuckles grazed and his school blazer torn. When I enquired the reason, he was for the first time curiously evasive.

But I gathered that a senior boy, the child of the American Cultural Attaché, made aspersions not only against the government of our country, but also against the dark complexions of many of our countrymen, comparing them to Egyptians.

'Wogs', Antol says—a term of opprobrium—was the word used. This occurred at the end of a history lesson after the master Ponsonby had departed. Antol immediately stood up for our glorious government and to his surprise, when he was outnumbered, found the boy Fulop by his side.

Evidently Mick Fulop had thought that only the complexion of his skin was being criticised, and ignorant of the political realities had joined the fight on the side of my son Antol. It seems that Antol, with the slight aid lent him by the Fulop boy, held his own in a corner for the space of several minutes before they were rescued by the master Ponsonby, who had returned from washing his hands.

May 28th

This morning came the great news. I have been appointed First Secretary to our embassy in Washington. At last I have got the chance I have always wanted. This promotion may mean all the difference to my career. Little Katzi was in a hysteria of joy. We cannot wait to see the look of excitement on Antol's face when we tell him the news, for he has always longed to visit America. And we will have to leave in three weeks' time . . .

This evening I was purposely writing in the reception room of the embassy when Antol came back from school, so that

Katzi and I could together break him the news. To our astonishment Antol did not seem pleased. But then, such is the way
of children. And how can he be expected to appreciate that his
father has now greater responsibility? . . . How can I expect
a child to understand the widened opportunity I now have for
serving our glorious socialist motherland?

June 2nd

This morning I received curious information from Swale.
It seems that last night he saw Antol give Micky Fulton, as he
calls the Fulop boy, a piece of toffee when they were leaving
the school building.

Katzi thinks this may have something to do with Antol's
reluctance to leave the school. But I cannot believe that Antol
would ever make friends with the son of a traitor. However,
I intend to discuss the matter with Antol next Saturday.

June 5th

This morning we drove out to the British-Soviet Society for
Cultural Relations' rally in Bognor Park. Once again the
Cadillac broke down, and we arrived late. I am beginning to
suspect that our chauffeur Harrington is not sympathetic to
The Cause. After the highly successful meeting was over I
had a long talk with my son Antol, who for the first time
seemed—I regret to have to put this down—definitely evasive.
He denied that since the episode in the park he had ever discussed politics with Micky Fulop. And when I taxed him, he
denied that he had any friendship for the boy. But I was not
wholly satisfied.

However, it is now only ten days to half-term, when we are
removing the boy, as indeed we must, because we fly to Washington the following Monday. Katzi considers it is a ridiculous
leniency on my part to allow him even to stay for the next ten
days.

June 9th

This evening Katzi was most annoyed because of a message
that Mrs. Glover has sent to her by way of Antol.

Antol has been desired to ask her whether she has an old hat.
This is obviously some sly joke of Mrs. Glover's at Katzi's

expense—because why should Katzi, of all people, have an old hat?

June 11th

This morning Mrs. Glover telephoned Katzi about the matter of the old hat.

It appears that—in typical bourgeois fashion—before half-term the boys of her school have a party at which they play a ridiculous game of 'Musical Hats'. Each boy dances round wearing one of his mother's old hats. Then, when the music stops he has to jump down to the ground, seizing the hat of the boy next to him. There is one hat short. Thus one boy is hatless at the end of each brief tune. Gradually the field is narrowed down to two boys. This may have some political significance, but at the moment it escapes me.

The half-term party is to be next Friday evening, and since Katzi does not possess an old hat, I have asked her to buy one from our chauffeur Harrington's wife.

June 14th

Only two more days to half-term. Only five more days before I leave this obstinately incomprehensible country for the greatest moment of my career . . .

Last night Antol seemed curiously excited. He spent a long time alone in his bedroom and when his mother went in to say good night to him, she found the door was locked. When she knocked it was opened, but she had a feeling that Antol was hiding something.

June 15th, Friday

Antol came in to me this morning while I was shaving, which is unusual. I shall be very glad when he has left England, which has had a definitely bad effect on him. . . .

At three o'clock Mrs. Glover telephoned to say how sorry she was to be losing Antol. And Mr. Glover offered to refund the remaining portion of the term's fees. This offer I declined after examining the contract.

7 p.m.

Harrington has returned without Antol. He waited outside the school for an hour and then entered the building. Mrs.

Glover informed him that Antol was no longer in the building and must have gone to the house of one of the other boys. I seriously disapprove of this. Antol *knows* that I do not allow him into strange houses.

7.30 p.m.
Still no sign of Antol.
Katzi is beginning to get worried.
I have telephoned Mrs. Glover, who informs me that after the half-term party some of the boys are invited to supper at the houses of others and Antol may not have told me.
This I discount utterly.

10 p.m.
No news. Antol has still not appeared. I have rung Mrs. Glover, who seems unconcerned.

11 p.m.
I have just put down the receiver from talking to Mrs. Glover. There is still no news of Antol. Mrs. Glover has now communicated with the police.
I can hear Katzi crying as I write. Our own agents have tried to contact Swale, without effect. My worst fear is that Antol has been kidnapped by our enemies who will use him for political purposes.

11.30 p.m.
The news has just been given to me by Mr. Glover that the boy Micky Fulop is also missing. I suspect that this is a bluff.

11.45 p.m.
Swale has telephoned from a call-box. Both the Fulops appear to be worried because their son has not returned from school. Swale has overheard them talking alone, and therefore this cannot be a clever bluff on their part. I have contacted the agents of our friends next door and informed them of what has happened.

June 16th, Saturday
Katzi and I were awake all night. No news of any kind. Both Mr. and Mrs. Glover now seem concerned, but think the children have left on some prank. They appear to place some

confidence in their local police, who have alerted other police stations.

11 a.m.

Still no news. Katzi and I are desperate.

6 p.m.

Mr. Glover has telephoned to say that the police think they have picked up a clue.

A pastry shop in Brighton was broken into in the small hours of this morning. Two small boys were seen escaping with some cakes.

I have discussed this with Katzi who thinks Antol might have taken the train from Victoria, because when we flew into London we arrived at Victoria Air Terminal.

Katzi and I are going down to Brighton in hopes.

June 17th, Sunday evening, Brighton

Although we have searched all day, we have found nothing.

An awkward incident occurred when we ran straight into the Fulops in the lounge of the Albion Hotel. Needless to say, neither Katzi nor I showed any sign of recognition, and walked clean past them. In their efforts to disguise themselves as British, the Fulops were wearing heavy, tweed clothing—though it was a warm evening.

Why are degenerate people so often tall?

June 18th, Monday

This afternoon we heard news from Mr. Glover. The police have traced Antol and probably the boy Fulop with him to Southampton.

It appears that early this morning two small boys went into a jeweller's shop in Southampton and the smaller one took from his pocket an Order of Stalin Second Class which he presented to the jeweller, saying his father had given it to him to sell.

When the jeweller enquired how much he wanted for it, the boy said seven shillings. The jeweller examined the Order and discovered that it was of solid gold (naturally). He asked the boys to wait for a while, went into the next room, and telephoned the police.

But while he was away, the boys must have taken alarm, for when he reappeared they had vanished.

I have now discovered by telephoning our embassy that my Order of Stalin Second Class is missing from the drawer in my bedroom, and therefore I am convinced that Antol must be in Southampton.

Harrington will drive us there immediately.

June 19th, Tuesday, Southampton

No sign of Antol although the local police have been alerted.

Our chauffeur, Harrington, had trouble with the police on the way for speeding, but I produced my card showing that I had diplomatic immunity.

Photographs of the Fulop boy have already been circulated to all police stations, and I have now consented to allow photographs of Antol to appear.

Wednesday

Still no news. But the police have informed my secretary that they are optimistic.

Thursday

The worst yet since the disappearance.

A woman from a village in Wiltshire saw two children walking along the lane near her house. Having read the reports in the press and seen their photographs, she recognised them. She therefore invited the two boys into her small cottage where she lives alone, persuaded them into a back room, and locked them in so that she could fetch the police, and gain the reward which the misguided Fulops have offered.

While she was away the two children, finding themselves locked in, must have suspected they were trapped, and panicked. For they broke out. One of them must have ripped open his arm or some limb, because a trail of blood was found leading from the broken window along the path for a distance of some thirty yards.

Katzi is desperately upset.

We drive to Wiltshire this afternoon.

Lower Ogbourne, Friday

We put up at the largest hotel we could find, but it was much smaller than the Albion at Brighton and very dirty. To our disgust we saw in the visitors' book the entry 'Mr. and Mrs. Arthur Fulton'. We were about to change our hotel when they appeared in the hallway.

My wife, resourceful as ever, turned on her heel and walked into the dining-room with me following her. But such people have no tact, and a few minutes later the so-called Fultons entered the dining-room, which contained only four or five tables, and sat down without even looking at us and ordered themselves a whole bottle of whiskey—as if one glass were not enough.

We took little notice of them, but later were forced to. Into the dining-room there suddenly walked two policemen who, with scant attention to us, walked over to their table and began interrogating the Fulops about the behaviour of Swale their chauffeur, who had caused an ugly incident in the local inn round the corner.

Lest Swale be dismissed, I was forced to intervene in the argument. I explained (perhaps not wholly truthfully) that the reason Swale had hit my chauffeur Harrington was because of some minor difference of opinion for which I would accept complete responsibility and over which I would claim diplomatic immunity. The police appeared entirely satisfied. And as soon as they had left I was able to break short my disagreeable encounter with Arpad and Ilona Fulop.

No more trace of Antol. He has now been missing for a week.

Saturday

A lorry driver has appeared at the local police station saying that he gave a lift to two children on his way to Exeter and only saw their photographs in the paper subsequently and realised their identity.

Katzi is grievously disturbed by the lorry driver's report that one of the boys had his arm in a sling, and seemed pale. The police do not seem to know which boy it was.

At breakfast this morning I noticed that both the Fulops appeared worried, and Arpad Fulop constantly asked the waiter for the time. I am surprised he has not got a watch of his own—perhaps for all his expensive tweeds and lavish drink-orders, his cargo boats may not be prospering.

Having arranged secretly with Joe Swale for him to take the Fulops to the Imperial Hotel at Exeter, I instructed Harrington to drive us to the Rougemont.

Both Katzi and I feel that we must get ahead of the Fulops because their fast driving and bungling with the police generally may get us into trouble. And we consider it essential that we should reach Antol before their contaminating hands draw near him.

Exeter, Sunday

Have searched the town all day without result. No news from the police, who seem rather hostile to us. I cannot think why.

Monday

This afternoon I was informed by the police that yesterday two boys approached a sailor in Plymouth, and one of them offered to sell him a gold wrist-watch studded with emeralds for seventeen shillings and sixpence. The sailor realised that he had found a bargain and bought the wrist-watch there and then for fifteen shillings.

The sailor was subsequently questioned by a jeweller to whom he attempted to sell the wrist-watch for three pounds ten shillings this morning.

It now appears that the wrist-watch was the property of Arpad Fulop.

We leave for Plymouth this afternoon. So, unfortunately, do the Fulops, who have heard the news from the police. But I have instructed Joe Swale to take sure the Fulops stay at the Duke of Cornwall.

Katzi and I will stay at the Continental.

Plymouth, Tuesday

No news.

But I stole a march on the Fulops by bribing Swale to introduce me to the sailor whom the boys approached.

The sailor was very stupid and uninformative and somewhat the worse for drink. He does not seem to have been able to distinguish between one child and the other.

Katzi is desperately worried in case it was Antol's arm in the sling.

Wednesday

The sailor appeared again this evening and says that he can remember that one child asked him the best way to get to Land's End, and he advised them to make the bus to Truro.

At last I have stolen a march on the Fulops, because this information is known to Swale and to Katzi and me, and to us alone.

Thursday

To my horror I have discovered that our chauffeur is a paid lackey of the fascists.

No sooner had I asked Harrington to look up on his map to make certain that Truro was indeed on the road to Land's End, than he asked himself to be excused. I allowed him a quarter of an hour for this purpose, only to discover that he had spent it in contacting the Fulops at their hotel and selling them the secret.

This I have discovered from Swale, who is now in hospital after assaulting Harrington. Swale in his turn has been grievously wounded by Harrington.

I am glad to hear that Harrington broke his ankle when the gallant Swale knocked him down the steps of the hotel. Harrington is also in hospital.

I shall drive the Cadillac myself. There is nothing else for it.

Truro, Friday

No trace of Antol.

We decided to stay at the Red Lion and found the Fulops there ahead of us, Fulop having passed my Cadillac on the road driving his Bentley like a lunatic.

We shall leave an hour before dawn in order to get ahead of him. But Katzi is feeling very tired, and I could do with some sleep.

Antol has now been missing for a fortnight.

I started this report, my last dispatch, by saying that I would begin with the entries in my diary. But here my entries end.

However, if you are to understand the reasons for my decision, I must tell you what happened that next day.

Katzi and I arose an hour before dawn, as planned.

We had paid our bill the night before, so it did not matter that there was no-one about in the hotel. However, being unused to driving the Cadillac, I knocked into the side of the garage door on leaving, which made a certain amount of noise. This awoke the Fulops, who, I learned later, looked out of their hotel window to see my car vanishing.

Immediately they gave chase, knowing from the infidel Harrington's report that my destination was Land's End.

Throughout that morning of desperate driving, our cars would pass and re-pass each other.

As we approached Penzance, I noticed that a policeman mounted on a motor-cycle seemed interested in our movements. And as we approached Land's End, the lanes grew narrower. Then came the accident.

In swerving to avoid a peasant, I braked violently, locked the wheels in a skid and punctured my front tyre. The peasant muttered at me in a strange dialect, and walked away, while Katzi and I got out to inspect the damage.

At that moment there was a loud noise behind us of hooting, and the Bentley driven by Arpad Fulop (Arthur Fulton) drove up.

Indignantly Fulop and his wife rushed out of the car and demanded why we were obstructing their progress on what they termed the 'Queen's Highway'.

Coldly and in our precise language, I explained what had occurred. Fulop brushed past me and examined my car, assuring me that he was an expert in motor-cars of every make. He discovered that I had wrenched my steering-wheel, that both my front tyres were punctured, and that in addition my Cadillac had run out of petrol, the unspeakable Harrington having forgotten to fill her up at our last port of call before his accident.

I explained to Fulop that there was nothing I could do about it or intended to do about it, and that if he wished to pass me he could do so.

'You clot,' he said. 'How can I pass you when your car is blocking the whole road?'

This indeed was the case. I therefore excused myself from him and his vile language, and suggested to Katzi that we should walk forward in order to find some other means of conveyance. At this moment, to my amazement, Katzi, for the first time in many years, lost her temper.

'You pig-headed old fool,' she shouted at me.

Then she rushed to Ilona Fulop (Helen Fulton), and dragged her to the back of the Bentley.

An instant later, both ladies reappeared, and—there is no other phrase to describe it—turned on their husbands.

'What do we care about your tiresome, beastly politics,' Katzi cried.

And Ilona Fulop added: 'You men have made such a mess of the world that it's time we women did something about it.'

When Fulop and I attempted to remonstrate, their excitement grew all the more intense. From the garbled and insulting words of our wives, we could sometimes glean phrases such as: 'Don't stand there just gaping.'

'Do something about it.'

'Get the car off the road.'

Arthur Fulop seemed as confused and amazed as I was.

'But how?' he asked. 'How do we get the car off the road?'

'By pushing it, you idiot. Pushing it into the ditch,' his wife cried.

I was amazed to find that Fulop (Fulton) responded to this. And immediately he and his wife, together with Katzi, began heaving at the car to push it into the ditch.

Suddenly I saw the point of their operation. If we pushed the Cadillac into the ditch, the road would be clear, and we could all drive on in the Bentley. I decided to lend my weight to their effort.

After three minutes of pushing, with one last heave, the car lurched slowly over into the ditch and the road was clear.

We were just climbing into the Bentley, when a large policeman appeared on a motor-cycle and addressed himself to Fulton.

'I've been after you for the last five miles,' he said. 'And now I've caught you. You've been speeding, you've damaged a lamp-post, and there's nothing for it. You will have to come back with me to the station.'

Fulton moved his face close to my ear.

'You've got to hit him,' he said. 'You've got diplomatic immunity.'

I am a small man. I looked up at the policeman. He seemed very tall and far away. But there was nothing for it. I stamped violently on his toe, and, as he doubled up in pain, I hit him smartly under the chin. He fell back into the ditch. We jumped into the Bentley and drove on.

When we reached the outskirts of the little village called Land's End, we asked a man outside the pub if he had seen two children wandering about.

'I've seen lots of them,' he said. 'Which ones do you want?'

We explained.

'I've seen two kids as might be foreigners,' he said, looking at us. 'They went down there.'

He pointed towards the west—where a line of fishermen's cottages straggled down to the Atlantic Ocean.

'Come to think of it, I think I saw one go into that last cottage right down there,' he said in afterthought.

We hurried on, and drove up outside a small, white, double-storeyed fisherman's cottage standing all alone.

We leapt out of the car and battered on the door and an old peasant woman with a shawl round her shoulders, came out.

'Have you seen our child?' I was going to ask, when Fulton interrupted me.

'Have you seen my child or this gentleman's child?' he asked.

The old woman looked him up and down, then looked at my city suit. Then she looked at the long Bentley.

'No,' she said.

'Then have you seen no children?' Katzi asked. And Ilona Fulton added: 'Haven't you seen two kids?'

'Two kids?' the old woman said. 'Why didn't you ask that first. I thought you said a gentleman's child. Why, yes. Two kids arrived this afternoon. Poor little mites, they were so tired they couldn't even eat. All they wanted was sleep. And my old man's out fishing with the boats, so I just put them upstairs to rest their poor tired little bones on our bed. They're up there now if you want to see them.'

I don't know what we said, or if we said anything. But I know that all four of us rushed up the wooden stairs, which led from their main room below and came into a long, low room lit by a single window.

And there, lying on the bed, right at the end of the room, sprawled out fast asleep, were our two children, stretched out flat in strange attitudes of exhaustion—with just their hands touching.

Now you will not approve of what follows. . . .

Our two boys were sleeping so soundly there was no point in waking them—though from the way Katzi and Helen Fulton cried at seeing them safe and well you would have thought they would awaken the dead. But the two children still slept deeply.

So we went downstairs to wait for them to wake up. And Arthur Fulton produced a bottle of whiskey from the back of his car. And we were so wrought up that even I needed a drink for once. So we all had a few drinks. And so did the old woman. And so did her husband when he came back from his fishing.

And then we started talking.

Well, Katzi and I have decided to stay in England for the time being.

I am a fully qualified accountant, as you know, so I can earn a living. And Antol can stay on with Micky at the Glovers' excellent school.

Arthur Fulton has kindly offered me a job in his shipping firm. But I'm not going to accept—because I don't quite approve of the way he's taken to running it now.

Ever since Arthur Fulton started to read the *Daily Worker*, the *New Statesman*, *Tribune* and the *Daily Herald*, he's introduced a lot of new joint-ownership and profit-sharing schemes into his business I don't approve of. So I think I'll accept this job they've offered me in the new firm of multiple stores they've started in Oxford.

Arthur and I still argue, of course. I can't think what he sees in Karl Marx. But he says that if I once believed the stuff, there must be something in it. And that's why I'm reading the works of Rudyard Kipling.

Night in Cassis

He put down his book and stared at the damp faces of the seven passengers in the train. I ought to have taken a first-class ticket, he thought. I might have had a compartment to myself. I've still got enough francs to last me four days, and Cassis isn't too expensive. Anyhow, we'll be there in half an hour. That girl sitting opposite me has wonderful legs, but her face isn't up to much, and I expect she's going on to Marseilles. If Cassis is dull or if the hotels are full up, perhaps I'll go on to Marseilles and find what I want.

For five minutes his mind soared with fancies of delight in Marseilles; it was recalled to the hot carriage by a tightness round his stomach. I must have my trousers let out, he decided, and I must eat less at mid-day. I ate far too much lunch. A man of forty is possible; a fat man of forty is impossible. Just remember that, Arthur my boy, he said to himself.

He left his luggage in the cloak-room and walked into the bright sunshine outside the station. The harbour was three kilometres away. There were no taxis.

'There'll be a bus perhaps in three-quarters of an hour,' the porter told him. 'You won't have to wait long.'

At last he got a lift in the back of a truck. It was a wonderful advantage being able to speak good French, he thought, while the truck clattered down the hill, but it was stupid to have dirtied his trousers when he had climbed in.

Round the little harbour, clusters of painted fishing boats lay glistening brightly in the afternoon sun. He walked slowly along the crowded quay. He stopped at each hotel to ask for a room.

'You'll never find a room, *mon vieux*,' they said to him. 'A room! Why, there's not even the spare half of a bed to be found in Cassis to-day.'

The sun beat down. He could feel his belly pressing against

the tight band of his trousers. Gloomily he strolled towards the sea-wall. Hundreds of brown bodies dappled with tiny bathing slips lay flat on the beach. I ought to have brought bathing pants, he thought. I ought to have booked a room ahead. I ought to take more exercise in London. I ought to be lean, even wiry. As it is I'm plump and forty and I'll take the very next train to Marseilles.

At that moment he noticed the body of a girl. She was walking slowly up the beach towards him. He thought she must be the loveliest young girl he had ever seen, with long brown legs, slender flanks, a flat stomach, small breasts and a well-poised head with flaxen hair. As she came closer he saw that she had wide blue eyes, a snub nose and wonderfully smooth skin. She was perhaps eighteen years old. The girl began to climb over the low sea-wall. He stretched down his hand.

'*Permettez?*'

'*Volontiers.*'

She stood beside him. His mouth was dry.

'Are you on holiday here?' he asked, still, speaking in French.

'Yes.'

She was not a bit shy.

'Are you from Paris?' His almost perfect French accent gave him confidence.

'Yes.'

'It's fine here, isn't it?'

'Oh, it's glorious. You're not French, are you?'

'No. English. I'm on holiday. *En ballade.*'

There was a pause. He could think of nothing to say, and he was afraid she would go away. He forced himself to speak.

'Will you, that's to say I wonder if you would care to come and have a drink.'

'*D'Accord,*' she said. 'But I'm waiting for my two friends.'

So that's the game, he thought. She wants me to buy drinks for all three of them and then she'll drop me.

'Can't you leave your friends?'

'You see, they'll be looking for me so that we can go back to the camp together. They're shopping.'

'To the camp?'

'Yes. We're camping right up there on the cliff. In the grounds of a half-ruined villa.'

She spoke hesitantly and slowly, as if she were mastering an impediment of speech.

'How many of you?'

'Only three.'

'All alone?'

'Yes.'

'Aren't you frightened?'

'I don't understand.'

'Three young girls alone.'

She laughed. 'But my friends are boys,' she said slowly.

He felt a surge of excitement.

'You camp alone with two boys?'

'Yes. Why not?'

'How old are they?'

'Roberto's twenty and Jo's twenty-two.'

'And you don't mind?'

'Why should I?' she said, smiling at his flushed face.

'How old are you?'

'I'm nineteen.'

'Don't your parents mind?'

'My mother's dead, and father's given me up as a bad job.'

He could see the golden down on the nape of her neck.

'Come and have a drink,' he said.

The girl did not seem to hear him. She was staring over his shoulder.

'Look. There they are,' she said suddenly.

He turned round. Striding towards them he saw two young men clad in scanty canvas shorts with satchels clamped to their naked chestnut backs. He gazed enviously at their lean hard limbs and broad shoulders tapering down to narrow waists.

'This is Roberto,' she said, pointing to the lithe, fair one, with a narrow, attractive face. 'His real name's Robert. And this is Jo.'

What idiotic names, he thought, as they shook hands.

Jo was solidly built with thick, black hair, deep-set eyes and a broad mouth. Jo's the better looking of the two, he decided. But somehow I think she prefers Roberto, with his slim body and the look of a faun about him—that is if she has any choice.

'Let's all go and have a drink,' he said.

'*Volontiers.*'

They went to a bar with a red and white striped awning.

'What shall we drink?' He tried not to stare at her smooth brown skin and the tilt of her breasts.

'*Tomates*,' she said. 'Let's all drink *tomates*.'

'Whatever is a *tomate*?'

'Anis with a dash of grenadine,' said Roberto, taking off his rucksack. 'Jeanne loves it.'

He noticed now and then that she glanced at Roberto's slender waist. But Roberto was only a boy. She must see that. Jo, with his heavy shoulders and thick neck, was a more serious rival, yet the girl hardly ever looked at him.

'Let's have the same again,' he suggested later. Drink lent him confidence and hope.

'Oh, but . . .'

'No, it's on me,' he said quickly. 'I'm celebrating.'

'Your birthday?'

'No. My freedom. I left my luggage at the station. I've got nothing but what I stand up in.'

'*Comme nous*,' the boy Roberto said.

'Just like you. And I've nowhere to sleep. All the hotels are full.'

'But you must stay with us,' Jo said. 'Mustn't he, Jeanne?'

'Certainly.'

'May I really?' he asked, looking into her eyes. 'Are you sure you don't mind?'

'But I would like it,' she replied gravely.

'Then you must all three of you dine with me.'

'We eat at the camp. If y'like we'll buy a steak. Roberto's a good cook,' Jo said in the quick slurred jargon of Paris. '*Un vrai cuistot.*'

'And I'm good at washing up the dishes afterwards,' Jeanne said. 'It's far better eating there than in a stuffy restaurant.'

'Then you must let me buy a bottle of wine and some brandy.'

It will be easier if we're all drunk, he thought.

Later he watched the three of them as they lay round the little fire they had made to cook the meal. Now that the sun had dipped below the mountain the air was cool, but they were still half-naked. Jeanne was lying on her side gazing through the pines at the sea stirring far below. Jo was sharpening a stake with a jack-knife. Young Roberto lay on his back looking up at the long pine branches which stretched out as if to hide them from the dark blue sky. The meal had been good. They had eaten the steak he had bought and then a sweet omelette—surprisingly well cooked by Jo. From a communal beaker they had drunk two bottles of strong red wine and half the bottle of brandy. The three of them were obviously happy; but he could only think about the girl and his longing to have her. And he was still uncertain of success.

He tried to recollect each event of the past three hours to discover a clue to their relationship.

Jeanne had led the way up the cliff-side, and he had followed, staring at the muscles in her lean thighs, staring at her small waist. He had clambered over rocks, up slippery paths, along perilous ledges, pausing and sweating, while the other two followed nimbly. Once he had thought of turning back, but as if by instinct she had turned and smiled at him with a radiance that gave him encouragement.

I still don't get it, he said to himself. Why did neither of them help her when we got to that hard stretch? It was quite a dangerous climb. At least I thought so. But they just stood watching her. I had dropped behind by then; there was nothing I could do. Yet Roberto helped me. I don't get it. She seems to belong to both of them equally. I can see they're both mad about her. Perhaps it's just one of those trios—which will make it all the easier to-night. That ruined villa they talk about sounds just the place.

At last they had reached the terrace on the cliff-side where the rest of their kit was hidden—two saucepans, a water-bottle, rags, three bricks for the fire, and a rucksack containing bread, eggs and olive oil. While the other two prepared the meal he walked with Jeanne to the derelict villa.

'We're not supposed to camp here,' Jeanne said. 'They don't like it. But they don't like us camping on the beach either. So there you are.'

The villa stood on a headland with sea on three sides. They looked at its crumbling red walls and shattered windows, the jagged hole in the side of the room, the litter of rusty bed-springs and broken glass.

'One day, if I'm ever rich, I'll buy this villa and make it lovely again and you must come and live here with me. Will you?' he asked.

'Oh yes. I'll be your housekeeper. *Je ferais le menage.*'

'You're very sweet. Do you know that?'

'You're sweet too.'

'You don't understand.'

'What don't I understand?'

He took her hand. In the silence they heard Jo shout out that supper was ready.

'I'll tell you later,' he said.

He still held her hand as they strolled towards the terrace. She made no attempt to withdraw from him, even when they approached the fire. But he released her fingers gently. He did not want the others to see.

And now he lay uncomfortably on a thin strip of canvas longing for the moment when he could take her slender body in his arms and kiss her lips and breasts and cheeks and stroke her tawny hair. Meanwhile he learned as much about the three of them as he could. They worked in various departments of an aircraft factory. They worked forty-eight hours a week, and lived with their families.

'What are you politically?' he asked.

'Politically?'

'I mean what do you vote?'

'*On s'en fiche royalement de la politique,*' Roberto said. 'We don't give a hoot.'

'What difference does it make to us s'long as we get paid?' Jo said, in his quick, slurred speech. 'Why should we care? Let the politicians wrangle it out amongst themselves, if it amuses them. We just don't bother about it.'

'We don't even read the papers,' Jeanne said. 'It only makes us gloomy if we do. If there's going to be another war what can we do to stop it? Poor Roberto begins his year of military service next October.'

Somehow, the slight impediment in her speech was exciting.

Suddenly he thought of the reason why. The impediment seemed to be caused not by her voice but by her whole body. Her pauses were rhythmic, and she spoke as if a man were slowly and deliberately penetrating her.

As he stretched out his hand for the brandy, Jo stood up.

'I'm tired. I'm turning in,' Jo said jerkily. 'Here's a blanket for you. There's one for each of us.'

'I thought you had a tent.'

'We have,' Jeanne said. 'But it's stuffy in a tent. So we just lie out in the open. It's not cold.'

'What about a stroll?' he said to her, trying to make his voice sound casual. There was no moon, and the night was dark.

'I'm too tired,' she said.

Jo and Roberto had rolled themselves up in their blankets and lay on the far end of the canvas strip which he now realised was their tent. He was lying between them and Jeanne. He was afraid she would move across to join them. But with a fierce thrill he saw her set out her blanket next to his.

'Have one more brandy,' he whispered a few minutes later.

'No more, thanks. Anyhow it's almost finished. And we could have made it last for a month.'

'Jeanne.'

'Yes?'

He took her hand and drew it to his body. He put his arm round her neck. For a moment they lay still. He began to tremble. He could feel he was losing control. He could hardly breathe. Then he stretched out both his arms and pulled her towards him and tried to crush her to his body. But suddenly she tore her hand away from him as if she had touched fire. She wrenched herself from his grasp.

'No,' she whispered urgently. 'Let me be. Leave me alone.'

'Jeanne.'

'Leave me alone, I tell you. I won't. I don't want to. Can't you understand? Don't spoil it all. Good night.'

'Jeanne . . .'

Abruptly she rose, picked up her blanket, and disappeared into the night.

He lay quivering with desire and rage. The bitch, he thought. I bet she's made some assignation with that little brute

Roberto. He rose quietly. He could see Roberto wrapped in his blanket. Both he and Jo were sleeping soundly.

She's probably arranged to wake him later, he decided. He took a long gulp of brandy. He lay trembling in the darkness. Presently he fell asleep.

He awoke two hours later, cold and guilty. His limbs ached from the hard ground. He got up. Roberto and Jo were still asleep. There was no sign of Jeanne. He was thirsty. He stumbled round to find the water-bottle which he placed by his blanket. He lay on his back, thinking. A slither of moon slid over the mountains and glittered in the sea. A star streaked across the sky. Bitter gusts of anger at the weakness of his flesh swept over him. I'm flabby and self-indulgent and sensual, he said to himself. I'm a gross parasite moving expensively over the face of the earth. Nurses, maids, tutors, cooks, laundresses, waiters—dozens of people have all striven for my benefit. And what have they produced? A plump, selfish creature that can't even sleep. And now it's middle-aged. Look at those two little beasts sleeping there. It's the young who are the capitalists of the world. They've got everything.

Then, as he stared sadly at the moon, Jeanne's remark about the brandy swung into his mind. 'We could have made it last for a month,' she had said. For the first time it occurred to him that the three of them were poor. He remembered their gratitude for the meat. He recalled the pathetic care they took of their shabby belongings. All through the year, he supposed, they must have looked forward to this holiday of two weeks with pay. He tried to think what it would be like to work all the year round, through heat and cold, forty-eight hours a week in a factory. He saw the train queues and the crowded journeys. A great weariness came over him.

He awoke at dawn feeling stiff and unrested. His eyes were sore and hard against their sockets. Roberto's blond head was turned towards him. He watched him wake and rise out of his sleep like a child from a refreshing bath.

'Where's Jeanne?'

'I don't know,' he answered, feeling guilty and apprehensive. Then she appeared.

'Good morning,' Jeanne said happily. 'I slept the other side of the villa. It's lovely there. How did you sleep?'

'All right, thanks,' he said, grateful that she was not embarrassed or angry.

'Wake up that lout Jo. It's his turn to make breakfast. I'll stay and help him if you like while you two go down for a swim.'

'Coming?' Roberto asked him.

'Sure.'

Together they climbed down the cliff. He suspected that Roberto went slowly to give him time to catch up.

They both dived in naked from the rocks. The green-blue water was very clear and cold. There was silence except for the splash of their arms as they swam. While they squatted on the rocks drying themselves in the sun he asked the question which was heavy in his mind.

'Are you in love with her, Roberto?'

Roberto turned his freckled face away and stared out to sea. His body was delicate yet he was obviously strong. Naked, the boy reminded him once again of a faun.

'Are you, Roberto?'

'Yes.'

'Do you sleep with her?' He tried to keep his voice even.

'No, of course not.'

'Why "of course"?'

'She doesn't want to. Naturally we'd both like to—Jo and I. We're both men, aren't we? But she doesn't want to. That's all.'

'But what's the point of it?'

'The point?'

'Taking her about with you, I mean.'

The boy swung round on his haunches and stared at him.

'But we're friends,' he said. '*Nous sommes des bons copains*. We've been friends since we were children. We'd be lonely without her.'

'Don't you find it painful?'

Roberto turned away from him and rose to his feet, and stood still for a moment. He could see the muscles of the boy's shoulders, the straight back and small buttocks. The whole body was taut.

'Yes. Sometimes,' Roberto said, and dived swiftly into the sea.

'I'm afraid we've only got some weak hot chocolate,' Jeanne said, when they got back. 'There's not even any milk. But if you dip bread into it, then it doesn't taste too bad.'

After breakfast, they climbed down to Cassis. All three of them strolled with him round the harbour to the bus stop. Jeanne smiled gaily whenever their eyes met. The station bus crawled in to the market-place with a raucous hoot. He thanked each one of them and said goodbye. He clambered into the bus. They stood solemnly watching him as he sat sweating against the shiny seat. Then they raised their hands in salute and wandered away. Passengers jostled against him. The air was fetid. He felt his stomach pressing against his waistband as the bus jolted up the hill to the station—in time for the train to Marseilles.

The Prodigal Son

The park was not crowded that cold Wednesday evening in Autumn. A few people clustered round the impassioned lecturer on Free Trade at Speakers' Corner. Fewer still loitered near the man in the shabby city suit. There were no flamboyant banners behind him, and he stood on a low wooden stool. His quiet voice and awkward gestures attracted little attention. He spoke in a north country accent, slowly, without vitality, like a child repeating a lesson, while his eyes flickered round his small audience.

'And this son gathered all together,' he was saying, 'and went into a far country, and there wasted his money with riotous living. And when he had spent all, he began to be in want. And he found a man who sent him into his fields to feed swine. And he was so hungry that he ate their food. . . .'

The typist clutched her companion, who was restive.

'He'll get all confused in a moment,' she whispered. 'Just you wait. It's quite a scream. He's here every Wednesday night, and it's always just the same. You must wait just to see. Then we'll go off for a cuppa.'

The man still spoke in a slow, dull voice, but his eyes, now lifted beyond his audience, were searching feverishly.

'And the son thought to himself: I will arise and go to my father, and will say unto him, father, I have sinned against heaven and before thee, and am no more worthy to be called thy son. So he began the journey home. But when he was still a great way off, his father saw him, and had compassion, and ran, and fell on his neck, and kissed him.'

'The father kissed him,' the man repeated, and then stopped.

The typist nudged her friend. 'They didn't half carry on in those days,' she tittered.

The man did not hear her laugh. His eyes were glittering, and when he continued his voice was no longer calm. Each word seemed to quiver with his emotion.

'And the son said to him: Father, I have sinned against heaven, and in thy sight, and am no more worthy to be called thy son. But the father said to his servants: Bring forth the best robe and put it on him, and put a ring on his hand, and shoes on his feet. And kill the fatted calf; and let us eat and be merry. For this my son was dead, and is alive again. He was lost, and is found.'

'Now he goes completely balmy,' the girl whispered.

The man's eyes were glazed as he stared straight ahead towards the passing traffic.

'The father forgave him,' he cried suddenly. 'He welcomed his son home. But he could have turned him away. He could have sent him packing. And he could have been perfectly justified. After all, the boy had behaved most wrongly. He could have turned him out. Or he could have delivered him to the authorities and let the law take its course. And let the law take its course . . .'

'The record's stuck. Put in a new needle,' the typist giggled.

'He could have delivered him to the authorities,' the man repeated stupidly, while his mind lurched back . . .

———————◆◆◆◆◆———————

His gaze always returned to the mirror with its curly green frame which seemed out of place against the dark panelling of the college room. In it he could see the two of them reflected: Sylvia, his wife, pale and fragile, leaning gracefully against the velvet cushions, and Rodney, his son, sprawling on the sofa beside her, his hand stretched out to clasp her hand.

He walked across to the long window and stared out at the great court while he listened to their conversation.

'Your father had to drive up to Hull for the launching of the new ship. She really is beautiful,' Sylvia was saying. 'So we decided to call in to see our son and heir on the way home.'

'Mummy, what a wonderful surprise!' Rodney cried eagerly. 'But just think if you'd arrived to find my rooms littered with chorus girls.'

Looking at his son's wavy hair and delicate features Charles Turner decided it was highly improbable.

'What a terrible son I have, to be sure,' Sylvia laughed.

'It was the pixies what did it,' Rodney explained gaily. 'I'm a changeling. Didn't you know?'

'You're a little horror,' Sylvia said, tapping his hand.

'I know I am.'

Charles turned. Suddenly the boy's voice was serious.

'But be patient with me. Please,' Rodney said quietly. 'Life's such fun just now. Those beastly years at school I never believed it was possible to be so happy. Each morning now when I wake up, at first I can't believe it's true. Let me be happy while I can. Let me be stupid and carefree. Just one more term. And then I'll start to work. I promise I will. I'll give up smoking and drinking and going to races. I'll work all day long, I swear it.'

Charles pretended not to see his wife's appealing look.

'When I was your age,' he said harshly, 'I was working twelve hours a day for three pounds ten a week in the dock-yard. Why should we pay our good money for you to gad about college with other young idiots like yourself?'

Even as he spoke he was conscious of his accent and rough voice.

'But Charles,' Sylvia said gently, 'because you suffered when you were young, why should Rodney?'

'Suffered? If I suffered, then ninety-nine per cent of the whole human race is suffering. I didn't suffer. I worked. And I'm proud I did work. If I hadn't we wouldn't be where we are to-day with a Rolls and a chauffeur waiting to take us back to London.'

'But Daddy, can't you see that I'm grateful?' Rodney said. 'I'm more grateful than I can say.'

'You're grateful for what you can squeeze out of me.'

The words had blurted out of his mouth before he considered them. He was now angry because he felt remorse.

'Charles, that's unfair,' Sylvia said quietly. 'You know Rodney loves you.'

'He doesn't know it,' Rodney cried suddenly. 'And he never will—whatever we say. Because he doesn't want to believe it. He owns a cargo line. He's a great man. Only that counts in his eyes. He can't believe anyone can love him just for him-self.'

'You mustn't speak like that,' Sylvia murmured.

'Let the boy say what he likes.'

Charles turned to his son. He was breathing heavily.

'I've made my own way in the world. Yes, I'm proud of it, I confess. But all along the line I've been limited because I'd no education. I know it. That's why I've given you this chance. So you should be better than me. But I tell you this right now. Rather than be known as a happy-go-lucky waster I'd prefer to have the reputation of an honest and hard-working man—even if I can't appreciate artistic stuff like that mirror you're both so daft about.'

'I agree, Daddy. But surely one can be honest and hard-working and still love baroque.'

'Precisely. But your tutor's dissatisfied with your work and you're overdrawn at the bank. That's why I've come here. This gambling's got to stop. You'll get not one penny more from me. And if you don't get down to work you'll leave at the end of this term.'

As Charles and Sylvia walked out into the great court, two undergraduates were standing beneath Rodney's window.

'Rodney, you old stick-in-the-mud,' the taller one was shouting, 'we're off to dine at Newmarket. Coming?'

'Sorry, I can't to-night.'

'Well, at least ask us up for a drink.'

'All right. But not for long.'

Sylvia turned to Charles. 'Try to understand,' she said.

'The boy's got to learn discipline,' he replied.

When a secretary showed the dapper, middle-aged man into his office, Charles got up to shake his hand and spoke briskly to conceal his disquiet.

'I understand from your card that you're the local manager of the National Industrial Bank at the university,' he said. 'What can I do for you?'

'I'm afraid I've come upon an awkward errand, Mr. Turner,' the manager said.

'Well, what is it?'

'Your son has an account at our branch.'

'I know, I know.'

The manager took out a smart notecase from his pocket. From it he took out a cheque which he handed to Charles.

'Is that your signature, sir?' he asked quietly.

Charles forced himself to look at the words on the cheque form.

'Pay Rodney Turner,' he read, 'one hundred pounds. £100. Charles Turner.'

The signature was a blatant forgery.

Then waves of fierce rage swept over him. The little idiot, he thought. Because I'd made out so many cheques for a hundred he reckoned I wouldn't notice. The fool. He only took the risk because he thought I'd protect him if he was found out. The spoilt coward. He wouldn't come straight to me. Oh no. He cheated like a common crook.

The room swayed before him. With a great effort Charles controlled himself.

'No,' he said coldly. 'That is not my signature.'

His voice seemed to come from far away. He gripped the desk hard. The room was steadier now, and he was aware that the manager was talking.

'I'm sure that you will appreciate that we will do our best to avoid a prosecution. Unfortunately, this bookmaker . . .'

'Avoid prosecution?' Charles interrupted. 'Why should you avoid prosecution?'

'But surely . . .'

'Surely I want to protect my son? Just supposing I wasn't rich? Suppose I only earned five pounds a week with a wife to support? Suppose my son was a docker, not an undergraduate? Would there be any chance of avoiding prosecution then?'

'Under the circumstances . . .'

'The circumstances don't change the fact that my son has broken the law like any other common crook.'

'If I may point out . . .'

'Does the boy's mother know?'

'Naturally, I came to you first.'

'Thank you, sir. You have acted properly according to your own lights. Now you must let me act according to mine.'

'And what am I to do?'

'Let the law take its course.'

They stood facing each other in front of the Adam mantelpiece in the long drawing-room. Sylvia was wearing the evening dress he had persuaded her to buy when they were in Paris. Even distress, he reflected, did not impair her beauty.

'It's no good,' he said. 'I've heard all you've had to say. But me mind's made up.'

Slowly she lowered her head.

'Charles, I've asked you for things often. But in all our years together have I ever asked you for anything for myself?'

'No, I can't say you have.'

'Then you can't refuse me, Charles.'

Slowly she knelt down.

'On my knees I beg of you for my own sake, Charles. Please forgive him.'

For an instant he looked down on her in pity. Then he remembered it was for Rodney she was pleading—not for love.

'No,' he said, and walked out of the room.

The law took its course. Rodney begged his mother not to attend the trial. He pleaded guilty and was sentenced to six months' imprisonment.

The next morning Sylvia received a letter he had posted on his way to court. This letter she did not show Charles until later.

'Darling Mummy. After what's happened I can't come home. Please try to understand. I'll always love you as long as I live. You know that. I won't write to you from prison even if I can. But you can find out from them the day I'm due to be released. Don't meet me. You must promise me that. And don't let Daddy see this. In return I'll make you a promise. I'll meet you the Wednesday after I get out, in the park at Speakers' Corner. In the evening at six. I'll explain everything then. Meantime, try not to worry. Bless you, darling. And please forgive me. Much love, Rodney.'

<hr/>

Rodney was released on a Monday four months later. He had gained two months' remission for good conduct. The following Wednesday at five-thirty Sylvia paid off a taxi at Marble Arch and walked across to Speakers' Corner. Feverishly, she scanned the faces of the passers-by. Perhaps he would be early. There were few people about because it was a bleak evening. She would find him easily. Time passed slowly. Towards seven it began to rain. Rodney must come soon. At seven-thirty she must leave the park. Charles would return from his club in time to change for dinner at eight, and he must not suspect. The winter rain was now falling steadily. Perhaps Rodney was ill. That was it. He was ill. He would telephone to her. Perhaps he had already tried to reach her at the house.

At twenty minutes to eight Sylvia took a taxi home. Charles was waiting for her in the hall.

'You're drenched. Whatever's happened to you?'

'I went to a cocktail party. I couln't get a taxi back,' she lied quickly, trying to stop shivering.

Charles looked at her curiously, but he said nothing more. He had not mentioned Rodney's name since the trial.

<hr/>

There was no message from Rodney that evening. Nor did Sylvia hear from him during the next five days when she was in bed trying to shake off her fever.

The following Wednesday she dressed as quickly as she could and hurried out into the cold darkness in spite of her maid's protests. For an hour she waited for Rodney in the empty park. When she reached home she collapsed and was carried to bed.

Then it was she who showed Charles the letter, when they both knew that she was dying.

'Find him,' she kept saying. 'Please find him.'

'I promise you I will,' he cried. 'Oh my darling, forgive me for all I've done.'

'Find him. Only find him.'

The full powers of determination and wealth were then employed to find Rodney. Private detectives, advertisements, rewards, patient enquiries at home and abroad—all were useless. It was known beyond doubt that Rodney left prison that Monday morning at six a.m. From the instant he left the prison, Rodney had vanished into oblivion, leaving not even a trace.

And that was three years ago. . . .

'He could have delivered him to the authorities,' the man repeated stupidly.

'Give the needle a shove, old cock.'

Desperately the man forced his mind back to the present.

'He could have delivered him over to the authorities,' he said, 'and he might never have seen his face again. Think then of his agony of remorse. Think then of the evenings towards sunset when he would have prayed that his son might once again be walking towards him across the fields so that he could run forward and clasp him to his arms.'

The man paused. His eyes seemed fixed on the light of a park lamp near by.

'What, then, can we learn from the story?' he continued. 'It is this. There will be more joy in heaven over one sinner who repents than over ninety-nine just persons who need no repentance. Fathers and sons, if we repent we shall be forgiven. Surely, surely, if we have suffered enough we shall be forgiven, even here in this world, before that day when there will be no more tears and no more bitterness. Thus should we pray in our own heart, saying: I have sinned. Pray God forgive me, let mankind forgive me, grant me only the chance to mend the evil I have done.'

The crowd had drifted away into the dusk. But by the lamp a young man was standing motionless. The preacher picked up his stool and moved slowly towards him, his hope dragging him towards the light.

The Last Gauguin

I have got the last Gauguin ever to be found in the world. I've got it for sale. Rupert Calloway owns it, but I'm responsible for selling it, and I'm taking a twenty per cent commission. In a foreword to our informal brochure, Professor Maximilian Sonnenburg, who everyone knows is one of the greatest experts on Gauguin alive today, has given proof of the picture's authenticity and has acclaimed it as the greatest work of Gauguin's second—and last—Tahitian period. But I have been asked to write these words to tell the true story that lies behind what is generally considered to be the most important art find of the century.

The story begins in Tahiti and ends in Tahiti. I'm not an experienced writer, so if I may I'll start from scratch.

I'm not a good publicity man, and I know it. First, to be successful at the job you've got to believe at least half the nonsense you hand out, and I can never believe a word of it. Then you've got to be interested in the people you write about, and I'm not. These film stars leave me cold—even in Tahiti. Take Anne Delabra.

Anne Delabra! What a name! I wonder what bright-eyed agent thought up that one. I'd have left her name as it was—Jane Fish. Short and unusual. But no. Fish didn't convey the vision of a twenty-three-year-old, peach-skinned, doe-eyed, fawnlike—here we go again—slender, slinky, dewy-lipped—surely that's wrong?—little creature. So Anne Delabra she became. And, of course, when it was discovered that she indulged in occasional little nips from the bottle, all the boys on the unit called her Canned-delabra. Her agent ought to have foreseen that one.

And what in heaven's name does Rupert expect that I can write about dear Annie Delabra? She has the mental age of a child of six and the morals of a slut. The very night she flew out here from Los Angeles she popped into bed with one of the Tahitian taxi drivers on the unit, and that didn't please Rupert for two reasons. First, he'd hoped she'd have a little romp with him—for old time's sake, as it were. Second, he was scared stiff she'd catch some disease and hold up the shooting.

Rupert Calloway, I should explain, is our film producer. He's come out to this island dump with a movie unit sixty strong to make an epic called *Hibiscus Tangle*. I have to put out a thousand words of copy a day about this original, entrancing, light-hearted, witty, passionate—turn over the record, Charlie —brilliantly conceived love drama, so I'm damned if I'm going to write about it here. I'll just say this. If the statisticians who tell us that the average age of the movie-going audience is eleven are correct, Rupert's film is going to make a fortune. And I only hope those clever statisticians are dead right, and we clean up, because Rupert is my boss, and as long as his films make money I reckon I'm all right.

Rupert employs me because we were in France together, and because he knows he can trust me to be sympathetic with his problems.

Rupert's main problem is his health. He believes that he's dangerously susceptible to germs in general and to skin diseases in particular. And this, of course, complicates his second problem, which is sex. Rupert loves women. He loves everything about them. But if they so much as sneeze he's convinced they've got virus pneumonia—and very catching at that. And if he sees the smallest pimple on their elbow he's determined they've got infectious dermatitis at the very least. So his love affairs are infrequent—and he's particularly restricted out here in Tahiti, or Devil's Island, as we've come to call it.

Tahiti, I'm here to tell you, is a snare and a delusion. I'd always thought of it as a simple, unconventional island paradise of love and innocence. Well, it's an island, I'll grant you that. But simple! It's about as simple as the theory of relativity. And unconventional? It's so unconventional that you're not even allowed to sit down at an open-air waterfront café in shorts or bathing trunks. The heat may be stifling but you must still wear a shirt. But it's certainly paradise—and your little hut by the lagoon will cost you eight pounds a day without food. As for love, the girls are wonderfully attractive and unspoiled and all for it. But you can't take a girl to your hotel unless she's got an identity card, and I've yet to meet one that has. As for innocence, the only innocent people around are the tourists.

Perhaps I'm biased against Tahiti, because from the moment we arrived everything went wrong. The first thing was that Rupert refused to shake hands with the mayor's deputy who came down to the airport to meet us. There stood the deputy with an enormous *lei*—a great garland of gardenias—in his left hand and his right hand outstretched. Rupert stared at him in horror for five seconds while our cameras clicked, then he stepped forward and patted him on the shoulder. The deputy's hand fell limply to his side, and he dropped his garland in confusion, muttered a few words of welcome, and turned round and left.

'Why in heaven's name didn't you shake hands with him?' I asked Rupert afterwards.

'But my dear Tom, you are unobservant! Didn't you look at his right hand?' Rupert asked.

'No.'

'There was a whole square inch of rash on it. It looked highly contagious.'

'Then you should have embraced him,' I said.

'Embraced him!' Rupert cried in horror. 'Surely you know that the skin on one's face is *far* more sensitive to disease than the skin on one's hand? At least one's hands have developed some degree of self-protection.'

'After such a scene at the airport, you're going to need some degree of self-protection,' I said nastily.

'Take the deputy's brother-in-law on as our liaison officer with the government,' Rupert replied.

'How do you know he's got a brother-in-law?' I asked.

'He will have,' Rupert said. 'French officials always do.'

And as usual, Rupert was right. So the brother-in-law was taken on and promptly make furtive advances to Mabel, our continuity girl. He pinched her in the car when we were on the way to shoot our lagoon sequence, and she slapped his face. He slapped her back, stopped the car, and walked home to Papeete. From that moment our relations with the government deteriorated.

Then came the episode of Annie Delabra's bath.

I live in a rickety old hotel on the waterfront at Papeete—I like looking out at the boats in the harbour, and as publicity man I feel I ought to be in the centre of things. Rupert lives in an air-conditioned, especially fumigated, mosquito-proof bungalow about ten miles out of town. One evening shortly after midnight, the concierge at my hotel battered on my door to say that I was wanted urgently on the telephone. So down I plodded to the hotel's only telephone, which is inconveniently situated in her bedroom on the first floor.

I took up the receiver, which was lying in a welter of old lipsticks and grease bottles on her dressing table.

'Hullo?' I said wearily.

'Hullo. Is that Tom?' It was Rupert.

'Yes,' I said.

'Tom? Tom? Is that Tom?' he kept asking. He sounded frenzied.

'Tom speaking,' I said. 'As I told you before.'

'Now you've got to keep calm,' Rupert's voice crackled in my ear. 'You mustn't lose your head.'

'As yet,' I said, 'I'm perfectly calm. What's it all about?'

'You've got to find Lebrun, and you've got to find him quick.'

Lebrun was the unit doctor. Rupert alone kept him pretty busy. Rupert had a routine check every morning, vitamin injections every other day, and a blood test twice a week.

'Have you tried phoning him?'

'Of course I have. But his number doesn't answer.'

'He's probably at Quinn's Bar.'

'Then get him. And bring him here quick. And tell him to bring an ambulance.'

'What's happened?'

For an instant there was a pause, and then Rupert said: 'It's Annie. She's ill. Dangerously ill.'

'Where is she?'

'In my bungalow,' Rupert said. 'Now don't waste time talking. Get Lebrun and get an ambulance.'

Far away in the background at his end I heard a moan, and a woman's voice in the distance said, 'You bastard!'

'Oh dear!' Rupert said. 'There she goes again.' And he hung up.

I dressed quickly and took a taxi to Quinn's Bar where I found Doctor Lebrun, festooned with garlands, dancing a hula with three deliciously pretty Tahitian girls.

'Can it not wait until tomorrow?' he asked, eyeing the youngest of them.

'No,' I said. 'It can't.'

The lights were all blazing in Rupert's bungalow when we drove up half an hour later.

Rupert was wearing the Chinese silk dressing gown he'd bought when we made *The Blue Dragon* in Hong Kong three years ago. His nose was twitching as it always did when he was distraught.

'She's a little calmer now,' he said to Lebrun, ignoring me completely. 'I've given her two grains of sodium amytal, three of my reinforced vitamin B tablets, and an aspirin dissolved in Vichy water.'

'The lady has been sick?' Lebrun asked.

'She *is* sick,' Rupert said. 'You must come and look at her at once.   She's in my bedroom.'

'First I would like to discover what you think is amiss with her,' Lebrun said firmly.

Rupert looked rather embarrassed.

'Well, she had a bath,' he said.

'Too soon after her meal? Is that the trouble?' Lebrun enquired. 'She has had an attack of the heart?'

'No,' Rupert said. 'It wasn't quite that.'

'Was the bath too hot?'

'Yes. In a way.'

'How do you mean—in a way?'

Rupert hesitated. The door leading to the bedroom next to the living room was open. The silence that followed was broken by a woman's voice.

'You bastard,' the voice said distinctly.

'It was what was in the bath,' Rupert said wretchedly. 'I'm afraid it burned her.'

'What was in the bath?'

'Disinfectant,' Rupert said. 'My special disinfectant.'

'You bastard!' said the voice from the bedroom. 'You ought to be disinfected yourself—right off the island. I shan't be able to sit down for weeks.'

'I'm afraid I put too much disinfectant into the water,' Rupert said.

As he spoke the bedroom door opened.

'I'll say you did,' Anne Delabra cried. 'You medicated monster. You sadist. You disinfected maniac.'

She was wearing the flowered kimono Rupert had bought in Tokyo when we made *The Treasure of Osaka*, and I could see that her legs were scarlet.

'That bastard's nearly burnt me to a cinder,' Annie said.

'Dr. Lebrun's come to give you a calming injection,' Rupert said.

'Muck the injection,' Annie said. 'I want a Scotch and I want a big one.'

And over her drink the truth came out. She had called on Rupert after dinner because she wanted a change made in the script. In the scene where Ludovic leaves her in despair and goes out to drown his sorrows with a hula girl, Annie wanted him to run into her accidentally in a nightclub. I could guess why. The dear girl didn't want to be off the screen for more than three minutes at a stretch. If Annie had her way she'd be on the screen non-stop from the first fade-in to the last fade-out. Anyhow, Annie had come round to Rupert's specially fumigated bungalow to exert her wiles on him, and she'd been successful. After she had cast languorous glances at his bedroom door for half an hour, Rupert caught on. And he was all for it—until he remembered the episode of the Tahitian taxi driver her very first night. And this worried him. What if she had caught impetigo? Or something even worse?

But Rupert is cunning. I'll give him that. He knew that if he could persuade her to have a bath all would be safe, because he'd got a new disinfectant reinforced with penicillin that was guaranteed to slaughter any virus infection known to the medical profession. So he mixed Annie another drink, and while she was swilling it down, the sodden slut, he crept up behind her and stroked her neck.

'You're a beautiful little thing,' he said. The dialogue is never brilliant in Rupert's films.

'Thanks, Rupert,' Annie said, taking another swig.

'Do you know what I'd love most in the world?' Rupert asked in a low, vibrant voice.

'No, what?' replied Annie.

'I'd love to see you lying naked . . .'

'Well, that's simple enough,' Annie interrupted. 'If you'll just unzip . . .'

'Lying naked,' Rupert continued firmly, 'in a delicious hot bath.'

'I had a bath before I came out,' said Annie.

Rupert's voice became softer and even more vibrant.

'You could always have another one,' he said. 'And then . . .'

He paused significantly.

'I get it,' Annie said. 'If that's the way you like it, you can go run that tub. But before we start any water sports, you're quite sure that I'm right about that nightclub scene?'

'Convinced,' said Rupert, and strode away to the bathroom and took the bottle of high-powered disinfectant from the medicine cupboard.

And the rest of the story we knew only too well, and Annie's scarlet backside was there as proof.

Anyhow, Dr. Lebrun covered her from head to foot in calamine lotion and gave her an injection to keep her quiet and I made suitable soothing noises, and at last she went to sleep, and Dr. Lebrun said that there was nothing more we could do so we'd better be off.

'You can go,' Rupert said to him. 'I want Tom to stay.'

This made me very nervous, because whenever Rupert makes a fool of himself he takes it out on other people. It's one of his little foibles.

'Then good night,' said Dr. Lebrun.

'Good night,' said Rupert. 'Don't forget my vitamin B injection to-morrow afternoon.'

'I shall not,' Dr. Lebrun said between clenched teeth and left the two of us alone together.

'Tom,' Rupert said, 'we've been friends for a long time.'

Then I was sure that trouble was on its way. But there was still a chance I could head it off.

'For a long time,' I echoed. 'Remember those days in France? Remember that little girl who served behind the counter at the fishmonger's? Wasn't her name Ethel?'

I tried hard to distract him. But my words—to use an Arab

expression I picked up when we were in Cairo doing a remake of *The Thief of Baghdad*—my words had no more effect on him than if I had belched on marble.

'So I know you well enough not to have to beat about the bush,' Rupert continued inexorably. 'I'm going to tell you straight out. So there it is. You can take it or leave it.'

He then became silent and glowered at the carpet. I got up and helped myself to a drink.

'What are you going to tell me straight out?' I asked.

'There are lots of people I wouldn't tell straight out,' Rupert went on. 'Some people I'd have to tell in a roundabout way. But not you. No. You're an old friend. So without any beating about . . . without any circumlocution I can just tell it to you direct.' Again he was silent.

'Tell me what?' I asked nervously.

'This picture's not getting enough publicity in the world press,' Rupert proclaimed in oracular tones.

'What?' I cried indignantly. 'Not enough publicity! Didn't the *Daily Mirror* carry a picture with you on its very front page with that man-eating shark you shot off Mooréa?'

'But they said I ought to have harpooned it instead,' Rupert complained.

'Didn't William Hickey's column carry five paragraphs about *Hibiscus Tangle*?'

'Only because Annie Delabra fell off that French frigate.'

'Didn't the *New York Age* say you were one of Britain's twenty most successful film producers?'

'We've only *got* twenty film producers. And it was on a back page anyhow.'

'I've never known such ingratitude!' I cried.

'Unless you think up some bright gimmick to put me and my film in headlines all over the world you'll never have known such an absence of pay cheques,' Rupert said unpleasantly.

So that was that.

But indirectly it was how we found our Gauguin.

At noon the following day in Papeete I was sitting at a little table outside the Café Vaima drinking a beer and looking at the masts of the yachts across the road on the waterfront when I saw a very odd figure of a man staggering toward the bar. He was about sixty-five, I reckoned, shabby and shambling, yet curiously distinguished. He was tall and lean and gawky. He wore an old straw hat, a torn shirt, a pair of patched trousers that were too short for him, and broken sandals. He had long ears and a long beaked nose set in a long haggard face. And I had an odd impression that I had seen him somewhere before.

I wanted another beer anyhow to help me forget Rupert's unkind words about the pay cheque, so by dint of ogling her as if I had an improper suggestion to make, I managed to attract the attention of one of the alluring but indolent waitresses. She swayed toward me gracefully and stood beside my table gazing down at me listlessly.

'*S'il vous plaît, mademoiselle*,' I began in the French that served me so well when we shot *Joan of Arc* in Beirut, '*l'homme qui vient d'entrer le bar . . .*'

'You no speak American?' the girl asked.

'Yes.'

'Then speak American. It is better.'

'Right,' I said. 'Who's that tall guy who's just come into the bar?'

'You do not know Armand?'

'No. Armand who?'

'Armand Gauguin.'

'Armand Gauguin?' I repeated.

'Yes. He is one of Paul Gauguin's sons.'

Then I knew why I felt I'd seen his face somewhere before. He looked exactly like the 1896 self-portrait that I'd seen on a postcard in the shop next door to the Café Vaima. Gauguin came over to Tahiti in 1891 and lived with a series of young Tahitian girls—or vahines, as they call them here. And it wouldn't be at all surprising if he had had dozens of children. I'd already heard about one of them—a plump, genial man called Émile who sold fish traps. This was yet another one. Gauguin didn't die till 1903. The gaunt creature at the bar looked about sixty-five, so the dates would fit, and the resemblance was fantastic.

'Do you think he'd come and have a drink with me?' I asked the waitress.

'If you pay for it,' she replied.

'I'll pay for several,' I said. 'Can you ask him over?'

A few minutes later Armand Gaugin shuffled across to my table and shook my hand.

'I am Armand Gauguin,' he said. 'I can speak a little English but not too much.'

'What do you drink?' I asked.

'Please, I will take a pernod.'

I ordered Armand Gauguin a pernod and then another and then another, for I had a hunch I was onto something that might get Rupert and his wretched *Hibiscus Tangle* mentioned in the beastly world press. By the third pernod I had discovered that Armand was a bachelor, that he earned a little money by fishing, that he earned more money by posing for photographs for tourists, that he had an inferiority complex and resented his father's fame, and that he was an alcoholic.

Over the fourth pernod he leaned forward and tapped my knee.

'I too am an artist,' he said. 'I too paint and make drawings.'

Then it was that I had my brainwave.

'Wait,' I said to him. 'Wait just where you are and don't move.'

I waved my hands wildly and succeeded in gaining the attention of the languid waitress.

'*Encore deux Pernods*,' I called.

'You two boys whoop it up,' she said.

'Now don't move,' I said to Armand again, and I rushed off to find Rupert.

That morning Rupert was taking a pretty shot in which Annie had to come tripping down the gangplank of a cargo boat. Inasmuch as Annie was lying flat on her face in a stupor of morphine and covered with calamine, they were using her stand-in. Just as I arrived the sun disappeared behind a thick bank of cloud.

'Break for lunch,' Rupert said wearily.

It was a bit of luck, because on the pretext that I'd spotted an attractive girl in the crowd of onlookers I managed to get him alone. Rapidly I told him my plot.

'But I don't see the point,' Rupert said. 'Why do we make the man draw a picture? Because his father could draw, that doesn't mean to say that he can.'

'It doesn't matter if he draws like an old boot. The whole point is that you buy the picture afterwards.'

'But why should I buy it?'

'Because we get a picture of you buying it. Can't you see the caption? "Rupert Calloway finds a Gauguin in Tahiti." And then will follow a bright little piece written by me. It'll get used all over the place. Mark my words. It's a winner.'

'All right,' Rupert said. 'Let's go.'

I got hold of Ernest Lush, our stills man, and I bought a large pad of writing paper and together we advanced towards the Café Vaima. And there still sitting at the same table was Armand Gauguin.

'He looks rather grubby,' Rupert hissed in my ear. 'Do I have to shake hands with him?'

'Bow to him instead,' I muttered.

So when I introduced Rupert he made a courtly bow and stepped back quickly out of the danger zone. The waitress came rushing towards us because she had recognised Rupert and hoped for a part in the film. And I ordered drinks for the four of us. Armand had already finished the two pernods I had ordered for him. His eyes were gleaming strangely, and I was afraid he might fall off his chair before we'd taken the photograph of him and Rupert.

'I was talking to my friend about your drawing,' I said to Armand.

'Yes, I can draw,' Armand said, swaying slightly. 'And I can draw very well. I have made many drawings. And I can paint. I can paint very well. I have made many paintings. I can paint as well as my father painted.'

Rupert raised his eyes in resignation toward the clouded sky.

'Better than my father,' Armand cried.

Hastily I produced the writing pad.

'Could you do us a little sketch now?' I asked.

'Certainly. I can draw at any time. Have you a pencil?'

I produced a pencil.

'And can I ask you for another drink?'

I ordered another drink, and we watched him with fascination as he began to draw on the pad, gripping the pencil tight in his tremulous gnarled hand, making slow laborious strokes, wrinkling his brow in an effort of concentration. But at last it was finished and he handed us the writing pad with a gesture of triumph.

The sketch might have been made by a child of ten in an off moment. It showed the inside of a hut that was completely bare except for a large chest in the left-hand corner. In the wall to the left was an open window with a hinged shutter above it fastened up to the ceiling. Through the window was a palm tree.

'I think it's fascinating,' I said, kicking Rupert under the table.

'So do I,' Rupert said.

'I don't suppose you'd be prepared to sell it by any chance?' I asked.

Armand Gauguin's eyes glittered.

'For how much?' he replied.

I glanced at Rupert who shrugged his shoulders.

'How much do you want?'

Armand's hand shook violently as he raised his glass to his full lips, and a look of cunning swept across his face.

'A hundred francs,' he said.

'Less than eight pounds,' I murmured to Rupert.

'That's fine,' Rupert said, taking out his wallet and producing a hundred franc note. 'I'd be delighted to buy it.'

Armand took the note and examined it carefully. Then he folded it up and put it in his pocket.

'You are lucky to have got the drawing for so little,' he said. 'My father would have charged more.'

'I'm sure he would,' I said. 'And now what about a picture to celebrate this happy occasion?'

Ernest Flush sprang up on cue and began focusing his camera.

'You want to take my photograph?' Armand asked slyly.

'Yes. We want a photograph of you and my friend Rupert Calloway.'

'Ten francs,' Armand said firmly. 'Ten francs a photo.'

Wearily Rupert took out his wallet and handed another note across the table. Quickly I adjusted Rupert's hand so that he held the sketch in position between the two of them. And Ernest took three shots of them from different angles.

'That'll do the trick,' he said. 'Anything more you want?'

'Nothing, thanks.'

'Well toodle-oo,' said Ernest and hurried off to get his lunch.

Armand stared at us with wild, haggard eyes.

'Now I go to eat,' he said. 'But this afternoon I will take you to my *faré*, to my hut, to see my painting.'

'I'm afraid we'll both be working this afternoon,' Rupert said.

'This evening, then. I will take you this evening.'

'I'm afraid we're invited to a cocktail party.'

'Can you not spare half an hour to see a painting that is a work of art?'

'Perhaps we could come to-morrow,' I suggested.

'To-morrow we're shooting on Mooréa,' Rupert said.

Armand glared at us.

'You do not think I can paint well. Is that it?' he asked. 'You are not interested in my work; you are only interested in my father's painting because he is famous and so people think that everything he did is a work of genius.'

'I can promise you . . .' I began. But Armand took no notice of me. He was quivering with rage, and his words swept over us like a torrent.

'They think that even pieces he did when he was sick and old are great works. Even pieces he did in five minutes to pay for bread or wine are said to be works of genius. But they will not even come to see the painting I have spent five years in doing. Why? Because no one has heard of Armand Gauguin. So no one cares about him. And yet his work is greater than his father's. Far greater, I tell you.'

Suddenly he seized the sketch from Rupert's hand.

'That is my *faré*,' he shouted, pointing to the childish drawing of the interior of the hut. 'And you see that chest in the corner? Do you see it? Can you see it?'

'Yes,' I said. 'We see it.'

'That chest is a seaman's chest,' he said. 'And it belonged to my father. And in that chest are many sketches by my father. Many. And I tell you that not one of them is as good as the work I do.'

I saw Rupert's nose twitch.

'You've got some sketches by your father?' he asked.

'Yes, I tell you. Many.'

'In your hut?'

'Yes. In that chest, I tell you.'

'Where is your hut?'

A look of cunning crept again over Armand's face.

'Not far,' he said. 'Perhaps an hour in a car. Perhaps less. You bring a car, and I will take you there.'

'We'll collect you at six o'clock,' Rupert said.

'What about your cocktail party?' Armand asked.

'We'll get out of it.'

'Good,' said Armand, rising heavily from his chair. 'I will wait for you here at six o'clock. But now I must go to eat.'

And he walked unsteadily down the street and turned off into an alleyway that led to the jumble of clip joints and shanties in the hinterland of Papeete.

Rupert leaned forward, wiped the rim of his beer glass with a handkerchief, and took a sip.

'What do you think?' he asked.

'There may be something in it. At any rate we're onto a good story.'

'How shall we know if those sketches in the seaman's chest were really done by Paul Gauguin or not?' Rupert asked.

'We won't,' I said. 'And he could easily forge the signature.'

But even as I spoke I thought of Max.

Max Sonnenburg was a painter *manqué* who was our art director. He was short, squat, and plump, with a round smooth face and rimless spectacles. He was very central European, very temperamental, and quite brilliant. And before he had got mixed up with the film world he had worked as art critic on a Paris newspaper for ten years.

'Max,' I said.

'Of course!' Rupert cried. 'The very man. Why didn't I think of it? Have him meet us here at six.'

'If the sketches are really genuine, what do you intend to do?'

'Buy the lot as cheap as I can and sell them in America for all they're worth. And I'll give you ten per cent of the profits.'

'Twenty per cent,' I said. 'After all, I did find Armand Gauguin.'

'All right.'

'And you'd better give Max ten per cent. We want him on our side.'

'That only leaves me seventy per cent,' Rupert said. 'But I suppose it's still worth it. Let's go and get some lunch at Chapiteau's. You can phone Max and I can phone poor Annie.'

When the three of us met him at the Café Vaima at six o'clock that evening Armand Gauguin was drunk. His eyes were bloodshot, and his long, haggard face was mottled. He could hardly stand up when Max arrived and we introduced the two of them. We told him that Max was a friend of ours who had lent us his car. And indeed Max, looking rather like an overblown cherub, did drive us off in the unit Chevrolet. By now Rupert was convinced that Armand was suffering from tuberculosis, so he sat in front with Max and I sat in back with Armand, who had fallen into a sodden silence. And on we drove through the dusk, past the airport and the turning to Faaa, past little villages of thatched huts and copra plantations with each palm tree encircled with a metal band like an umbrella to keep the rats from climbing up them, past the Iaorana Villa hotel and the site of Paul Gauguin's hut by Punaavia, past the Club Mediterranée and the Maraa Grotto. On and on.

Darkness had fallen when Armand stirred himself and told Max to take the next turning to the right, and we left the road to Faratea and clattered slowly along a narrow, bumpy track that led towards the beach. The moon was hidden by clouds, but perched on the end of a small promontory ahead we could see a hut.

'That is my *faré*,' Armand said. 'From here we must walk.'

The thatched hut was built so close to the edge of the cliff that it looked as if it would topple down into the sea at any moment. Armand unlocked the padlock on the wooden door.

'Wait,' he said. 'I will go in first and light the lamp.'

'Lots of insects about,' Rupert said. 'They're not supposed to be harmful, but I've taken my tablets in case. Can I lend either of you my insect repellent?'

'No, thanks,' we both said hastily, for we had smelled Rupert's insect repellent all the way there in the car.

'Now please come in,' Armand said.

We entered a long, narrow room, such as he had drawn in

the sketch, with two open apertures, square in shape, that served as windows on either side. Hinged to the wall above each window was a wooden shutter, which was held back by a cord that ran over a hook fastened to the rafters, so that if the cord was loosened the shutter would fall into place over the window. Two oil lamps and a pressure lamp hung from the crossbeams. To the right of the door was a low divan covered by two grey blankets and a stained bolster. The wall at the far end of the room was completely concealed by a greasy red curtain. In front of the curtain were two chairs and a table made from packing cases. To the left of the door was the brass-bound seaman's chest that we had seen in the sketch. Otherwise the dusty room was bare.

Armand unwrapped the brown paper parcel he had been carrying and produced two bottles of brandy.

'First we must have a drink,' he said. 'I have no glasses but we can drink from the bottles.'

'I don't think I'll have a drink just now,' Rupert said quickly.

'But I will,' Max said firmly, taking one of the bottles. 'And my friend Tom will drink with me.'

'Splendid,' I said.

Rupert glanced at his gold wrist-watch.

'I don't want to hurry anybody,' he said. 'But I have to be back in Papeete in time for dinner with the governor.'

'You would like me to show you the pictures now?' Armand asked.

'If you don't mind, I would.'

'Very well.'

Slowly Armand fumbled in his pocket and produced a key. Then he knelt down and unlocked the dark wooden chest with a shaking hand. Slowly he rose to his feet and pulled back the heavy lid.

There was silence in the room. Rupert was twitching his nose like a rabbit. Max had put down the bottle of brandy and was standing very still and taut, gazing at the chest intently. And I must admit I was excited. Without really knowing it, I was twirling the cord of one of the shutters round in my fingers. But Rupert frowned at me, so I stopped.

Armand took out a torn blanket from the chest and laid it to one side. Then he took out a stack of thick sheets of white cardboard mildewed around the edges, and walked across to the table. In silence we followed him, and in silence we watched while he held up the sketches, one after the other, for our inspection.

After the first five of them I did not even dare look at Rupert. Gusts of rage swept over me. It was monstrous. We had been taken for complete mugs. He'd played the cheapest trick imaginable to lure us all the way out to his flyblown hut. Sketches by his father indeed! Even I could tell who had drawn them. The childish curves, the crude blunt lines, the spiky palm trees, the wobbly rafters—I'd seen them that very morning. The drunken old idiot had made those sketches himself. Suddenly the silence was broken.

'And when are you going to show us some work by Paul Gauguin?' Max asked.

Armand glared at him. His long, raddled face was twisted in anger.

'Those sketches are by Gauguin,' Armand said.

'Not by Paul Gauguin, they're not,' said Max.

Armand took a swig of brandy.

'They are by me,' Armand cried. 'They are by Armand Gauguin. They are the work of genius. Admit it. They are far better than the work of Paul Gauguin, do you not think? Speak. Do you not agree?'

'No,' said Max. 'Quite frankly, I don't.'

'You do not think my work as good?'

'Not quite,' said Max.

'Then you are a fool!' Armand shouted. 'And I will prove you are a fool. Stand back and look.'

Frantically he tore aside the long red curtains at the far end of the room. Then he stood proud and erect, breathing heavily, staring triumphantly at the three of us as we gaped in awed silence.

The whole of the end of the room was a window—or rather it was a series of some twenty panes of glass joined together by thin wooden frames so as to form one huge tall window as one sees in a painter's studio. And on this great window had been painted what I can only describe as the most thrilling picture I've ever seen. In the background was a Tahitian village with blue pandanus trees and green-crowned palms that cast odd curling shadows of a darker green. Beyond the shadows were thatched huts with roofs of pink and walls of purple. In the foreground, riding white horses, were three naked girls, their bodies painted in bold orange and chrome yellow. The paint had faded, and two of the panes of glass had been broken and showed as empty squares in the picture. But the composition was magnificent, and the effect of the picture was shattering.

'Now are you convinced?' Armand cried. 'Now will you believe that I can paint? Now do you admit I can produce a work of genius? Do you admit it?'

'You are right. It is a work of genius,' Max said very quietly. 'It is probably the only work by Paul Gauguin that is unknown in the world to-day.'

There was dead silence. Armand stared at him with such hatred that I was afraid he would fly at Max and kill him. I began to play nervously with the cord again. Somehow it gave me confidence.

'You lie,' Armand said softly. 'Armand Gauguin painted that picture.'

'No.'

'You lie,' Armand repeated louder.

'I know the work of Paul Gauguin,' Max said gently. 'I studied it for ten years.'

'But I painted that picture.'

'Never.'

Armand tilted back the bottle of brandy and drank quickly.

'I painted it with my own hands, I tell you.'

'No. I'm afraid you didn't.'

'Will you sell it to us?' Rupert asked, smiling at Armand pleasantly.

'Sell it? Never. That is my painting. I will never sell it as long as I live, because it is my masterpiece. I painted it with my own hands. It is mine.'

'You could never compose that picture,' said Max.

Armand glowered at him.

'Why? Why could I not?'

'Because you're not Paul Gauguin.'

Suddenly Armand began to scream in a high-pitched, mad voice. It was horrible, and I tried not to listen, but I couldn't help hearing the words that emerged between his screams.

'I am *not* Paul Gauguin,' he shrieked. 'I am *Armand* Gauguin. *Armand* Gauguin. And I made that painting. I and I alone. And it took me five years. Five whole years.'

For a moment he was silent. Then he stumbled toward the bottle.

'You've had enough to drink,' Rupert said quickly and stretched out his hand for the bottle. But Armand moved faster and sprang back with the bottle clutched triumphantly in his hand. But as he sprang back he lost his balance, staggered and reeled heavily backward into the painted window. There was the ghastly sound of splintering wood and breaking glass. Then with a loud screech he toppled through the shattered window and disappeared into the darkness.

'That's torn it,' Rupert said.

I rushed to the empty socket where the window had been and looked down. For an instant I could see nothing. Then my eyes grew accustomed to the darkness, and I saw what had happened.

When I turned back into the room Rupert's face was pea green and he was popping pills into his mouth.

'Is he dead?' he asked.

'No,' I said, taking a quick nip of brandy to steady my poor nerves.

'Dying?'

'No.'

'Then what's happened to him?'

'At present,' I said, 'he's floundering around in three feet of water. He's lucky that the tide was in.'

'Isn't he even hurt?'

'He doesn't look it.'

'Oh, well, that's that,' Rupert muttered.

'You sound disappointed,' I said.

'Well,' said Rupert, 'for a start we've lost the chance of buying a Gauguin, and you must confess that if he'd been *slightly* hurt it could at least have made a story.'

Sometimes Rupert shocks me, and I told him so—which unexpectedly enraged him.

'The trouble is that you're a prig,' Rupert snorted angrily. 'And you always *were* a prig. Even in France. Who was it who refused to put aphrodisiac in Ethel's lemonade?'

'Why should *I* put aphrodisiac in *your* girl's drink?' I asked indignantly.

We were still wrangling when Armand walked into the room. He was dripping wet, but the shock and the sea water had sobered him up a little.

'I am sorry,' he said, 'I became excited and I lost control of my head. But now I am better. And I think I will take some brandy from the other bottle.'

'Don't you think you've had about . . .' Rupert began when Max interrupted.

'Give him the brandy, Tom,' he said.

We turned to him in surprise. Max had been so silent that we had forgotten all about him. He was standing at the end of the room examining the solitary pane of painted glass that remained unbroken. He looked utterly distraught, and I thought he must be mourning the loss of a fine work of art. As we stared at him Max crossed over to me, took the bottle of brandy from my hand, went over to Armand and handed him the bottle with a low bow.

'Allow me to offer you your own brandy,' he said. 'And allow me to offer you my deepest respect. I realise now that you are a profound artist.'

This change of attitude surprised me so much that I started playing with the cord again.

'Yes?' Armand said dully.

'I owe you an important apology,' Max said. 'I can only hope that one day you will find the generosity in your heart to forgive me for the terrible wrong I have done you. But I must ask you to believe that it was the composition rather than the painting on the glass itself that misled me. The composition, if I may say so, had what I could only believe to be the very hallmark, the distinctive stamp, of your father's work.'

'What on earth are you talking about?' Rupert asked.

'I simply could not believe that any artist in the world except Paul Gauguin could have composed that painting,' Max continued in tones of reverence.

'No?' said Armand.

'What?' cried Rupert.

'But I was wrong,' said Max, pointing to the solitary pane. 'And the paint on that piece of glass proves it. For I am willing to swear that that paint is not more than ten years old at the most.'

'You mean . . .' Rupert began slowly.

'I mean that Armand Gauguin painted that window,' Max said in a solemn voice of awe. 'I mean that we stand in the presence of a great genius.'

This turn of events startled me so much that I must have given a violent tug at the cord. Anyhow, the cord suddenly unwound from the hook and the wooden shutter fell down over the window with a startling crash. Our nerves were on edge and we all jumped violently.

'You idiot!' Rupert said. 'You . . .'

But the words shrivelled on his lips, and the three of us gasped and then were silent.

On the inside of the shutter, covering the whole back of it was nailed a canvas. And on the canvas was painted the picture of the Tahitian village we had seen painted on the window before it was broken. It was the same picture. But the colours were more vivid and the lines were more assured. And in the bottom right-hand corner was the signature: P. Gauguin.

Instinctively we turned toward Armand. For a while he was motionless. His gaunt face seemed racked with pain. Then slowly he nodded his head.

'Yes. That was the original,' he said. 'And my father, Paul Gauguin, gave it to my mother when they were living together. And she hid it away from the men who came searching for his work after his death. But before she died my mother gave it to me. And I have kept it here in my *faré* ever since. That is the original,' he repeated, turning toward Max. 'But I painted the window. You believe that now, don't you?'

'Yes,' said Max. 'I do.'

'First I sketched out the design in small squares to represent the panes of glass in the window. Then working inch by inch, I copied it onto the panes of glass. Sometimes it would take me a whole week to get the right colour. Sometimes I would go wrong and have to remove the pane and start again on a clean glass. But I never gave up. I went on with my work. And little by little I began to forget about the original and to believe that the work was my own. And as the years passed by I began to hate the original. Once I nearly destroyed it.'

Armand gave a dry laugh.

'But I'm not a fool,' he said. 'I'm a poor man, and one has got to eat. *Il faut vivre.* So I kept it.'

I'm glad you did,' said Rupert, fingering his chequebook. 'How much do you want?'

As Rupert spoke those words the sorrow appeared to vanish from Armand's face, and the old look of cunning returned. The transformation was surprising but complete. A moment ago he had been a sad, defeated old man. Now he stood there slyly rubbing his long nose with his finger. It was amazing.

'It will cost you quite a lot,' he said. 'Because I intend to charge you for the loss of the window.'

'And as your expert friend admitted just now,' he added, 'it was a work of great genius.'

Well, they haggled away, and finally Rupert got the picture for what he now hopes is less than a third of its market value. At any rate old Armand was delighted and went on a spree with a bevy of vahines that lasted a week and ended up in the Papeete jail and had to be bailed out by Max.

Armand now talks of going to Paris to study at an art school. But I doubt if he will, because one of the vahines he met on his spree has taken a fancy to him and moved into his *faré*. There's even talk of their getting married, and Armand has grown quite merry.

So there you are! And that's my story of how Rupert got hold of this Gauguin that we're now on our way to America to sell.

Or at least that's my story so long as I get my commission.

Stolen Tune

One evening a year ago I went into a Chelsea pub where a man was playing the piano. He was obviously a professional and he was playing with wild brilliance because—as I soon noticed—enthusiastic customers were pouring drinks down his throat to refresh him for the next number, as if he were a human juke-box.

I moved closer to look at him. He was about thirty, with a sensitive face and wide-set, staring eyes. He was wearing a stained tweed jacket and faded corduroy trousers. He needed a shave and a hair-cut, and from the nervous tic that twisted his face I reckoned he also needed a month in a nursing-home.

A fat man with a smooth face was leaning against the top of the battered piano. He winked at a girl with obviously dyed hair who was holding his arm and turned towards the bar.

'Another drink for the maestro!' he called out in a loud voice.

Then he bent down to the pianist.

'Play "Follow the Sun",' he ordered.

The pianist glanced up at him and began playing 'Buttons and Bows'.

The girl laughed.

'I said "Follow the Sun",' the fat man said crossly.

The pianist stared up at him dully and went on playing 'Buttons and Bows'. Now and then his fingers slipped on a complicated run, but he had a wonderful sense of rhythm.

'It's the smash hit from that show at the Royalty. You must have heard it,' the fat man insisted.

The pianist did not look up.

'I don't play to order,' he said.

'No play tune, no get drink. Isn't that right?' the fat man asked, turning to the people clustered round the piano.

'That's the form,' one of them said with a titter.

'I'll play any other tune you like.'

'What's wrong? Don't you know it?'

The pianist looked up at him.

'Know it?' he asked scornfully. 'You fool! I wrote it.'

'Don't try to kid me,' the fat man said. 'Maxie Palmer wrote "Follow the Sun", and you're no more Maxie Palmer than I'm Boadicea.'

'I wrote that tune all the same.'

'Naughty, naughty,' the fat man said. 'We mustn't tell fibs, must we?'

Suddenly the pianist crashed his hands flat on to the keyboard.

'I wrote it!' he shouted. Then his head tipped on to his hands, his shoulders began to shake, and he started to mumble in a low, trembling voice.

'He's drunk,' the fat man said.

No one else spoke. In the silence we could hear some of the words the pianist was muttering:

'Smash hit . . . smash hit I was certain . . . But she stole it . . . Joan stole it and sold it to him . . . She must have . . . She was the only one who'd ever heard it . . . There was no one else . . . And she was the only girl I ever loved . . .

The barman walked over and stood beside him.

'Shall I get you a cab?' he asked quietly.

Slowly the pianist raised his head and nodded. The barman helped him up and they walked out of the swing doors together.

When I went into the pub a fortnight later neither the drunken pianist nor the fat man was there. A placid woman in a green blouse was thumping out 'Tea for Two' with her foot on the loud pedal. Glass beads clinked round her neck as she played.

I walked across to the bar and ordered a pint of bitter. Standing next to me at the bar was a small, stout woman clutching a glass of port in one hand and a shopping-bag in the other. Her grey hair was crimped into tight curls over her broad head. She turned to me and smiled confidingly.

'I always think there's nothing like the old favourites,' she said.

'Nothing,' I agreed.

'Now take that new show at the Royalty,' she said, waving her glass in the air. 'I expect you've seen it?'

'Not yet.'

'Well, there's only one tune that's worth anything in the whole show. And do you know who wrote it? My Doreen's son, George. And do you know how old he is? Seven last birthday.'

I decided that she was tipsy.

'You wouldn't believe a kid like that could write a tune, would you?' she asked.

'It's a bit surprising,' I said cautiously.

'I thought you'd say that,' she said triumphantly. 'You see, I was working for Mr. Max Palmer at the time. I'd come in for two hours in the mornings to do out his place. And my Doreen works full time in a shop, so I'd have to take young George along with me in the holidays when he wasn't at school. Not that he was any trouble. He'd just sit downstairs in the kitchen whistling to himself and not worry anybody. I've never known a kid so keen on music. And that's how it all came about.'

'I don't understand.'

'Well, one day Mr. Palmer came down to the kitchen to get some ice out of the fridge. And there was young George whistling. Of course, Georgie stopped as soon as Mr. Palmer came in, but Mr. Palmer must have heard the tune because he asked Georgie to go on with it. So Georgie whistled it again.

'And Mr. Palmer went running upstairs to his piano to write it down. The next day he gave Georgie a pound note. But he's a mean one, that Mr. Maxie Palmer. Because do you know what the tune was? "Follow the Sun." I swear it.'

I stared at her as she drank her port. The muttered words of the young pianist slipped back into my mind. 'Joan stole it and sold it to him . . . She must have . . . She was the only one who'd ever heard it . . . There was no one else.'

But was there no one else?

I ordered drinks and made myself wait until the barman brought her a glass of port before I asked her the question which was haunting me.

'Did you ever work for another composer, a young pianist about thirty?' I asked, and described as best I could the drunken pianist I had seen in the pub.

'Why, that would be Mr. Corrie,' she said. 'Such a nice young gentleman, he was. I was really sorry to leave him. But he just couldn't keep me on. "Mrs. Roach," he said, "I'm down and out and that's all there is to it." '

I tried to keep my voice steady as I asked her my next question:

'When you were working for Mr. Corrie, did you ever take young Georgie along there with you?'

'Why, heaps of times. Of course, Mr. Corrie's place wasn't anything like Mr. Palmer's—just one great big room with a piano in it and a kitchen and bathroom downstairs. But Georgie would be that quiet when Mr. Corrie was playing he never worried him. I told you Georgie liked music. Sometimes he'd sneak upstairs while Mr. Corrie was playing and sit there all morning, and Mr. Corrie wouldn't even know he was in the room.'

At last I had got it. Corrie believed that Joan was the only person to whom he had played his tune and that only Joan could have sold it. But he'd played it to another person— someone who stayed curled up so quietly in a corner of the sofa that Corrie had never even noticed him—a small boy with an ear for music who had unconsciously picked up the simple tune and had whistled it to Max Palmer and had been pleased to get a pound note.

I sank down my drink.

'Can you remember where Mr. Corrie lived?' I asked.

'I should do. . . . Yes. It was Number Seven, Elvering Mews. Runs off Smith Street.'

'One more question, Mrs. Roach. What's your address?'

She fished in her shopping-bag and produced a typewritten card.

'I always keep them handy,' she said. 'But can I ask why you want it?'

'Because I think it's just possible that Mr. Corrie will be very grateful to you,' I said.

And so will a girl called Joan, I thought, as I walked round to Elvering Mews.

Le Père Auguste

As I had a week to spare before sailing from Marseilles to New York, I went to stay with some friends in Grenoble. The evening I arrived they took me to a restaurant called *Chez le Père Auguste*. There were half a dozen tables covered by pleasant chequered cloths in the small whitewashed room. There were no tourists. All the tables were occupied by stolid French businessmen and their yet more stolid wives. They ate with rapt attention—though now and then their faces would relax into a smile of deep satisfaction. The place was attractive and pleasantly unassuming, as was the old *patron*, 'le Père Auguste', who came to take our orders.

With his broad, heavily creased face, vast paunch, and deep laugh, you would have thought that, apart from his devout preoccupation with the food he so excellently prepared, he hadn't had a care in the world in all his seventy years.

'There goes a contented man,' I thought to myself as we said good night to him after our first meal and walked out into the fresh evening air. But I was wrong. I found it out the night before I left for Marseilles.

By that time we knew him quite well. He would come and join us for a *fine* at the end of the meal and he would describe to us the fabulous dishes and wines he had known in his life. But that last night—after my friends had told him that I was off to America—he became oddly restive and gloomy. I also noticed that he drank more than usual. After a while he came and sat down beside me. Suddenly he asked me, with a strange look of intensity, if I were going to New York. When I said that indeed I was, his story came out. This is it.

Thirty years ago le Père Auguste had quarrelled with his son, Maurice, then a boy of twenty. Le Père Auguste's wife had died the previous year. And at that instant his only child—Maurice—wanted to leave him to go to Paris because, said le Père Auguste, the boy was in love with 'some kind of worthless girl who lived there.'

Old Auguste said 'no'. Maurice insisted. Auguste told his son that if he married the girl he would be completely disowned. There was a violent scene. Young Maurice rushed hysterically out of the house, vowing never to return. He went to Paris. The girl *did* turn out to be worthless, and Maurice emigrated to the United States where—le Père Auguste told me—his son now worked as a waiter *'dans quelqu' espèce d'estaminet.'*

'But I am now an old man,' Auguste continued. 'The doctor tells me I have not many years to live. I think I should forgive my son before I die. So I ask you this my friend, could you find my son in New York and give him a message from me?'

'Certainly,' I answered. 'But have you got his address?'

'I can tell you where he used to work,' Auguste said. He shuffled into the kitchen.

He came back carrying a piece of paper. He carefully unfolded it and handed it to me.

'Maurice Godet,' I read. And then the name of one of the most famous hotels in New York, which I will call the *Savoy-Waldorf*—hardly what I would have described as an 'estaminet.'

'I'll try to find him,' I said. 'And if I do, what message can I give him?'

For a moment le Père Auguste sipped his *fine* in silence. Then he said, 'Tell him that I forgive him. I forgive him altogether.'

'Can I tell him about meeting you and about this restaurant?' I asked.

'Certainly,' le Père Auguste replied.

Suddenly his broad face creased into a smile and he added: 'And you can also tell him this. If he is really a true son of mine, he will cook you as good a meal as I have done to-night.'

Then le Père Auguste blinked as the tears pricked his eyelids, and he turned away.

The following day I sailed from Marseilles to New York.

When I had been in New York for a few days, an editor asked me to lunch with him at the *Savoy-Waldorf*. Immediately I remembered le Père Auguste's errand. I therefore arrived half an hour early. I went to the reception desk. Rather nervously I asked them if I could get in touch with a Mr. Maurice Godet who must now, I calculated, be about fifty. I explained that he had once worked in the hotel as a waiter.

The receptionist was kind and very helpful. He rang through to the restaurant, the grill-room, the Champagne Room and the night-club. But not one single person had ever heard of a Maurice Godet. I was about to give up in despair when another receptionist, who must have overheard our conversation, leaned across and said, 'He couldn't mean Mr. Maurice, could he?'

There was awe in his voice.

'Who is Mr Maurice?' I asked.

'The manager of the whole Savoy-Waldorf,' the assistant receptionist replied. At that point I decided that this character could not possibly be Père Auguste's son. And yet . . . and yet . . . perhaps. . . . I decided I might just as well have one last try.

Then, 'Please put me through to Mr. Maurice,' I said. And when they seemed doubtful I added, 'I may have an important message for him.'

The receptionist hesitated. Then he took up the telephone and dialled. A secretary answered, then yet another. At last I was put through to a man who spoke with a firm, rather cold voice, devoid of any trace of a French accent.

'Mr. Maurice?' I asked rather nervously. By now I was beginning to feel rather like a con-man.

'Yep. Speaking,' the voice replied.

'Does your father run a restaurant in Grenoble?' I asked, now feeling like a complete fool.

There was a pause, and then the voice said, 'Yep. Why?'

'I've got a message for you from him,' I said.

For an instant there was complete silence.

'Where are you now?' the voice asked after this pause.

'At Reception.'

'I'll have you sent right up.'

The elevator shot me up like a rocket to the top of the vast building. I was met and shown past ante-rooms full of secretaries. Then I entered one of the smartest penthouses I have ever seen. There, at the end of a long, pale green room, behind an enormous desk, littered with telephones and files, sat a smooth-faced, dark-haired, plump man. He was alert and very confident.

'Mr. Maurice Godet?' I asked.

'They call me Maurice around here,' he answered. 'It's easier. Pleased to meet you. Have a cigarette. Sit down. Well now . . . So you met my father? How is he?'

Something about this man, who obviously saw himself as a powerful tycoon—together with his deliberate calm irritated me.

'How is he?' the man repeated.

'Not too well,' I replied. 'The doctors have told him he doesn't have many years to live.'

The large man swung away from me. Suddenly he pressed a small lever on the complicated intercom system on his desk.

'I don't want any calls until I tell you,' he said into it. Then he looked me up and down as if he were trying to guess my weight. After a pause he said, 'You mentioned you have a message from my father?'

'Yes,'

'What is it?'

At that instant I felt uneasy.

'Your father asked me to tell you that he forgives you,' I said.

Mr. Maurice's bland expression did not alter.

'Did he tell you what I did?' he asked.

'He said you'd run off to Paris.'

'Did he tell you he'd chucked me out of the house?'

'No.'

Mr. Maurice smiled. For a brief moment he reminded me of his father.

'Proud old bastard,' he said. 'He never would admit himself in the wrong.'

Mr. Maurice stood up and walked over slowly to an elaborate cocktail cabinet.

'Drink?' he asked.

'No thanks. I'm meeting a friend here, and I'm late already.'

'Mind if I have one?'

Mr. Maurice poured himself out half a glass of bourbon and

added some ice. His back was still half-turned to me when he next spoke.

'Was there any other message?' he asked.

'Yes,' I replied, after a moment of hesitation.

'Let's have it.'

'With the set-up you've got in this hotel, I'm afraid it will sound rather ridiculous,' I muttered.

'I'd like to know it, just the same.'

'Well,' I said, 'Your father told me to tell you that if you were really a true son of his . . . no, it's really too stupid.'

'Come on.'

'If you were a true son of his,' I continued nervously, 'I know it's perfectly ridiculous—but he said, "you'd be able to cook me as good a meal as he did." '

Mr. Maurice swung round and stared at me. Then he put down his glass of bourbon.

'Right,' he said. 'Give me a week to get things organised and we'll see what this hotel can do.'

'But my editor's invited me to lunch here to-day,' I told him.

'Oh, no you don't,' Mr. Maurice said firmly. 'You get him to take you to *Twenty-One* or some place like that. I need warning for this.'

I thought of his vast hotel, with its various grill-rooms and restaurants and nightclubs. Then I thought of le Père Auguste in his little whitewashed room with its six tables.

'I suppose you're right,' I said doubtfully.

'Listen, you've eaten my old man's cooking, haven't you?' Mr. Maurice asked. And for the first time there was some truculence in his voice.

'I certainly have,' I replied.

'Then I know I'm right. I need warning. You lunch with me here to-day week. Is that a date?'

I nodded. 'Thanks enormously,' I murmured.

For the first time he relaxed and chuckled.

'I reckon it's me that's got to thank you,' he said.

———◆◆◆———

I never lunched with Mr. Maurice because I had to leave for Charleston three days later. But as I left his magnificent penthouse—elegantly set upon the roof of the *Savoy-Waldorf*—only a little late for my luncheon date—I experienced an instinct which made me turn round. At the instant that I opened the door of the elegant apartment, I looked back. Mr. Maurice was crying. I shall never forget the expression on his face as he reached for the telephone.

I hope the line between New York and Grenoble was clear that day.

Broken Cellophane

Though he was not ugly, Leslie Warren had a face which made policemen look at him twice and Customs officials open his suitcase to turn out the contents. Examined separately, his nose, eyes and mouth were pleasant, but something had gone wrong in the assembling process which gave a strained, lopsided effect. When he was young, even in happy moments, he had appeared melancholy or worried. At school, in the streets and later, when he was an office boy, he made few friends. But it was not until his mother died that Leslie Warren, aged twenty, realised he was lonely.

By the time he was thirty Leslie had grown used to being alone. The other clerks in the office where he worked might chuck him a few words from pity or civility, but they would not invite him to join them round the corner for a drink. The lodgers in Number Five, Adelaide Row, were happier when he had left the sitting-room. His landlady, Mrs. Blaker, only welcomed him because he was clean and sober and paid his rent regularly. Leslie was aware that he was not popular.

Therefore, on the evening of September 14th when he left his office and walked down Victoria Street, Leslie planned to spend the evening as usual. From East Finchley Underground station he would catch the bus to the tobacconist shop on the corner where he would buy a packet of ten Players from the pretty girl who avoided looking at him. Three minutes' walk brought him to Number Five, Adelaide Row, where he would go up to his room to wash. He would then change into his brown suit and descend into the sitting-room five minutes before supper was ready. Afterwards he would retire to his room to read a detective novel.

Leslie stopped in front of the brightly-lit window on his way home that evening, partly because toy shops reminded him of his mother and partly because a white horse caught his eye. It was a young carthorse with a gold mane and cobby legs standing so firm that at first he thought it must be carved from wood. When he peered closer at the gentle swell of the flanks and the up-flung nostrils he was amazed to see that it was made of rubber. Though only nine inches high there was something solid and satisfactory about it, yet there was also a charming delicacy which reminded him of a horse he had seen in the windows of a shop which sold Chinese porcelain. As he admired it he remembered that he had heard Mrs. Blaker tell Mr. Tulse the hairdresser that her daughter Thelma would be ten years old next week. He did not like Thelma. She was a noisy, podgy, emotional girl and he felt that her intense devotion to her mother was rather unnatural. Moreover, he was aware that in her unreasonable and violent way Thelma hated him, although he had tried to be pleasant to her. However, she was the only child he knew with a birthday next week. In fact, now he came to think of it, she was the only child he knew at all. And he wanted an excuse to buy that horse—if it was not too expensive. After all, it wasn't your tenth birthday every day of your life, and it was a most attractive horse.

He walked in nervously and found an assistant, a slim girl with dyed red hair who looked at him with hostile eyes.

'Excuse me, but how much is that little rubber horse in the window?'

'They come out at fifteen and six,' the girl said, taking down a box from the shelf behind her.

The price was more than he could afford. Leslie hesitated. The girl looked at him scornfully. A man in striped trousers, evidently the manager, was strolling towards them. The girl's face changed.

'They squeak and move their legs,' she said quickly, almost desperately, he thought.

'I see,' he said.

'Let me show you.'

Her voice was now beseeching.

'All right.'

She turned the box round, and he saw that the lid was a painted cardboard frame covered with cellophane so that it seemed as if the horse was in a stable. As soon as she removed the frame and stood the horse on the counter Leslie noticed that it was not exactly the same as the one in the window.

'I like his stable-mate best,' he said, trying to smile.

'They're all the same.'

The man in striped trousers took three brisk steps towards them.

'If the gentleman prefers the one in the window, get it,' he said, and turned away.

'Yes, Mr Lucas,' the girl replied, and hurried towards the window.

By the time she returned Leslie had decided that he could not avoid a purchase.

'I'm afraid the rubber on this one is a bit perished,' she said. 'That's why it was put in the window, I expect. It only shows on one side.'

The paint on the right flank had flaked off so that it appeared mottled. But this was the horse he wanted. In the stance and twist of the neck, in the expression of the painted eyes and nostrils there was a coltish charm the other lacked.

Suddenly he noticed that he was the only customer left. The shop was closing.

'I'll take this one, please, if the box goes with it.'

'Certainly, sir.'

Hurriedly, Leslie put it in the box, put on the lid, and fumbled for the money.

It was only after he had left the shop that he realised he had forgotten to ask for the parcel to be wrapped up.

———◆◆◆◆———

In the Underground he held the box cunningly with the cellophane side pressing lightly against his coat. Perhaps it was his concern to conceal its contents which made the tall man standing beside him curious. After peering down for a while he looked Leslie full in the face.

'That's a horse you've got there,' he announced with idiotic satisfaction.

'Yes,' Leslie replied.

'Can we have a look?'

'Certainly.'

With embarrassment Leslie turned round the box.

'It's got something, that horse has.'

'That's what I thought.'

A woman sitting beside them leaned forward to look.

'Why, Margaret, just look at that sweet thing,' she shouted to her companion who must have been deaf.

'Bought it for the kiddy?' the man asked, beaming at him stupidly.

'Not exactly,' Leslie mumbled. 'It's for a little girl I know.'

'What a nice present, isn't it, Margaret?' the woman bellowed. 'Made of rubber, isn't it?'

'Yes,' Leslie said. 'Sorry, but this is the station where I get out.'

In the bus he sat with the box turned resolutely upside down. Next to him was a shabby old man with white side-whiskers who seemed asleep. After a while Leslie began to long to have a quick look at the other side to make sure the cellophane was intact. Furtively he turned over the box.

'T'ang,' the old man said suddenly.

Startled, Leslie looked up.

'I beg your pardon?'

'T'ang,' the old man repeated, nodding his head. 'The makers of that horse must have been influenced by horses produced by the artists who flourished during that remarkable dynasty.'

'Oh, indeed.'

'Yes, indeed. Little can those craftsmen in that inspired and sunlit land have known that two thousand years later they would influence rubber manufacturers in the land of fog. Do you not agree?'

'Yes. Certainly.'

'Fog and a damnable government. Yes,' the old man said, getting up and glaring along the bus. 'Yes, I repeat it, a damnable government. You sir,' he continued, tapping Leslie on the shoulder, 'are evidently a man of taste and culture. That I can see from your features and your purchase. Never abandon your struggle against the dictatorship of the rule of the majority. Never bow down to the tyranny of the mob. I get off at this stop. Good night to you. We need a second Plato. Farewell.'

————◆◆◆◆————

As he approached the tobacconist shop Leslie was surprised and half-pleased to think that Tang, as he now called the horse, had been responsible for two complete strangers talking to him. He no longer felt ashamed of carrying him; and he put down the box on the counter with the stable door upwards.

'Good evening. Ten Players, please.'

'Ten Players,' the pretty girl repeated, mechanically stretching out for a packet, and avoiding looking at his face.

Then she saw Tang.

'Oh, but isn't that lovely. Where did you find him?'

'In Victoria Street.'

'What's he made of? Rubber?'

'That's right.'

'He really is a duck. Mind if I take him out and look at him?'

'Of course not.'

She took out Tang and pressed his belly. There was a loud squeak which disturbed Leslie. He felt that somehow it was beneath Tang's dignity to squeak.

'Isn't that cute!' she cried, looking up at him for the first time. 'I bet your kid will go mad about him.'

'It's not for my kid,' he said, trying to grin.

'Don't tell me it's for yourself.'

' 'Course not. It's like this. My landlady's daughter has got a birthday next week.'

'How old?'

'Ten.'

'Not Mrs. Blaker's kid?'

'That's right. How did you guess?'

'Mrs. Blaker often comes in here for her Woodbines. So you live at number five. Single, I suppose?'

'That's right.'

'Well I never.'

The shop bell rang loudly as the door was pushed open and a customer walked in. The girl gently put back Tang in his box. Leslie paid for his cigarettes and edged towards the door.

'Good night, miss.'

'Careful of the Derby winner,' the girl called after him.

———◆◆◆———

Leslie walked out happily into a street which now seemed alluringly bright. She had talked to him. She had even smiled. Perhaps his mother had been right when she maintained that with a bit more confidence he could get on with girls as well as anyone. As he turned the corner he saw the lights of the pub. By the saloon door he paused. He had never been inside. Suddenly, he pushed open the door, walked resolutely up to the bar, and put down Tang on the counter, stable door upwards.

'A pint of bitter, please.'

As the barman turned he caught sight of Tang. When he came back with the beer he smiled at Leslie.

'What's it made of?' he asked.

'Guess,' said Leslie.

'Wood?'

'No. Some kind of rubber.'

'Now would you believe it,' said the barman. 'Here, Joe, come and look at this.'

'Have a drink on me,' Leslie said, as Joe approached.

Three rounds later Leslie was the centre of an admiring group. Tang was beside him standing on the counter outside the stable door. By this time the landlady's daughter had become a touching and pathetic character who was longing for a present, and Leslie was the modest benefactor who had searched London for a suitable gift.

After the fifth round Leslie realised that he was late for supper and ordered a cheese sandwich. He stayed in the pub until closing time.

———◆◆◆———

The next morning he awoke for the first time in his life with a hangover. Miserably he stared at the dark red flowers on the greasy brown wallpaper. Then he remembered. Anxiously he looked towards his dressing-table. Tang was still there.

Wearily, Leslie forced himself to get out of bed and face the tedium of the day ahead. Then a plan came into his mind.

That morning he left the boarding house with a square box wrapped up in newspaper under his arm. Throughout the morning he allowed the other clerks to tease him about its possible contents. Shortly before the office closed Leslie showed them Tang in his stable. Once again the strange charm worked. Fred, who played centre forward for the firm, asked him out for a drink. Once again Leslie did not return home until after closing time.

When he woke up the next morning Leslie lay in bed wondering. It was obvious to him that Tang was his only means of contact with his fellow men, his passport to comradeship. Luckily he had not told Mrs. Blaker's horrid little daughter that he was giving her a present. There was no reason why he should not keep Tang. And as long as he did not show him twice to the same person, Tang's charm would work.

The following evening Leslie returned from his office by a different route. In the first pub at which he stopped the audience, consisting of an old woman with a moustache and two commercial travellers, was not sufficiently impressed. But in the saloon bar of *The Anchor*, Tang's success was immediate. For three hours Leslie talked and laughed and drank with a friendly circle which changed as the evening wore on.

For the next three nights Leslie explored London for comradeship and found it in abundance. Tang's stable was stained with beer, and the cellophane cover was broken, but Tang still stood firmly and proudly immaculate.

When Tang had been in Leslie's possession for five days, Mrs. Blaker stopped him as he was leaving the boarding house. For a moment Leslie expected she would mention his late nights, but when he saw her sulky face break into a warm smile he suddenly felt apprehensive.

'Oh Mr. Warren,' she said. 'You reely shouldn't have done it, reely you shouldn't. Now don't pretend you don't know what I'm referring to,' she said, seeing his blank face. 'Miss Lewis, that nice girl that works at the tobacconist shop, has told me all about it. And Thelma's that excited she can hardly wait until to-morrow.'

'You haven't told her?' Leslie asked, clutching the square parcel under his arm.

'Well, I didn't like to reely, but Miss Lewis kept teasing the poor girl about it, telling her what a lovely present she was going to get, so that finally I just had to. I thought you knew. I thought that was why you took it out each day in case she looked into your room. Fancy going to all that trouble to give her a surprise. You reely are a gentleman, I must say. But don't worry, Mr. Warren, I can keep it until to-morrow. I know the very place to hide it.'

Leslie was so amazed that he could think of no excuse. Wretchedly he handed his parcel to Mrs. Blaker and stumbled out into the dismal street. It was not until he reached his office that the solution, like a searchlight, pierced his gloom. It was very simple. He could buy another.

He was kept late at the office that night, but as soon as he could get away he hurried along the street to the shop. It was still open. Nothing resembling Tang was displayed in the window. Nervously he walked inside. The cross-looking girl was still serving behind the counter.

'Good evening, miss,' Leslie mumbled. 'Do you remember me buying a rubber horse here a week ago?'

'Can't say that I do,' the girl replied. 'Why, was there something wrong with it?'

'No, no. I wanted another, that's all.'

'If you can tell me what it was like I'll see what we can do.'

Patiently Leslie described Tang. His embarrassment was increased by the approach of the smart sales manager in striped trousers.

'Were you wanting something?' he asked Leslie suspiciously.

Leslie realised that his earnestness had been misunderstood. Apprehensively he began his explanation once more.

'Sorry, but we're out of stock,' the man said coldly.

'Can you tell me where I could possibly find another?' Leslie stammered. 'You see, my little girl was so fond of it,' he said, lying wildly, 'that she showed it to the little girl next door, and I've promised to get her one.'

The man's suspicion appeared to increase. Leslie could feel himself sweating.

'It really is important,' he added lamely.

'I'm afraid we can't help you,' the man said. 'When we ordered a further supply we were told the firm that made them had gone out of business.'

'Have you got anything like it?'

'I'm afraid not.'

'Thanks,' Leslie said, and walked sadly out of the shop.

That night he returned home by his usual route, but he felt so dejected that he could not even bear to stop at the tobacconist shop.

At breakfast the next morning he found Mrs. Blaker presiding at the end of the table, which was unusual.

'I wouldn't let Thelma open it till you came down,' she said, beaming at him.

'Happy birthday,' Leslie forced himself to say.

'Thank you, Mr. Warren,' Thelma said, her beady eyes gleaming with excitement. 'Thanks ever so. Can I open it now?'

'Of course you can.'

Feverishly she ripped open the parcel and took Tang out of his box. For a moment there was silence. Thelma's dumpy face had grown sullen.

'Isn't it lovely?' her mother prompted.

'You said it looked like a real horse!' Thelma blurted out.

'But it's a lovely horse,' Mrs. Blaker said, determined to be cheerful. 'Look, if you press it here it squeaks.'

'Real horses don't squeak,' said Thelma. 'It's a kid's toy.'

'Now don't be a silly girl. Say thank you to Mr. Warren.'

'Thank you,' Thelma said in a flat voice.

Leslie finished his coffee quickly and left. His great sacrifice had been in vain. Years of solitude lay ahead of him.

That evening as he returned home he decided that he must go back to his old routine. Wearily he pushed open the door of the tobacconist shop and heard the bell ring. He walked up to the counter.

'Ten Players, please.'

'Hullo, it's you,' the girl said. 'Where have you been these last few days?'

'I was kept late,' Leslie lied automatically.

'Did she like him?' the girl asked.

'Like him?'

'Wasn't it the kid's birthday to-day?'

'Yes.'

'Well, did she like him?'

Suddenly Leslie decided not to lie. There was no point in it. Lies had only been useful when Tang was about.

'No,' he said.

'Why ever not? I know I'd have liked him myself.'

'Would you?' Leslie took a deep breath. 'Would you really?'

'Why, of course I would,' she said, smiling at him.

'There aren't any more,' Leslie said wretchedly. 'I found out.'

'I'd like anything you gave me,' she said quietly.

Then, as Leslie stared at her, while happiness swept over him, she blushed and turned away.

The Guide

I knew they would be late, late in arriving, but I was not quite certain I knew the reason for their delay. The streets of Italy are cluttered with cars in summertime nowadays, yet few of the visitors whom I am here to greet and to escort round the ruins ever bother to allow for the delay caused by the congestion on the roads. Moreover, the hall-porters of the big hotels—especially those at Amalfi, from whence the four clients I was expecting were setting forth—never tell their guests the amount of time it will take to drive from Amalfi to Pompeii for fear of daunting their clients' eagerness to see the place.

It was in the burning heat of noon that the large open Cadillac which I was expecting drew up, and the four of them alighted. There was no point in telling them that in southern Europe it is an error to go sight-seeing after 11 a.m., for by that time the colours and dimensions are seared out of the landscape and the sensibilities are dulled. As they left the car the noonday blaze struck down on them.

I shook hands with each of them in turn.

'I am the guide your hotel has appointed to show you the ruins of Pompeii,' I told them, speaking in English. 'You may call me Mercurio, for that is what they call me in these parts. I must apologise for the heat, but this summer has been unusually warm. In the days when Pompeii flourished, fountains were placed at almost every street corner for the use of the inhabitants. But now I suggest you should take what refreshments you need at the gates.'

There was a pause. Then the younger of the two women turned to her companions and said, in a soft and pleasant voice: 'Perhaps we can see the ruins first and have a drink later. What do you think?'

Her three friends nodded in assent.

While I had spoken, I had watched them observing me and I knew what they were thinking about me. A man of about sixty-five, they were thinking. Evidently a gentleman. Probably some kind of impoverished Italian Count from one of the many crumbling and dissolute Roman families.

Meanwhile, as we moved towards the ruins, I was examining them as they appeared to me at that moment. And, of course, I was listening to their conversation. The girl who had spoken first was called Ann. She was about thirty years old and very beautiful, with naturally fair hair and wide-set blue eyes. Her features were soft, and her expression was gentle, yet she gave me the impression of being high-spirited and impetuous. I felt she was warm-hearted and had a generous nature. That morning she seemed intensely alive. But, of course, she was nervous. She was bound to be nervous—I knew it.

As we walked through the ruins of the Forum, with Vesuvius covered in a blue haze in the background, I examined her husband. His name was Mark; he was tall, heavily built, and of about forty. He had a stern expression, except when he smiled. Then he would look like a mischievous boy. To my surprise, he seemed perfectly calm and at ease that morning. Indeed, he asked me some pertinent and intelligent questions about the Temple of Apollo which we now visited.

But the other three remained silent. I was not surprised for I knew that it was not only the heat that was oppressing them.

The second woman in the party was the actress Diana Price who had recently been making a film in Rome. Her husband had been killed in a car crash in Los Angeles three years previously. She had never married again. I knew that her age was forty-one. But her makeup and style of clothes she wore tried to disguise the fact. Traces of glamour still remained. Though she was putting on weight, she moved elegantly, and her prowess and technique as an actress were sufficient to enable her to disguise—for the time being at least—the anger she undoubtedly felt that morning.

The other man in the party was attractive, and well built, and possessed of great personal charm. His name was Alec Costa; he was half Greek and half English, but had been educated wholly in England. One read of him quite often in the gossip columns. He had a large private income which came from shipping, and he led an extravagant 'playboy' existence which was unusual in these modern times of heavy taxation. Ann's husband, Mark Hartfield, was not only his banker, but one of his oldest friends—as indeed the actress Diana Price was one of Ann's oldest friends.

So you would have thought they made a perfect quartet, and indeed, on the surface their manners towards each other were friendly and affectionate. But as we moved along the stone-paved streets in the torrid heat, cracks began to appear in the smooth veneer which covered their relationship. For instance, Diana relaxed her efforts to disguise the fact that she was very much in love with Alec Costa. Their names had been linked together in various newspapers and glossy magazines, but Alec was known to have had many affairs in his life and to have taken none of them seriously. But now, as we wandered around the Temple of Isis, Diana would glance towards Alec from time to time with an expression of wounded arrogance and pathetic rage. Further, if Ann addressed a remark to her she would now refuse to answer. Meanwhile, as the noonday heat blazed down mercilessly on the five of us, I took them round those parts of the town I intended them to see. I showed them the great theatre, and the covered theatre. I showed them the public baths, and the private baths, and every single one of the temples. By this time, the plain facts of what had occurred in Amalfi the previous night had become clear to all three of them—with the exception, it would seem, of Mark Hart-field.

In their suite at the big hotel in Amalfi, Ann and her husband, Mark, had separate rooms. Alec had a suite on the floor above. Diana had a suite on the floor below. When Mark had retired to his room for the night, Ann had gone up to Alec's suite. They had made love together.

At midnight Diana, who had attended a charity performance of one of her films, returned to the hotel. She spoke briefly to the hall-porter and then went up to Alec's suite. She found the door locked. She knocked loudly on the door, but there had been no answer. Diana had then gone down to her own suite and dialled the number of Alec's room. There had been no reply. But the hall-porter had assured her that both

Signore Costa *and* the Hartfields were in their rooms. Diana had poured herself a large drink and had then dialled Ann's room. When there was no reply, she became suspicious.

When they all met in the morning, she had examined the expressions on Ann and Alec's faces. She guessed what had happened.

You may ask how I know all this. Of course, I gleaned much of it from listening intently to their conversation. But I could only perceive the true answer when I led them towards the former residential quarter of the old town. By then the atmosphere between the four of them had become taut and ominous. Mark could no longer pretend to ignore the tension, and was making rather strained jokes in an effort to ease the dangerous mood that was spreading over them. But his easy manner and assured poise only seemed to infuriate Diana all the more. Her makeup now seemed garish, and I could see that her shoes were hurting her feet. I knew that at any moment her self-control would snap and she would speak the fatal words which might destroy the friendship between the four of them for ever. There was no time to be lost. I led them to the ruins of the private house I knew so well. We crossed the garden and passed through the main entrance with its powerful pillars and elegant capitals. As we reached the central court flanked by broken pillars, the four of them became silent. All four of them were staring at a half-broken column which had a particularly beautifully designed base. Slowly and unwillingly, as if they had lost control of their movements, they approached this column and stood staring at the base of it in complete silence.

'This was the house of Marcellus,' I told them.

But still not one of them uttered a word.

It was Diana who at last broke the silence.

'I have been here before,' she said.

Quietly, and with almost imperceptible gestures, the other three nodded their heads in assent.

'Perhaps,' I told them. 'Perhaps we all have. Who knows? But allow me to tell you a little of the history of this residence. Perhaps if you will follow me into the living-room which has been restored you will be more comfortable. The room has a roof and it contains chairs in which we may sit in the shade.'

'Thank you,' Ann said. 'I'm sure we'd all be grateful for the shade and to rest for a while.'

They followed me along a narrow corridor which led to a large area of garden surrounded by colonnades of a portico and surmounted by a gallery. Further along the corridor were the bathroom, the kitchens, and the dining-rooms. To the left was the living-room which had been restored. I ushered them into the room and we sat down.

For a while I let them admire the beauty of their surroundings. On the floor was a mosaic of the wolf suckling Romulus and Remus worthy of appearing in any royal palace. The walls were covered with mosaics—Bacchus riding on a panther; white doves drinking; a festoon of grapes and fruit, a dancing faun.

————◆◆◆————

As I told you, this house belonged to a man called Marcellus, I began. He was a wealthy man of business from Rome, married to a beautiful girl named Antonia who was both proud and virtuous. At the moment at which my story begins the two of them were sitting here in this very room, planning a banquet to be given in honour of a close friend of Marcellus, one Alexander, who was returning from five years' duty as Pro-Consul in Africa. Antonia had never met Alexander. The preparations for a banquet in those days—and, remember, I am speaking of the year A.D. 79—were enormously complicated. Not only had more than a dozen courses to be planned, but dancers and singers had to be engaged. The town's Censor had to attend the dress rehearsal and the banquet itself to make sure no flagrant indecencies would be performed in word or deed.

On the night of the banquet Antonia was standing between two Corinthian columns at the far end of the partly covered main courtyard greeting the arriving guests. The illuminations of the courtyard flickered and threw shadows against the famous frescoes of Venus and Adonis, and against the fine statues of marble. The guest of honour, Alexander, was one of the first to arrive. Marcellus embraced him warmly and introduced him to Antonia. At the moment Antonia and Alexander looked at each other for the first time the strange light of love appeared in their eyes. I suppose you could use the phrase 'love at first sight' to describe their reactions. From that very instant they became desperately in love. But, of course, by no gesture did they reveal the fact. Their conversation throughout the evening was as formal as befitted the situation of a wife meeting her husband's closest friend for the first time.

Alexander was a slender man of about thirty, very handsome in a lean kind of way, endowed with great vitality and charm. Many women and, indeed, many men, had been in love with him since he was little more than ten years old. But he himself, until that evening when he met Antonia, had never been in love. In Athens, six years previously, he had met an actress who —later in Rome—became a protégée of Ann's. He had enjoyed a brief affair with the actress, pretending to himself, for a while, that he was in love with her. However, he quickly came to recognise his self-deception.

An hour after the banqueting had started, the actress made her entrance into the banquet room. She had known that her former lover was to be the guest of honour and had taken even greater care than usual to make herself especially attractive. Slowly and gracefully she moved across the room to greet Antonia and Marcellus. Then she waited to be greeted by Alexander. But as soon as they spoke she sensed that his attitude towards her had changed.

I paused in my story and looked round at the four of them as they sat in the shade of the mosaic-lined walls. I have forgotten to tell you the name of the actress, I continued. Then I paused again, and carefully avoided looking at Diana Price. Her name I said, lying, was Julia.

Though Alexander's attitude towards her was friendly, Julia knew immediately he was no longer attracted to her. She realised there was no hope of his visiting her villa some way out of the town later that evening—or of his inviting her to his own villa situated further up the hills from that of Marcellus. Nevertheless, Julia could not prevent herself from making a constant effort to entice her former lover. When she was asked to sing, she chose a love-song, and her eyes were fixed upon him all the while she sang. All present declared her performance was even better than ever. The banquet was a great success.

Now Pompeii was not a large town, and people in the class of Marcellus and Antonia moved in a small community. Thus Antonia was almost certain to meet Alexander at every dinner party she attended. But from loyalty to Marcellus, neither Antonia nor Alexander would confess to each other the deep passion which had overwhelmed them. However, one evening at a party given in the house of some rich friends of theirs from Rome, Antonia and Alexander found themselves alone in one of the many living-rooms off the main courtyard. It was the first time they had been alone together for an instant. At first their conversation was stilted. But what their voices refused to utter their eyes proclaimed. At last their self-possession and cool manners crumbled and vanished. Alexander confessed his love, and took Antonia in his arms. Thus it was their great love affair began.

You have heard the Roman saying that those whom the Gods wish to destroy they first render mad. So it was with Antonia and Alexander. Their discretion and wits seemed to have left them completely. At night in Pompeii the slaves left the main town and slept in a quarter of their own. At night, accordingly, whenever she could leave her villa, if Marcellus was sleeping or away in Rome on some business matter, Antonia would find her way to Alexander's villa a little further up the hillside. There they would make love together until the hour before dawn. Each time they met they seemed to love each other more frantically.

One night Alexander was alone in the villa. He had dismissed his slaves: he was expecting Antonia. There was a knock at the side door. He went to open it. Standing outside was Julia. She was wearing clothes more suitable for a girl than a woman. She looked desperate and tired, but managed to smile at him.

'I've come here at this late hour,' she said, 'because I need your advice. May I come in?'

Alexander hesitated. But he could think of no reason for refusing her admittance. He closed the door behind her and escorted her to a chair in the hall. For he thought the hall would be less intimate than one of his living-rooms. He poured out two goblets of wine and handed one to Julia.

'What can I do to help you?' he asked.

'It's to do with the land I've bought out at Herculaneum,'

Julia began. Then she started to tell some rambling story about a dishonest lawyer. Suddenly, to Alexander's dismay, Julia broke down and began to sob violently. Hysterically she cried out that she loved him and had always loved him. She made him wild promises of gold she would bring him. She described obscene details of acts which she would perform for him.

Alexander listened in disgust. When she had finished her wild babblings and was sitting crying quietly with her face buried in her hands, Alexander spoke. With brutal frankness he told her he no longer cared for her. Indeed, in his revulsion at the unseemly proposals she had made to him, he told her she now sickened him and that he intended to have nothing more to do with her. Julia lifted her head and stared with frantic eyes at him. She was completely silent.

At that moment there was a knock on the side door. For a moment neither of them moved.

'It must be my neighbour from the adjoining villa,' Alexander said. 'He sometimes stops by here if he's had too much to drink and wants a little more. If I don't answer, he'll go away.'

'Those weren't the footsteps of a man,' Julia said.

'Nonsense,' Alexander replied.

Then Julia ran across the hall. But Alexander was too quick for her. He leapt to the door and stood with his back to it.

'I'm not letting anyone else into this house tonight,' Alexander cried out loudly.

Julia glared at him. 'Please may I be allowed to leave?' she asked sarcastically.

'When you've finished your wine,' Alexander answered. 'And when you have composed yourself.'

A few minutes later Julia left the villa. Alexander watched her as she moved down the hill, then turned back into his villa and closed the door behind him. But Julia did not go home. She remained in the side street and, as soon as she heard the door close, hid herself in the portico of an empty house. Presently a woman appeared, walking swiftly towards Alexander's villa.

At first Julia watched the woman with complete disbelief. Then, as she realised the truth, she began to quiver with anger. For as the woman passed by her hiding place, Julia saw it was Antonia. She watched as Antonia approached the side door of

Alexander's house. She waited while Antonia knocked on the door. She watched as Alexander admitted Antonia to the house. Then she turned violently round and stumbled furiously down the hill.

Early the following morning, when Antonia had returned to her villa and was sleeping, Marcellus was told by his steward that Julia was waiting in the outer courtyard and wished to see him alone. He received her coldly; for he had never liked Julia; he only tolerated her for the sake of his wife who had seemed in days past to enjoy her company and to be amused by her. It was a hot, sultry morning. Marcellus and Julia sat by a column in the courtyard beneath the shade of the red-tiled roof.

'There's something I think you should know,' Julia said to Marcellus. 'Your wife is having an affair with Alexander. I saw her enter his villa late last night.'

Marcellus stared at her calmly as if he had not heard a word she had said. His tranquillity enraged her.

'Don't you believe me?' Julia asked. 'Or does it stun you to think your noble and virtuous wife should be sleeping with your best friend?'

'I believe you,' Marcellus answered quietly. 'I believe you because I've known for the last seven weeks what was going on. I've known, in fact, they had fallen in love with each other on the evening they first met.'

Julia gaped at him in amazement.

'Then what are you going to do about it?' she asked.

'Nothing,' Marcellus replied. Then he paused, and in the silence as he gazed at her his eyes seemed to be making a summary of the lines on her over-painted face, of the dye in her hair, of the vulgar jewellery she was wearing, and of her garish style of dress.

'What would you have me do?' he asked softly, almost as if he were speaking to himself. 'Divorce the woman I most love in the world and never see her again? Kill the man who is my best friend?'

Julia looked at him in astonishment.

'This thing there is between the two of them won't last,' Marcellus explained. 'It came like a flame, and like a flame it will die and be forgotten—*if*, and only if, I wait and give it time.

Therefore I must never seem to know about it. They must never even begin to suspect that I know about it. You must never tell them that you came here this morning, and I shall act as if you had never visited me.'

As Julia listened to him, her rage increased, for she realised that the scene she had hoped to create would not take place. Furiously she turned towards Marcellus.

'And I always thought you were brave,' she sneered scornfully. 'But obviously you're afraid of Alexander. You're afraid to kill him.'

Until that moment Marcellus had controlled his temper, but now the reins on his control broke. Bitterly, he reminded Julia of his wife's generosity towards her and the support Antonia had given her career. He attacked her lack of loyalty and gratitude.

'You're cheap and vulgar,' he concluded. 'No better than a common whore.'

Suddenly Julia rushed at him in a frenzy of hysteria, clawing at his face and throat. In a gesture of revulsion Marcellus flung out an arm and struck her to the floor. For an instant, Julia lay motionless. Then she scrambled to her feet and began to stagger across the courtyard, her face bruised and bleeding, her clothes torn and stained. Unfortunately—or so it seemed at the time—at that moment two events occurred. Alexander appeared in the main doorway, and from the other side of the courtyard Antonia appeared from her bedroom and stood watching the scene in consternation.

I paused and examined the intent faces of my four clients as they sat by the mosaic-covered walls of the living-room beneath the red-tiled roof.

'Please go on,' the actress called Diana said to me. 'What happened then?'

It's easy to say what might have happened, I explained. So many things might have occurred. Julia might have screeched out the truth. Alexander and Marcellus might have fought. Antonia and Alexander might have run away together and lived out the rest of their lives in Athens or in Egypt. As in every small group of human-beings whose lives are entwined, there could have been innumerable permutations and countless combinations of action that might have taken place—because the strength of each person's love and of each person's hate is so strong and so extremely variable. I have heard it said that unless the poor human race learns to adapt itself to the factors of the world it inhabits then it will perish. Perhaps that process of adaptation has taken place to a small degree. One can only hope so.

Once again I was silent.

'What happened?' Mark repeated. 'We want to know.'

As I have told you, the air was warm and sultry, I continued. At that moment from far away there was the sound of thunder. Then, suddenly, came a blinding flash, followed by a deafening explosion which shook the whole villa. In fear, the four of them raised their eyes to the distant horizon. Then, from the peak of Vesuvius, there arose a vast cloud of mist and vapour—a cloud which the historian Pliny described as being shaped in the form of a gigantic pine tree—which, of course, in its turn strangely resembles the shape of the mushroom cloud of an atomic explosion. Next there was an ear-splitting noise as thousands of tons of rock were shattered by the volcano and hurled into the air. The earth trembled, and there was the sound of the crash of falling masonry. Rivers of molten lava began to pour down from Vesuvius, forming a torrent which moved inexorably towards the town of Pompeii. A cloud of ash settled into a thick fog. The sun was obscured; and presently the town was in darkness. And the grey ashes began to fall— steadily covering every villa and street and alleyway, muffling all sound. And still the ashes fell heavily until the whole of Pompeii was covered by a thick carpet of ash.

Antonia and Marcellus, Alexander and Julia, rushed out of the villa, followed by the frightened slaves. Immediately they were caught up in a swirling multitude of screaming people rushing desperately to get away from the city—people rushing against each other, hurrying to escape, some of them carrying bundles and others loot. But as the noise of Vesuvius in-creased, so the shrieks and cries of humanity grew fainter, because now the ashes had formed a heavy layer above the town in the shape of a large and monstrous dark cloud. This dark mass was growing lower in the sky each moment, so that the air was becoming stagnant and foul like a close and dark narrow room. But still the four of them staggered forward in the crowd, all of them now knee-deep in ash. They were panting and gasping for breath. They were slowly suffocating.

Soon the whole town was quiet—for every single person within its confines was now dead. The wind-blown flakes of ash still fell heavily on the town, and the lava streamed over the streets.

———◆◆◆◆►———

The four of them sat perfectly still, without speaking. I rose from my chair. My work was done.

'Would you like me to show you another house which has now been *completely* restored? I asked. 'It is called the House of Mercurio, and it is only next door.'

For a while they remained silent.

'I don't know about the rest of you,' Mark said after a pause, 'but I think I could do with a long, cooling drink in one of those cafés we saw on the way in.'

'That's an excellent idea!' Ann exclaimed.

Mark looked towards Diana. She was sitting huddled in her chair; her expression was dazed.

'Besides,' Mark added in a very gentle voice as he looked towards Diana, 'haven't you got to make another appearance at the Film Festival tonight?'

Diana looked up at him in surprise, and I knew that the reason for her astonishment was the tenderness in Mark's voice.

'You're right,' she answered. 'I have. In fact, I was hoping the three of you would accompany me.'

'I'd love to,' Alec said in a voice of sudden enthusiasm. 'And if you're not too tired afterwards, I'll take you to that new nightclub.'

Diana smiled. At that instant she looked young again.

'Thanks. It would be lovely,' she replied.

Together they moved out of the house and wandered back through the ruins towards the entrance. And I followed them as they strolled along, talking contentedly to each other.

When they had sat down at a table beneath an awning outside the café and had ordered their drinks, they looked round.

'Where's the guide?' Diana asked.

'Where is he indeed?' Mark demanded. 'We haven't even given him a tip.'

But though I could still hear their conversation, I had departed a few seconds ago. I was already on my way to my next assignment.